DEADLY
LESSON

S. J. Butler is a writer and teacher from Co. Mayo, Ireland.

Also by S. J. Butler

Between the Lines

DEADLY LESSON

S. J. BUTLER

ACCENT

First published in 2021 by Headline Accent
An imprint of HEADLINE PUBLISHING GROUP

3

Cataloguing in Publication Data is available from the British Library

ISBN 978 1 7861 5968 7

Typeset in 11.25/15.25 pt Bembo Std by Jouve (UK), Milton Keynes

Printed and bound in Great Britain by Clays Ltd, Elcograf S.p.A.

MIX
Paper from
responsible sources
FSC® C104740

Headline's policy is to use papers that are natural, renewable and recyclable
products and made from wood grown in well-managed forests and other
controlled sources. The logging and manufacturing processes are expected
to conform to the environmental regulations of the country of origin.

HEADLINE PUBLISHING GROUP
An Hachette UK Company
Carmelite House
50 Victoria Embankment
London EC4Y 0DZ

www.headline.co.uk
www.hachette.co.uk

For Teresa and Louis

Prologue

A fresh, crisp, sunny morning: the kind you want to wrap yourself up in, to drink hot, steamy, sweet tea while watching your breath slowly rising, each gulp making you warm inside as the sun hits the side of your face. The terraced streets alive with sounds of activity, gates squeaking then clanging shut, children shouting, dogs barking; the early part of the day when you expect nothing bad to happen. The potential of another day – a new experience, the beginning of a chapter.

That was how it should have been, could have been if only you'd stayed in bed.

Prologue

Chapter One

'Is here fine?' Sally said, pulling up outside the run-down launderette.

'Couldn't have done better myself,' said Tom cheekily, taking off his seat belt and checking his hair in the passenger mirror. 'What was that song you were playing?' he added casually, pushing his greasy fringe off his face with a flick of his head.

'Pulp: "Common People".'

'Can I borrow it a sec?' he asked as she nodded, still dabbing at a wet fleck of mascara in the corner of her eye. She took the tape from the cassette player.

'Haven't moved on to CDs yet then?' He almost snatched the piece of musical plastic from her outstretched freckled hand.

'No, I'll stick with the cassettes for now – only just replaced all me LPs,' she added, hoping he'd soon get out of the car as she removed the last trace of stray make-up from her eye.

'Won't be a minute,' he said, placing the tape in his Walkman, which he stuffed down the front of his trousers as he got out and gave her a wink and wave.

Glancing back at the waiting car he quickly disappeared

down the alleyway beside the launderette. As he did, a noisy black mass of crows and jackdaws took flight in an untidy cluster, squawking and arguing as they rose and fell on the wind, no doubt complaining at Tom's sudden entrance into their world.

Spying a phone box a few yards away, Sally grabbed a few coins from her bag and made a dash for it, mistakenly racing against a man with a dog who she was sure was going to make a call before her, but walked on by.

'Pete, it's Sally, I didn't wake you up this morning, did I?' she began breathlessly. 'I tried to creep out,' she added, fumbling with the receiver.

'No, I'm fine, Sal, slept in till twelve.'

She loved the way he called her Sal; loved his accent too. It seemed as if everyone at university either wanted to sound northern or London; his accent was definitely the latter. It was as if all the posh kids had jumped ship and squashed themselves into Oxford and Cambridge.

'Shall I come around tonight?' she enquired affectionately.

'Yeah, come round.' Pete wasn't one for talking and it was one of the many things that attracted her to him. 'Where are you now?' he asked sleepily, still waking up to the world of daytime living.

'I'm driving up to East Ham to see Sarah. Oh, and I'm dropping that Tom bloke off in Stratford,' she added casually, feeling that she should at least mention it.

'Oh, right,' said Pete in his usual laid-back way, 'the one at Jean's party.' In truth he'd paid little attention to Tom at the party and only remembered him saying something about Social-Darwinism that wasn't very interesting and a bit contrived. Apart from that he'd seemed an all right type of guy.

'*Rio Bravo* is on in a bit,' he said.

Pete was clearly flicking between channels. 'So, I'll see you tonight then,' she said, eventually having gone over the other finer details of her morning and more of his TV-watching schedule.

'Yeah, tonight.'

'Love you.'

'I love you too. Bye, Sal.'

'Bye.'

Where the fuck is he? Sally thought, now safely back in the car but desperately needing a pee, and wanting to see Sarah and get back to Pete before nightfall. Looking at her watch and noting that twenty minutes had already passed, she cursed her travelling companion once more as she pressed her hands deep between her legs.

'Sorry about that,' said Tom, appearing out of nowhere and throwing himself down in the passenger seat with what appeared to be his T-shirt rolled up in a plastic carrier bag. 'Me mate's gran was there, and she wouldn't stop yakking,' he added, pushing the bag deep into his hoodie and zipping it up quickly.

'No problem,' she lied, starting up the engine with urgency and trying not to think of her bursting bladder. 'Shit!' Suddenly defeated, she turned off the ignition. 'I'm sorry, Tom, I've got to go and pee.'

'Go down the alley, no one takes that short cut,' he said casually, his smile returning. 'Go on,' he added, sensing her trepidation, 'no one will see yer.'

'Is it safe?'

'Of course it is. I'll keep a look out for yer. Go on!' he repeated in a playful tone, nearly pushing her out of the door.

'OK, but don't move; stay there; promise?'

'Promise; cross my heart.'

Once he was sure that Sally was safely out of sight, Tom reached over to the back seat, grabbed her handbag, and began sifting through its contents. Finding her purse, he opened it; nothing, only money he didn't need; a photograph of the boyfriend, and her driver's licence. Further down her bag there were a few stray Tampax and some chewing gum. Glancing up nervously at the alley, he continued. Bingo: a telephone bill. Scanning the information for a brief second, he had it all: full name, telephone number, and address. Placing everything neatly back in the bag he looked up and saw her flushed face move into the light of day as the already excited jackdaws swooped overhead, clattering into one another like an undisciplined gang of psycho–bandits, as Sally too looked up to see the commotion. In that split second, he had the bag placed safely on the back seat and was now intently reading the back of the Pulp cassette as she opened the door and got in.

'Hey, you were supposed to be watching the alley, yer daft git,' she said, smiling again in an attempt to hide her embarrassment.

'I was, you just didn't see me.' He wanted to say, *but I saw you*, though thought it sounded a bit creepy. 'Brilliant album,' he said, putting the cassette back in its case.

She was about to say that he could borrow it, but decided not to when she thought about all the tapes and LPs she'd lent to friends over the years and not got back.

'Funny creatures,' he said nodding towards the birds, who were now landing on each other's heads, scrapping over some imaginary feast.

'Loud,' she replied.

'I reckon those ones there, the smaller birds with the grey hoods,' he began pointing at the jackdaws, 'they're embarrassed by the crows.'

'Well, the din they're making is like a record being played loud and backwards,' Sally said as she turned on the ignition and the birds flew off again.

Moving on now with certainty, and with the need to be rid of her travelling companion firmly on her must-do list, she drove seamlessly and effortlessly towards her destination.

'Don't you think that it's strange how birds are given negative labels?'

'What?' She really was tiring of the birds now.

'I mean an unkindness of ravens or a clattering of jackdaws, and of course a murder of crows: not a good advertisement, is it – you really wouldn't want to be a bird.'

'I suppose not,' she replied, finding it hard to concentrate on driving and wishing he would just stop. Relieved to be seeing more signs for Stratford, she took the town centre exit.

The earlier part of the journey hadn't been so easy. Before the sudden detour, she had nearly run over a drunk in Whitechapel who'd stepped out into the road, sending his shopping trolley of belongings spinning to the other side of the street as the wino shook his fist and pressed his filthy, beery face against the glass of the driver's side, smearing snot its entire length as Sally screeched to a halt.

'Where did you learn to drive like that?' had been Tom's unhelpful response as she pulled cautiously away, only for the car to stall again, which seemed to happen every time she touched the brake.

'There must be something wrong with the shitty thing!'

'Or maybe the London roads – you could blame the roads,' Tom had added sarcastically.

Well, as roads went, there probably wasn't one as long and straight as the Mile End one. From Whitechapel to Bow, there wasn't a curve or squiggle to be found. Take the traffic and wandering drunks out of the equation, it was the perfect road for a learner.

'I think I'm getting the hang of it now,' she'd said ironically, managing a smile which seemed to temporarily calm things down a little.

'You must be the only student in London with a car; didn't have you down as a posh bird!' he'd laughed.

She'd ignored the *bird* jibe – knew it was deliberate. 'Oh, yeah, mad about me pony riding and hockey,' Sally had replied dryly, her unsullied northern accent reverberating through the yellow Fiat Panda which now roared with new-found enthusiasm past the Globe pub, skimming the pavement and ironing out a dead pigeon as they jumped the lights at Mile End tube station.

'If your driving etiquette is anything to go by, I'm guessing you could be the daughter of a getaway driver?'

'Yeah, me dad robs post offices,' she joked.

He seemed serious for a few seconds as if he'd just captured a passing thought and given it serious attention.

'So, what do your mum and dad do?'

'Dad's a builder and Mum works in a local bakery.'

'Builder, baker, candlestick maker,' he laughed.

She didn't appreciate his jokes. Talking of her family in such a whimsical way didn't sit well with her.

'They must be very proud of you.'

He was like a dog picking at a scab. Sally couldn't put her

finger on it, but she felt as if she was being toyed with in an unpleasant, intrusive way. Letting the comment linger, she merely nodded, blushed, and consciously said nothing. Getting the message, he didn't pry any further, but kept up the jokes.

Further on and many odious quips later, there was now an obvious awkwardness and a silence.

'It's good of you to give me a lift,' he said, seeming to relish the drop in temperature.

'It's no problem; I have a friend in East Ham I'm going to visit, so I'm going this way anyway. Where do you live again?' she said, less out of a need to know and more the fact that her guest needed to be dispensed with ASAP.

'Stratford, but it's fine, you can drop me at the shopping centre, I need to buy some shampoo and a tin of baked beans.'

'Chopped-up soap goes better with beans,' she added, flicking a stray lock of pink hair from her eyes.

As they headed further east towards Bow and Stratford, the landscape became less colourful and a far cry from the strangely enticing, eye-catching chaos of Brick Lane and Whitechapel Market. Now the road appeared wider, enclosed by a dull outline of sad greys and depressing, drizzling blues, as if the whole changing scene was being wrung out, squeezed of life by a toothless washer-woman.

'So, you've got a boyfriend then?'

'Yeah, you met him last night at the party, didn't you?'

'Oh, yes: the tall, quiet one.'

She was sure that there was a hint of spite in the 'quiet one' comment but decided to overlook it. After all, she hardly knew Tom and was unlikely to bump into him again. If anything, it was perhaps a compliment of sorts.

'If I knew you better, I'd think you were envious of him.' There, she'd said it, exactly what was going through her mind as they hit a bit of traffic at the second set of lights; though she hadn't revealed the other evolving fact that she thought Tom was quite good-looking. Remaining silent, he just shrugged his shoulders, and grinned, though it had been more of a smirk. This she had missed, once again stalling the car at the lights.

'So, where are you a student again?'

'The London School of Fashion.'

'Arts and Crafts then,' he'd laughed.

'Is that funny?' she'd asked playfully. 'I suppose to you, being an artist is an example of someone who's lacking; like someone who's good at potato- and hand-printing?'

'Well, you said it.'

'You fucker,' Sally laughed. 'I suppose you're a computer science-maths-psycho-freakoid?'

'No, English and History actually.'

'I thought only thick posh kids did that,' she'd joked, his 'posh bird' jibe still fresh.

'If you're working class like me,' he'd started, his northern accent thicker than earlier, 'then you should know what the bastards did to us and wrote about us.' He said it with a serious face, before letting it crack and bursting out laughing.

Getting nearer to Bow they'd talked and listened to music, made judgements, and tried to be as cool and happening as was humanly possible for students to be.

It was then, out of the blue, that he'd asked if she minded taking a slight detour to lend a friend some money. She'd been a bit annoyed to begin with, but at least the call to Pete had relaxed her a bit and now that they were mobile again, heading towards where Tom lived, she was more than relieved.

The Stratford arcade loomed, dilapidated, like a Soviet shopping centre: dark, dank, drab and unattractive – though housing the only decent supermarket in the vicinity. If you knew the area, you'd walk around it at night rather than through it, the potential for violence ever present. Sally knew it well, having got lost there once when trying to locate the local theatre.

'You said you wanted the shopping centre?' said Sally, pulling up just past the tube station and the entrance of the bus station.

'Here's great,' Tom said, suddenly dropping a flat tin on the floor.

'Is that yours?' Sally pointed towards the object, which had flown open to reveal what looked like an ink pad. Not replying, he quickly scooped it up and returned it to his pocket as if it were nothing.

'Well, it's been good to see you again,' concluded Sally, pleased that she at last could see the bright lights of the shops.

'Likewise.'

'Right.'

'So, you want me to go then, you want me to leave?' he said seriously, with a hint of menace, while looking straight ahead. The air between them suddenly became thick and oppressive.

It was an odd thing to say all right. Was he just going to sit there, she thought as a sudden surge of weird scenarios entered her mind, making her grip the door handle, ready to run, as she temporarily saw her name in grisly headlines in the Sunday papers.

'Er, yeah,' she said, making a dumb expression in an attempt to lighten the growing tension.

'Well, so do I,' he said at last, turning towards her and delivering an enticing smile showing a good set of pure white teeth. 'I had you there, didn't I?' he joked, pulling up his hood ready to leave.

'Yeah.' It was all she could manage. Feeling relieved and a little foolish she managed a weak, 'Bye then,' as she consciously released her sweaty grip from the door handle.

'Bye, Sally,' he said, opening the door. 'See yer soon.'

Before she could reply, he'd gone. Instead of driving off, Sally sat there for a few seconds watching him in her rear-view mirror as he headed towards the shopping centre. After several steps he stretched out his arms like a bird in flight and continued spread-eagled towards the bright lights, only to suddenly stop and turn around abruptly, as if aware of being observed.

Pushing the gear stick into first, Sally uncharacteristically slowly pulled away, hoping she hadn't been seen. As she got up speed, she made another quick check of her mirror to see if he was still there and saw him: rooted to the spot, standing legs apart, violently stabbing his forehead with his finger, while appearing to be talking to himself.

Watching Sally drive off, Tom spat with disgust. He tapped the side of his nose, continuing to stare straight ahead until the car was out of sight. Sure she was gone, he didn't turn round and head for the shopping centre, but quickly began walking the way he'd come: past the bus depot and information desk, until stealthily disappearing from view, taking the chewing gum-spotted steps which led to the warmth of the underground and the waiting trains below.

12

Chapter Two

'You see over there, Jake, just to the right of the pond; have you got it? Well, that's a sparrowhawk. What do you think? She's a beauty, isn't she?' said Jack Hogan, holding his own binoculars while guiding his son's small hands as he scanned the trees and the forest beyond. Jake expectantly took his father's lead and nodded quietly in agreement.

'Look there, quick, Jake: a skylark. Can't believe it; haven't seen one in years,' he said, ruffling his son's blond mop.

'Dad, quick, he's flying away,' Jake said proudly, now directing his father's gaze.

'You're right, he is. What a spectacle,' Jack added, wiping his brow. 'It's what life is all about.'

'Who are they?' his son said, suddenly pointing to two heavily clothed women with headscarves and long skirts, who had temporarily slipped out into the clearing then dipped back into the forest.

'They're Romanies, been coming here for years. Ever since I was a boy they've been coming and going.'

'What, they live there?'

'Yeah, deep in the forest. Look, see that smoke there, in the distance above the trees? That's their campfire.'

'Wow, a real camp! Just around the corner from where I live,' Jake said, trying to see more through his binoculars.

Jack looked at his beautiful fair-haired ten-year-old boy intently viewing the landscape and wondered if his son would ever really get over the death of his mother. On the surface he seemed OK, and Jack always chose to keep Mandy's memory alive, saying things like, 'Your mum would have loved this' and 'Your mum used to say that you're just like her'.

Four years ago, on a self-catering holiday in Devon, it had happened. The three of them had finished their breakfast, having decided to head for the beach early, when Mandy said that she needed some fresh air before clearing up. Jack had readily volunteered for washing-up duties instead, and she had walked out into the morning sunshine.

Finishing off the last plate and placing it in the rack, Jack had asked Jake to give his mum a call. And that's when they found her, Jake first, turning blue and taking her last breaths. In the seconds that her heart began to falter and slow to a shuddering halt, Mandy had tried her hardest to remain in the world for the son she had dreamed would maybe one day study law and have a family of his own.

Sudden death: breaking like a wave on a rock, smashing in an instant their secure, happy family. After the pain of losing the love of his life and the sadness of seeing his son trying to come to terms with the loss of his mummy, the episodes began for Jack. The constant replaying of events in his mind, over and over again: his son collapsed, sobbing, at his mother's side; the ambulance man trying to resuscitate her; the coffin being carried into

14

the church. The pills that swiftly followed, hastily prescribed by his doctor, and taken more for Jake's sake than his own, only temporarily numbed the feeling of loss and total despair.

It had seemed an eternity before he was able to find himself again. Men like Detective Chief Inspector Jack Hogan couldn't just break down. It wasn't in their DNA. You just bloody got on with it. That was his view, although he struggled to keep up the pretence.

'Maybe we could visit them some day?' Jake continued, tugging at his father's sleeve to gain his attention.

'What? Who?' said Jack, lowering his binoculars and refocusing his attention.

'The Romanies,' Jake replied emphatically. 'And then if we got to know them, they could come to our house; maybe have a cup of tea?'

Agreeing to think about it, but not committing himself, Jack marvelled at his young son's innocence and wondered how long it would last. At times he could be strangely grown-up and tipping the scales of precociousness, and then it was as if he would suddenly slip and scurry back to the safety of his earlier childhood. At the moment he was somewhere between the two – trapped in the middle of a lullaby and a gritty news story.

'Do you get lonely, Dad?' said Jake suddenly, catching his dad by surprise.

'No,' he lied. '*You're* not lonely, are you, Jake?' he asked, concerned that his son may have been really speaking about himself.

'Of course not,' laughed Jake cheekily as Jack smiled with relief.

'What do you reckon, Jake: pub lunch?' said Jack, looking at his watch as a flock of gulls settled around them, frantically digging their beaks into the soft, moist ground.

Not a strange thing to ask a ten-year-old when you considered their close relationship: not just father and son, but good mates as well. It was their joke. Every time they rounded the corner and saw Epping Forest laid out before them and then the Sir Alfred Hitchcock Hotel to the right, Jake would instantly say, 'Pint, dad?' And his father would love him a little bit more every time he said it. But it hadn't always been that easy, passing the Hitchcock. Not after the Wanstead stand-off . . .

Flat B, 30 Elgin Road: an address not easily erased even after years of constantly trying to forget it.

Nine a.m., Mile End police station operations room. The call came that their man, double-murder suspect Paul Ryan, was holed up at an ex-girlfriend's ground-floor flat in Wanstead and had taken a pot-shot at the armed response unit already at the scene. With an urgency to get to their man before the bullets did, Jack and Detective Sergeant Christine Peters, known as Chris, had rapidly scrambled to the address. Chris was a young single working mum. A worthy companion who you could count on not to abandon the foxhole when the fighting got dirty.

They were relieved to be informed on arrival that Ryan had given up on the shooting practice and was at last talking.

'Lads, no John Wayne stuff – not unless I say. We need to find out more from him,' had been Jack's first frantic words to the response officers.

After a matter of minutes, they'd established that Ryan was alone and was prepared to come out if the armed officers stood down. After careful consideration it was agreed that Jack and Chris would both wait for him at the entrance to the flats. They would be armed, of course.

'Guv, we don't have to do this, you know?' Chris had said, clearly not fully convinced that it was the right course of action. 'If he gets himself shot, then he gets himself shot.'

Jack was sure that Ryan wasn't going to go for the blaze of glory shootout (he'd had his chance already) and would relish the mind games of the interview room instead. That aside, he still had to respond to his partner's fears.

'Chris,' he'd said, moving in closer, almost whispering in her ear. 'You stay here. I can go alone. It doesn't have to be the two of us.'

It was as if someone had given him a quick glimpse of the future and he hadn't recognised it, his words merely a natural response to his colleague's concerns; a conversation he'd live to regret; a doubt he should have acted upon.

Before she could speak, he already knew the answer. As police etiquette went that wasn't going to happen, and deep down Jack knew it, as Mandy's blue, ashen face flashed before him, in what was becoming a frequent episodic nightmare. Brushing it aside as quickly as it had gained passage, he accepted Chris's insistence that she wasn't going anywhere. They both waited for the nod, which came in seconds as the unit stood down and signalled that they were ready.

In all his years of being in the force, Jack had thought he could smell a bad omen and knew when not to act. Glancing briefly at Chris, he was sure that his judgements were the right ones, as he gingerly knocked on the entrance door and waited. Patting the right side of his raincoat for the shape of his gun he winked at Chris as if she were his son, and she did the same, softly tapping her piece and mouthing 'Ready!'

The door suddenly burst open and Ryan came bundling out, brandishing his firearm. He pointed it directly at Chris, who had instantly drawn hers.

In the split second of guns being bandied around, Jack had wrestled with Mandy's image once more, and the heartbreaking crying of his young son, as he too drew his gun and aimed at Ryan.

'Put the gun down, sunshine!' Jack roared. It was purely old school, but he was still one of a dying breed who liked a bit of drama to add spice to what was otherwise a thankless profession.

'You heard him! Put it down!' Chris shouted, her hand visibly shaking.

Read the face; look for the change of expression: the twitch, eye recognition. It was all there in the manual. Jack searched Ryan's shark eyes with all his years of experience for the answer and came up with a blank as Mandy's coffin came into view again, he and Jake slumped at its head as it was lowered into the ground.

Ryan remained focused on Chris, his hand steady and determined.

Chris was the first to see it: the flicker of the eye, the impulse encrypted on the face of a man who kills for thrills. She recognised the twisted hate and the intent rearing itself up as his gaze flitted to Jack and then back to her. She knew it was coming.

'Jack!' she'd cried as the armed response unit reappeared assembling their arsenal. 'Jack! Just do it! Do it, Jack! Jack!'

The last earth had been thrown on top of his wife's lowered casket . . .

18

Jack had turned towards his colleague as the left side of her face was blown away from her head, held together only by a string of sinew and muscle as it went in the opposite direction. At last opening fire, Jack hit Ryan in the shoulder as another bullet from a police sniper zipped past, hitting him cleanly in the forehead.

Rooted to the spot for some time, sick to the pit of his stomach, Jack had closed his eyes and dropped his head as he felt the sudden urge to turn the gun on himself.

'Fuck,' was all he could say, as he heard Chris pleading with him again and again to shoot.

'Sir, you need to move,' the officer softly placing a comforting hand on Jack's shoulder had said. But he couldn't move; couldn't leave his dead partner, who was now covered in a red blanket, her buckled black-shoed right foot the only reminder of her, sticking out beneath a warm-looking cloak. He knew it; they all knew it; it had been Jack's call; his delayed reaction to pull the trigger – this and much more mixed together in his toxic mind, which fought and sought to send him completely crazy.

In the madness that had unfolded, he'd lose his partner and his Mandy time and time again. During the months that followed, he had self-medicated, increasing the dosage of his medication and drinking more heavily than usual, as he now had the constant recall of both Mandy's and Chris's deaths repeating on a loop throughout the day and night. He was a total mess for two years after. A barely functioning, pill-popping boozer, who as soon as his son was put to bed and the au pair, Skuld, had retired to her room, would venture out into the night, usually placing himself in the Hitchcock, where he'd drink until the numbness set in and his mind became blank.

Because he thought it was his nirvana, it quickly became his nemesis, as the blackouts followed, when the bingeing continued after he'd staggered home and he'd wake up delirious on the sofa with the TV blaring. It was after Jake had found him slumped, fully clothed, covered in vomit, in the shower one morning, that the change took place. Ashamed and petrified, he had apologised to his son, emptied the overflowing drinks cabinet, got rid of his medication, and had taken up birdwatching and clean living again ...

'So, pint is it, Dad?' Jake said, taking his father's large guiding hand as they headed for the Hitchcock.

'Why not?' beamed Jack, who loved the ritual of it all: the ordering of two pints of orange squash; the round of ham and mustard sandwiches, the game of pool which he would always let his son win.

Always the dreaded call came at the most inconvenient time.

'Yes,' said Jack gruffly, picking up his new mobile phone as they stopped at the steps of the hotel.

'Sir?' It was Detective Sergeant Alan Sharpner, known as Pencil due to his tall, skinny frame as well as his surname.

'Pencil, what is it?'

'Guv, we've got a DB, a dead body: Dean Waters, student, Bow area. His gran found him this afternoon.'

It wasn't just the call that irritated Jack, it was the fact that every time his sidekick spoke, he thought of Chris.

'Sir?' The reception wasn't very good, and Jack was breaking up a little.

'Yeah, right; I can hear you now. What's the address?'

Jake eyed him suspiciously as he took the details. It didn't take a degree in Communications to know that their afternoon together had been ruined.

'Right, see you there,' were Jack's parting words on the matter as he looked into his son's mournful blue eyes.

'Sorry, Jake.'

'It's all right, Dad.'

It was complicated, as it often was at the weekends. Being the second week of the month, it was Skuld's day off and she was sightseeing with her childhood friend Jelka, who was visiting from their native Iceland and had been staying with them after commencing on a European trip.

'Jake, you'll have to come with me,' he began apologetically. 'Is that all right?'

'Don't worry, Dad, I've got my *Guinness Book of Records*.' Jake knew his dad's job was tough and understood that he needed a helping hand now and again.

Retracing their steps, they reluctantly got into the car. 'John Coltrane or Blur?' said Jack, putting on his seat belt.

'Blur,' said his son knowingly as his father pushed in the ready CD. 'Girls & Boys' began to play as they took off for Stratford, which had changed little over the years, apart from the renovated shopping centre and new bus station.

Turning off for Bow, they slowly pulled into Langley Road where they were welcomed by the usual array of Forensics vans, patrol cars, ambulances, and black unmarked cars congesting the quiet street.

'Jake, sit in with Detective Sergeant Evans,' said Jack, gesturing to the tall blonde woman who had moved swiftly into view as he slipped on his blue rain mac. 'OK, Pencil, walk and talk me through it,' he continued, acknowledging his other colleague who was soon at his shoulder. With Pencil giving much of the same information as before and annoyingly littering his dialogue with too many *sirs*, Jack was soon tiring of his sergeant's presence and was relieved to be at last inside the cordoned-off front garden of the crime scene.

Entering the small terraced house, they were instantly met by an officer who let them into the draughty front room which smelt of sweet tea and tobacco. Craning their heads to avoid what was a low ceiling, they stumbled upon an upturned bookcase of *Reader's Digest*s and a knitting basket, looking as if it had been hurled across the room, the different coloured threads covering the carpet like a woolly spider's web, in the middle of which sat the mutilated head of Dean Waters.

'Christ, it looks like they've tried to get into his skull through his eye socket,' said Jack, crouching down by the corpse and touching the detached eyeball with the tip of his pen. 'And what's this?' he asked, pointing to the smudge on the forehead.

'Sir?'

'On his head!' snapped Jack impatiently.

'Oh, sorry, sir,' began Pencil, correcting himself. 'Looks like a stamp gone wrong; you can just make out a triangle of sorts on the right side,' he added, pointing at the lines. 'The rest of it is a mess.'

'And the twenty-pound note?' Jack said, nodding towards the wrinkled paper which protruded out of the young man's mouth.

'Maybe some kind of drug money – a payback of sorts?'

'Yeah, could be making him choke on the money he owes?' said Jack, tapping the end of the note. 'And why the outstretched arms?' he asked, letting his sergeant take the lead and at the same time testing his skills of deduction.

'Well,' began Pencil, scratching his head, 'until Pathology has a look for bruising, I suppose we can assume the murderer was sitting on his chest, with their knees holding down his arms.'

'Old-fashioned beating.'

'Yes, sir.'

'Almost of a different time: a bit like an extreme version of *Tom Brown's Schooldays*.'

Pencil looked baffled, but agreed again.

'No weapons; just fists,' added Jack. 'Primal: one man sinking his hands deep into another man's skull. Some sick bastard. Might be a little bit more than the drugs angle, though I certainly wouldn't rule it out.'

'Sir?'

'Usually they'd use a weapon: a quick, retaliatory, teaching-a-lesson kind of crime. This is deeper than that; intense, more than just a message. This is a statement. It's been thoroughly thought through,' added Jack, getting to his feet and taking off the latex gloves. 'And of course, there's the stamp.'

'Never seen anything like that before, sir?' said Pencil, because he couldn't think of anything to say as he struggled to slip his gloves off his huge shovel-like hands.

'See if you can get more on the stamp. Also find out if Dean Waters had a housemate, a girlfriend; the usual enemies, local gossip, any record of drug misuse – anything. Then get me the forensics.' At this stage Jack always rattled off the obvious potential leads as a matter of course. He never took anything for granted. Although textbook stuff, it made him feel in control at the beginning of an investigation. 'And, Pencil?'

23

'Yes, sir?'

The constant *sirs* had become a bit of a thing, making Jack bristle with annoyance every time the sergeant opened his mouth. The odd *sir* was fine. He just needed to vary it. Of course, he couldn't have Pencil call him Jack, but there were different ways to answer a question or address someone!

'It's only an observation, but try a little bit more than *sir* now and again – maybe leave one or two of them out and see how you get on,' he said stolidly, before turning and making for the door, as Pencil fought with the urge to say 'Sir' but said 'Yes, guv,' instead. Jack shook his head and sighed deeply.

Outside, the good day had turned into a bad one as dark clouds rolled up off the Thames, the heavens opening up to a heavy downpour. 'Thanks, Evans,' he said to the retreating detective, as he slumped down beside his son.

'Coltrane, I think,' smiled Jack as they drove off, pressing the play button as a sweet, smoky saxophone ballad oozed out of the speakers in time to the wipers and driving rain.

'And a pizza?' said his son.

'And a pizza,' he repeated as Dean Waters' mutilated face flashed before him.

Chapter Three

His mobile was vibrating in his breast pocket as if it had just been awaiting their arrival home to taunt him. Just as well they hadn't ordered the takeaway, thought Jack, not bothering to take off his wet raincoat.

'You better answer it, Dad, it might be important,' Jake muttered.

Christ, even his son could sense his despondency!

'Sir, I think we may have something,' chimed Pencil as Jack took the call.

'Oh,' said Jack, glancing at Jake, who sighed deeply, shrugging his shoulders and knowing the protocol all too well.

'Man arrested coming out of the Forestdale Estate in Bow.'

'Just around the corner from Langley Road.'

'Yes, sir. Bloodstains on his clothing, concealing a hammer in a plastic bag.'

'When?'

'When?' mirrored Pencil.

'When was he arrested?' snapped Jack grumpily as his belly rumbled.

'Literally, twenty minutes ago.'

'Right, hold him there. Don't do anything,' he added, still not fully trusting his colleague to do the right thing.

Poor Jake. Why couldn't he have a bloody teacher for a dad?

'Do you mind going in next door – play with Mark for a while until Skuld gets home?'

He didn't have to ask; Jake had already gathered up his box of football cards from the front room and was making for the front door with his swaps.

'Mark's got Dennis Wise and Ruud Gullit and I want them,' he was saying, pulling his coat back on.

'If I'm late – pizza tomorrow.' It was all he had.

It was going to be a long night. He'd always hated evenings, even when a constable, it was when madness happened and unpredictability danced more freely. Even more unappealing was the night-time interrogation: worse for the suspect, but hard on the concentration of the questioner too.

'So, you'll be all right?'

'Of course – go!'

Jake was getting more grown-up by the day, thought Jack, as his son ditched the box and stuffed the bundles of cards like stolen banknotes into his pockets.

'It's babyish,' he explained, throwing the empty box back into the hall as they walked back the way they'd come.

Checking everything was all right with Mark's mum, Jack was soon on his way, briefly making a quick stop at a petrol station for a takeaway coffee and a cheese sandwich.

'Police food,' said Jack solemnly to himself as he expertly drank, ate, and drove back to the station with the odd feeling that they might just have got lucky.

It was another wet London night, cars whizzing by; a frenzy of people in motion, racing towards destinations – life in its entirety on the move. *Perhaps never content nor happy*, thought Jack, looking in his rear-view mirror at a sad-looking young man and his female passenger who kept turning towards him in what appeared an irritable exchange.

Pulling into the compound, he watched a couple of young constables coming off duty, their fresh faces yet to be scarred by a profession which took no prisoners, that often left you emotionally disabled or, if you were lucky, a reluctant actor who was able to manage an on/off switch. As two of the officers jostled one another, laughing as they got into their cars, he remembered the banter he used to have in the early days with his colleagues and how it slowly began to ebb away as you moved up the chain of command. Maybe he'd try a bit harder with Pencil, he thought as he got out the car and stepped in some discarded chewing gum.

Pencil was already there with two boxes of KFC and three freshly poured coffees waiting on his desk.

'For me?' asked Jack, catching his detective on the hop.

'Well, not the KFC, one's for me and the other's for . . .' he nodded towards the interview room, 'the suspect,' he added cagily. 'Hasn't eaten today.'

Christ, Jack wanted to rip shreds off him. The 'trying a bit harder' with his detective sergeant was definitely off the table.

'But the other coffee is for you,' said Pencil as if it were a consolation prize.

'Are you bloody serious? Are you having me on?'

His blood pressure on the rise, Jack took a deep breath. 'Christ, man! We're at the start of a murder investigation and you order a possible suspect a KFC?' he roared.

'Sorry, sir; it's just the desk sergeant is on his break and wouldn't be able to sort anything out until later . . .'

Sighing heavily, Jack downed his coffee in one, watching Pencil all the way as he fiddled with the doorknob before disappearing red-faced into the next room.

OK, think; play it simple, thought Jack, basic logistics, observations, no conjecture. Start with appearance.

Putting down his mug, Jack glanced at Pencil's notepad on the desk. It detailed pretty much what he had said on the phone. The poor bastard, he thought, he had read it word for word. In the left-hand corner, he'd written *notes for Jack* and in parenthesis had put *don't say sir – vary it!* – he'd even put a tick by the side of it.

'What's his name?' said Jack as his detective slunk back into the room like a wounded dog.

'You said to wait—' Pencil started.

'It's just basic police procedure, DS Sharpner – you should know. Anyway,' he continued, 'where's DS Evans?'

'Night off.'

'Just you and me, then. Better you just watch and learn for now,' he added, his tone slowly softening.

'His name's Brian Edwards, sir, the arresting officer took his name. I was just going to say before you . . .'

OK. He had jumped the gun a bit, thought Jack, but it was late, and he was grumpy.

Greasy shoulder-length hair, wisp of a moustache, Spurs football shirt (bloodied), black hoodie (undone), grimy jeans, nails bitten to the quick, blue Adidas trainers, head lowered, cigarette burning itself out in the ashtray, staring into an empty polystyrene cup.

'Brian Edwards – is that right?' asked Jack as Pencil pressed the record button.

'Yeah.'

Local: Cockney accent, pondered Jack, pretending to check the notes in front of him.

'And I understand you don't want a solicitor sitting in – is that right?'

'No; why would I?'

'Well,' said Jack, briefly turning to his detective and smiling, 'you do seem in a bit of a mess; I mean literally,' he added, nodding at the bloodstains.

'Well, that's a story.'

'Is it? Do tell,' said Jack, surprised by the early admission.

'No – fuck it!' said Brian, sitting upright and folding his arms protectively. 'You tell me!'

Thinking the sudden change odd, Jack went along with it anyway.

'So, Brian, you were arrested leaving the Forestdale Estate, covered in blood and with a concealed hammer in a plastic bag?'

'That's good; very fucking good.'

Maybe mental problems, thought Jack, deciding to keep things calm.

'Thanks for that, Brian.'

'No fucking problem.'

'Edwards: is that Welsh?'

'My dad; he's Welsh – the old shite.'

'Oh.'

'Bastard's back in Cardiff with some old slag.'

'Not a good relationship then?'

'No! So, tick that! End of! Change the subject, please.'

'OK, Brian,' said Jack, pausing briefly. 'Tell me what this is all about: walking through a council estate with a hammer – not going on a picnic, were you?' Maybe a bit sarcastic, he thought before continuing. 'I mean, it's a bit strange, isn't it, Brian?'

A hot head, impulsive and not too bright, thought Jack, awaiting a reply which seemed to take aeons coming.

'I like the idea of a picnic: clever,' he replied, annoyingly drumming the table. 'And that reminds me.' He was facing Pencil now. 'Where's my bloody KFC?'

'Later,' said Jack before his detective could reply. 'Well, Brian, what's your story – why were you there? Simple. That's all we want to know?'

'Really, you want to know about that?' He seemed to find this funny as he buried his head in his hands and said, 'I don't fucking believe this.'

Looking to Pencil and then back at Edwards, the anticipation of a spill had somewhat increased.

'Yes, about that . . .' replied Jack, the sweat on the back of his neck trickling down between his shoulder blades and soaking his shirt.

'Three pieces of chicken or one?'

'Three,' said Pencil before Jack could stop him.

'And dips?'

'Just sachets.'

'Sachets are fine. Ketchup?'

'Ketchup,' replied Pencil for the last time, having received one of Jack's hardest stares.

'OK!' Raising his voice just high enough to get things back

on track, Jack felt as if his detective and suspect had somewhat formed a promising comedy double act in his absence. 'Why all the blood, Brian?'

Lowering his head, Edwards seemed to be weighing up his options. Watching him tick, tock, the pendulum getting faster, Jack read him completely: a crazy, possibly psychotic guy who was going to make a full disclosure on the promise of a waiting KFC, which at this place in time was more important than anything else to him – including freedom.

'Look,' began Brian slowly, 'he had it coming.'

This could be it, thought Jack, having to stop himself from jumping in.

'Crossed me too many times.'

'Who?' asked Pencil, feeling brave and ignoring Jack's irritated turn in his direction.

'He used different names. Sometimes Barry, Steve, Martin, Deano,' he laughed.

'Dean,' said Jack with perhaps too much urgency.

'No, fucking Deano. I said Deano, didn't I?'

It's Dean, thought Jack, narrowing his eyes, as he sensed the winning goal was on the way. 'OK, Deano,' he replied.

'Yeah, but mainly Barry, or Steve, or Martin.' Again, he laughed at the mention of their names as if they were a joke only understood by a select group of people.

'Why did he have it coming, Brian?'

'Drugs,' he said flatly. 'He owed me.'

The rolled-up money in Dean Waters' mouth – maybe it *was* a debt? thought Jack, his mind racing. He had to get this right.

'He wouldn't pay you then?'

'You got it, Columbo. Christ, he's quick!' he said, addressing

Pencil. 'Now, it's not big stuff,' he added, 'just a bit of weed-dealing.'

'But you wanted to pay him back, show him who's boss – right?'

'Sure, of course – reputations and all that.'

'So, you killed him.'

'Who?'

'The one you left beaten to death with a rolled-up twenty stuffed in his mouth. That's how you paid him back – didn't you, Brian?'

'I wouldn't do that! I killed Bernard.'

'Bernard?'

'His dog: smashed its head in with the bloody hammer. That'll show the bastard.'

'What?'

'Barry, Steve, Martin, Deano, whatever his fucking name is, loved that stupid dog, was always out walking his mutt.'

'Are you kidding me?' His face reddening, Jack tried to hide his anger as his drenched shirt made him shiver.

'Nope.' Edwards was grinning now. 'Send someone round to 76 Elmore Gardens if you don't fucking believe me. End of.'

'Give him his bloody KFC,' said Jack, handing the file back to his detective as he made for the door and the evening which should have been his, but had come to a crushing, disappointing end.

Chapter Four

'**O**i, piss bag! Give us a bit of your Special Brew!'

'You'd have to wash your lips for a month, sharing a can with a penny stamp.'

Hot and sweaty; six o'clock on the Central Line heading west, the two inebriated youths began jeering and pushing the Scottish wino, who up until the arrival of the likely lads had been doing his own fair share of abusing passengers on what was proving to be a very slow, arduous journey.

'Yee fucking Cockney pricks.'

'Oh, yeah, fucking Rab C. Nesbitt, you want some?'

'I'd leave him alone; you don't want to catch anything,' said the least pissed of the two as the carriage slowly pulled into Mile End tube station.

'*There will be a brief delay while we change drivers,*' came the crackly intercom message as those who'd been stupid enough to remain in their seats, instead of changing carriages, watched on as the tramp reluctantly gave one of his cans to the nastier of the two youths, who after opening it and pretending to drink it, proceeded to pour the contents over the head of the growling

Scotsman. The youths laughed hysterically, the bigger one pushing the smaller one on to the lap of a young woman who blushed, got up, and moved further down the carriage to a safer seat.

Scared, sickened, embarrassed, unable to handle a frightening situation, the superficially superior City workers in their identical suits looked on, or, more to the point, didn't. They had instinctively avoided eye contact since the first arrival of the tramp, who had been doing the rounds screaming 'English bastards!' into the faces of those who would normally have dropped the odd pound into the polystyrene cup of a beggar. Now it was every man for himself. Even the couple of square-jawed young men, who had been full of bravado and 'Swing Low Sweet Chariot' at Stratford, were now tucking their chins in beneath the collars of their England rugby tops and wishing they'd stayed quiet, as the pleading eyes of expectant women passengers filled them with emasculating shame.

As the red-eyed, muttering tramp opened another hissing can, a temporary hush descended upon the train. An eerie, unwanted silence, the kind that spelt danger, that the next sound would somehow ignite extreme violence.

'The swinish multitude; the great unwashed,' came the crisp northern accent. 'The common people: a natural contempt for the lower classes, based on the supposition that their hygienic habits and behaviour are inferior to the upper and middle classes'. Tom, who was standing face to face with a large, distinguished solicitor-type in a pinstripe suit, his hoodie still up as it had been since leaving Stratford, was now rhythmically rocking on his heels as he muttered the last words of wisdom to the stranger. '*Abschaum*,' he said as the man briefly smiled, acknowledging the German for *scum*.

'Who the fuck are you?' barked the bigger of the two Cock-ney lads, as Tom ignored him, continuing his steady stare into the face of civility towering above him.

'Scared?' said Tom to the man, who swayed in the warm underground breeze. 'No?' he continued as the man remained silent. 'Well, you should be, oh, you should be.'

'English bastards!' shouted the tramp to no one in particular, as the two lads got ready to pounce; the smaller one nervously searching for something in his trouser pocket.

'You want me to sort it out, don't you?' said Tom inquisi-tively, looking deep into the man's soul for a spark of recognition. 'Yes, you do,' he laughed to himself, seeing for a split second the glint of a blade now in the hand of the little piece of shit to his left who wanted to cause misery and harm.

It wasn't just a brief scuffle. It was timed, deadly intent, deliv-ered effortlessly in a calm manner. A kick to the balls of the fool with the knife, bringing his face crunching down on to a pointed knee. Then a leaden punch to the stomach of the other one, and a shattering kick to the shin. He was soon face down with Tom's boot on the back of his neck, waiting to snap it, while the cowering wino scrambled for cover.

The eyes; always in the retina, that flash of excitement and fear. Now it was approval, a look that said: 'Go on, finish the bastards off!' The many men around them now wishing it had been them who had dished out the violence, as they sighed with relief and pumped out their not-so-manly chests. The women who'd looked to the 'Swing Lows' for an answer now found a superman and they didn't try to hide their smiling appreciation.

'Get the fuck off the train,' said Tom almost comically as he bundled off the two Cockneys, and the tramp as well, who was shouting for his cans. Tom retrieved them and threw them out on to the platform. One or two exploded before the cursing Scotsman.

As the doors closed, there was an unprecedented round of applause from the rest of the passengers; a few slaps on the back and whispered 'Thank you's from many of the commuters who'd lowered their eyes back to their crime novels and newspapers. The train doors temporarily opened again to a few disgruntled sighs as more passengers who'd just arrived on the District Line train opposite piled on. Taking his cue, Tom jumped off and made it across the platform to the waiting carriage, which magically pulled away as soon as he boarded.

Changing trains at Bow for the Docklands Light Railway, he raced with urgency towards the Thames-bound trains. After another laboriously slow ride, he alighted at Island Gardens. His heart pounding with elation and adrenalin, feeling as if he'd just won the war single-handed, Tom made for the exit, springing, running as if he was the fastest mammal on earth.

'Hey, where's your ticket?' yelled the inspector as Tom jumped the barrier and ran for the foot tunnel which led to Greenwich on the other side of the river. Faster and faster. Blood pumping, pushing him deeper into the cavernous hole. It was as if the world of the living had breathed on him, as the trapped air in the white-tiled tunnel smacked against his face the more he accelerated. Eventually reaching the end, he galloped up the spiral staircase and then jogged in an exaggerated way, saluting the *Cutty Sark* as he went.

On this side of the river, it was like he'd travelled back in time into Georgian England. The surrounding naval buildings and old Jack Tar bars were still very much the tapestry of the place. Even Tom's one-bedroom flat above the Blue Thunder chip shop had a plaque dedicated to the old seamen of the area who'd travelled and died in the far reaches of the Empire.

Letting himself in, Tom sniffed the air like an animal making sure a predator wasn't in its lair. Quickly scanning the sparse confines of his home, he stripped, dispensing with the previously concealed T-shirt, his gloves, jeans, and hoodie in a black bin liner. Making for the bathroom he stepped into the shower and waited for the cold, soon-to-be-warm water to hit his face. As it did he felt as if he'd just been slapped, as the jet began washing away the red stains of blood, turning them pink as they ran like slug trails down his legs. Closing his eyes he swayed to the rhythm of the pumping spray, warm, content, and satisfied.

As he dried himself, he thought of a lioness, standing triumphant as she proceeded to rip into the flesh of a defeated antelope, her mouth and whiskers caked in the blood of her victim. Tom licked his lips as he felt a longing for roast beef and Yorkshire pudding. Where was his victory feast? Were the images in his mind enough? Wiping a spot of blood from his thigh he examined it for a moment and contemplated licking it.

Dressing in a flurry he rushed to the kitchenette, where he snatched a slice of cold beef from the fridge and slapped it between two pieces of bread, wolfing it down in between long gulps of milk from the carton. Hunger satisfied, he proceeded to check the locks of the windows, look in the wardrobe and under the bed, while counting backwards from a hundred. Reaching number one, he opened the front door and was soon back outside in the winter chill, sporting a long navy overcoat, black trousers, and crisp white shirt. With his hair greased back, donning a red paisley scarf and black leather gloves, he stopped briefly at a newsagents where he bought some cigarettes and a five-pound bunch of flowers, then began to retrace his steps to the bright tunnel which led back to Island Gardens and the DLR.

Passing the ticket inspector again he winked and cheekily smiled, happy that the man's memory of him skipping the barrier had deserted him. After several changes and a minor delay at Bow Road, he found his way to Hackney, where his evening would, hopefully, begin.

Chapter Five

'If you ever get caught up in why people do terrible things, then you are probably someone who thinks a lot about your own personal security and what may happen or is possibly going to occur in the course of your lifetime. The problem is, you will more than likely get stuck in some kind of ethical backwater in which you will no longer know your arse from your elbow when the broken bodies begin flying at you with great speed from a conveyor-belt just above your head, twisted, ripped, bruised, and battered. And it doesn't really matter that it's not always the person you've marked down as the bad guy or woman who's going to commit the terrible — no, grotesque — deed. You see, we've all got pretty good at it and some of us are just a little better than most. Innocence only exists to be crushed, corrupted, and capitalised upon in the cruellest of ways. Isn't that how they see it — the ones who enjoy and are good at it?'

'Oh, shut up!'

Sally Drayton turned the car radio off. She was running late, and she couldn't listen to that self-entitled, pompous crime writer Penelope Watson any more. She certainly drew you in, and made you sit up and listen, as if what was being said was naturally of great importance and interest given the delivery and antiquated intonation of her oh-so-wonderful, upper-middle-class voice – but it really wasn't.

If only she hadn't volunteered to give that cute weirdo Tom a lift, she thought. Why, why, why? Just sometimes, just *once* – could I just say no? This she kept up as a continuous inner dialogue, almost a mantra, as the traffic slowed, sped up, then stopped again.

And then there was the other situation. What she referred to as her *betrayal of Pete* and one which she was fighting tooth and nail to keep a stand-alone, secret thing. Naturally, she played it back time and time again in her mind, and at the end of each painful re-run her mind routinely and predictably threw back up the word: *Betrayal! Betrayal! Betrayal!* On better days her mind was kinder as her intellect rationalised it as an innocent mistake, committed – no, fallen into – with no intention of causing hurt or betrayal. Sally Drayton: ordinary girl, dazzled by the bright lights and high culture of London's Art World – someone who'd fucked up.

Andy Murrow. I mean really, had she *really* heard Andy Warhol in her head as he deliberated and pontificated, as he showed her his art portfolio and later his studio in Chelsea?

Installation art – Jesus, how could she have been so easily taken in by his video of a sobbing Joseph Stalin? Stalin having ice-cream spooned on to his head, face, and uniform by a doctor as he was being licked clean by a cluster of Dalmatian puppies wearing hammer and sickle neckerchiefs – all as a red spotlight flashed on and off to the strains of Jimi Hendrix's 'Hey Joe'?

'You know, Sally?' he'd kept saying as they sat on huge Union Jack beanbags facing each other. 'All I see, hear, and feel is beauty when you're caught in my viewfinder.'

She should have thrown up then. Instead, she did that later, after the realisation of what she had done hit her.

At least she'd kept her top on, she tried to fool herself, and it had been quick – the beanbag having a mind all of its own, slipping, collapsing, and sliding every time they moved in unison, as if they were trying to untangle themselves in a tent on the side of a steep cliff.

Unison: a word she quickly decided should not make it into her vindictive word bank any more. She hadn't even been that drunk; just tipsy, though over-dosing on the compliments of Murrow, an accomplished artist who'd been their stand-in tutor in Media Installation Art. One drink in the pub had led to an invitation to a wine bar on the King's Road, and then the studio . . .

'But *Pete*,' she kept asking herself, 'how could I have?' She was in love for the first time, with a kind, uncomplicated giant who was literally always there for her. They had similar backgrounds, working-class parents – there were no Andy Murrow pretensions with Pete.

'But you had only been seeing him a week before the Andy Murrow thing,' Sarah had said. 'So it had only just started, you and Pete,' she had added, strangely pleased that Sally had joined her in the having-casual-sex department.

I suppose it was only a one-night stand. It was enough for her, Sally reasoned. *I'll never tell Pete*, she resolutely decided, *and I'll live with my guilt*. As she drove across London, she knew though that it would remain an unwanted soundtrack to her life.

When she eventually arrived home, Penelope Watson's cold observations resonated in her mind. She slapped the flat of her hand against her forehead, as if squishing an unwanted mosquito. '*And it doesn't really matter that it's not always the person who you have marked down as the bad guy or woman who's going to commit the terrible — no, grotesque — deed . . .'*

'It was a stupid one-night stand,' she snapped. 'So, fuck off!'

Wiping the tears from her eyes and taking a deep breath, she decided, as she had done many times before, to draw a line under it all.

Parking precariously, half on and half off the pavement outside 22 Spencer Drive, she naturally stalled the car as she thought of how her so-called friend Sarah had arrived back late from college with a new potential boyfriend in tow. It had soon become obvious that Sally was really in the way of whatever business they had in mind. Not only that, she'd lost an earring given to her by her late grandmother, which she was convinced she must have misplaced when startled by the noisy jackdaws at the alley by the launderette. Deciding to drive back to where she had stopped with Tom, she had been denied access by a police road block and told to move on. Then she'd hit the relentless traffic trailing back into the City. Now the only saving grace was the sure, reliable fact that she'd be seeing Pete, even if her joy at the thought had had to be hard fought for.

It was dark now. Struggling to peer into her bag for her house key, she cursed the council, who after a string of complaints from residents still hadn't fixed the streetlamp outside. Putting the key in the lock she was instantly met by Grunge the cat, who zig-zagged through her legs, nearly tripping her in the process as she entered the dark, damp-smelling hallway. Turning on the lights, the odour didn't quite match the brightly decorated orange and yellow walls of the one-bedroom ground-floor flat. At least the timer for the heating was working, thanks to Pete, who had worked it out on his last visit. Happy to be home, she made herself a cup of tea and ran the bath. Pulling the BT extension lead into the bathroom she placed the phone on a stool.

'Pete, it's Sally. Can you come over here tonight? I'm completely knackered,' she said, pulling off her leggings and stepping out of her mauve, hippy dress as she struggled with the receiver.

'Sure,' was Pete's lazy reply as he flicked over to *Can't Cook Won't Cook.*

'First there was that twat Tom, doing a detour, and then to top it off, Sarah decided she wanted to play happy couples with her new man and I lost my earring,' she ranted, now completely naked and checking the temperature of the bath.

Through her window Tom marvelled at the sight before him, there beyond the living room and the brightly lit orange hall to the open door of the bathroom where his Venus stood: the deathly white porcelain skin, her backbone sticking rigidly out as she arched her back to check the bathwater. The pink hair untied and draped, fallen like autumn leaves around her pearly white angular shoulders . . .

'So, you'll come round,' she said, pulling the extension lead of the phone nearer and sliding down into the bath. 'Oh, and bring some wine,' she added, dragging up her pink mane and pushing it behind her as it hung heavy over the back of the tub.

'Will do, Sal,' he said, watching Ainsley Harriott beating the living daylights out of some peppercorns in his pestle and mortar.

'Oh, and Pete?'

'Yeah.'

'Maybe leave Ainsley at home,' she laughed, closing the call and bringing her knees up to her chest as she slid down the bath, contented, until completely submerged. In the seconds that the pressure of the water held her head as if a cradle, she struggled with her betrayal of Pete. Holding her breath a little longer, she commanded it to leave as Andy Murrow's image threatened to drown her and then miraculously, in a *whoosh*, it temporarily disappeared.

Choices; actions; desires; calculations. Tom's eyes flitted back and forth from the cheap flowers he gripped in his hand to the top of Sally's pink scalp as he leaned heavily on the windowsill, his elbows wanting to sleep. 'Should I Stay or Should I Go?' by the Clash played in his mind as he smiled for the first time since he'd arrived, enjoying that quiet moment of contemplation prior to plucking an idea and turning it into either a nightmare or a normal convention. The impulse is always worse than the desire, he mused.

'Flowers or power?' he whispered as Sally rose from the bath like Venus, cloaking herself in a royal blue towel which made her appear paler.

In the bedroom, out of view from prying eyes, Sally quickly dressed, throwing on some old, ripped jeans and a black cap-sleeved T-shirt. Knowing Pete would be there in minutes, she applied some lipstick and pulled on a black hair band.

★

Taking off his tight leather gloves and briefly smelling them, Tom returned them to his coat pocket and ran his fingers through his greased dark hair. Whistling the tune of the Clash song, he turned Sally's silver earring between his fingers, before clutching it in his fist and blowing on it, as if about to throw some dice. 'Flowers or power?' he said again. As if his mind was suddenly made up, he softly stroked the tips of the limp flowers as he walked with intent down the side of the house towards the beckoning front door.

'Pete, thank God. What a shitty day,' Sally said, opening the door and flinging her arms around his big, rounded shoulders, as he stepped from the dark into the warm glow of the hallway, a bottle of wine sticking precariously out of his donkey-jacket pocket.

Outside, the hedge ominously shook as the Victorian paned-glass door slammed tight against the looming darkness. Tom crouched beside the foliage. It had been a near miss. If it hadn't been for his black attire, he'd surely have been spotted by the towering, broad-shouldered Pete Brown, who had spontaneously lurched into view just as Tom was about to make for the buzzer. Moving back down the side of the house to his original viewing post, he waited, watching as Sally now wrapped her body around the Herculean whose shadow quickened and spread across the ceiling. Turning away, Tom threw the flowers to the ground and mashed them with his heel into the mossy stone path. Taking his gloves from his pocket and slipping them back on, he reluctantly had one last glimpse of the lovers as they headed for the bedroom door, closing it dramatically slowly behind them as they went.

Feeling disappointed and spurned, he left the front garden. Instead of turning right and going back the way he'd come, he hesitated for a moment and turned the other way. Stopping by Sally's yellow Panda, poorly parked outside, he took a small piece of metal wire from his pocket and proceeded to fiddle with the driver's side lock until it magically flipped. Getting in, he hot-wired the ignition, gave it a soft rev, and gently pulled away with the lights turned off until he reached the main road, where he switched the main beam on and roared away aggressively at high speed, heading east. Reducing his speed, as if the acceleration had been a way of releasing the anger he'd felt back at Sally's, he calmly retraced much of the same route as earlier in the day. Within half an hour he was back in Stratford, the place he knew all along he'd be visiting that night. Although of course if Pete hadn't arrived it could have been all so different . . . Thinking of how fate tended to work perfectly for him whichever path he took, he marvelled at the power he perceived to be at his disposal.

Parking outside the East London University campus, he removed his crisp white shirt to reveal an *Eat the Rich* T-shirt underneath. Putting his overcoat back on, he left the car and headed for the Students' Union bar.

Ten o'clock, not bad, he thought to himself, checking his watch as he entered the dimly lit bar, which was pounding out Alanis Morrissette while showing highlights of Arsenal versus Newcastle. Pulling his hair back down into his usual scruffy quiff, he scanned the various tables of students, most of whom sported black garments in one form or another; mainly young men in hoodies and women wearing short flowery dresses with leggings and Doc Martens boots – it was a recognisable uniform of sorts.

'Dave!' he said, at last having located his evening's entertainment.

'Tom,' said the small, spotty, shaven-headed student, who gave the impression he'd only just managed to grasp or barely remembered Tom's name.

'Mind if I join yer?' Tom said, not waiting for a response as he sat down and nodded in the direction of a cosy pair who were sitting jammed tight together, as if joined at the hip. 'Were you two at the meeting as well?' he started, addressing the girl and boy he didn't know.

'No,' they both said. It was obvious they were a couple.

'Oh, I just thought . . . because you're with Dave . . . that you were?' he said, taking off his overcoat to show off his *Eat the Rich* T-shirt. 'What are your names?'

'I'm Lucy and this is Luke.'

'What meeting?' Luke asked as they all looked up briefly to the flashing TV screen to catch Ian Wright celebrating a tap-in.

'The SWP,' he said finally with a hint of menace, as if seeking out a traitor in their midst.

'No, we're anarchists,' said Luke as they both giggled. So, it was probably a lie and an attempt at flippancy, which Tom instinctively latched on to.

'I suppose that's why you're both at university then?' said Tom as he winked at Dave, who stared uninterested into his pint. 'Do anarchists accept purchased drinks?' he asked Dave, who didn't answer, as the couple ceased their irritating *tee-hees*, a little thrown by the sarcasm of the enquiry. 'Do you all want a drink or not?' he finally announced, smiling broadly as the others followed suit. Pints bought, they engaged in the usual student shit-speak: secondary reading lists, and pompous statements stolen from the mouths of their God-like lecturers, as they peppered their conversation with expert criticism of just about everything: feminist, Marxist, classicist, even existential theories as to whether Britpop actually existed at all.

'You two live on campus?' asked Tom after a lull in the conversation and aware that last orders was well and truly past, as the barman began to annoyingly clear away empty glasses around them.

'No, in a shared house across the road,' Lucy said innocently.

'And Dave: where do you live? Can't believe I've never asked you before,' he said, playing with his fringe.

'I've got to get me bus,' Dave said solemnly before saying, 'Upton Park.'

'Oh, that's not too far away; I'm at Stratford, I'll give you a lift,' he said firmly, to which Dave just nodded. 'Hey, look,' he continued, addressing the other two. 'I've got a couple of spliffs. Do you want to go for a smoke?' he said, tapping his breast pocket, thinking that they'd jump at the chance.

Tom had already captured the glance of the girl and spotted the nudging of her boyfriend's knee with hers to know the answer, as he simply said, 'Another time.' Rather that than listening to them concocting an elaborate lie.

'Dave, you ready?'

'Ready.'

Outside it was clearly past throwing-out time as distant shouts, manic drunken laughter, and singing could be heard, accompanied by a chorus of distant dog barking and a long drawn-out cry of 'Shearer!'

'Here, jump in,' said Tom disguising the fact that he was using a piece of wire to open the driver's side. 'So,' he continued, climbing in, twisting the end of a spliff and popping it into his mouth, 'you hate the Tories as much as I do?' He knew he sounded like a baddie out of a Bond film. Lighting the end, he waited for a reply that seemed ages coming as he inhaled deeply.

'Yeah, fucking Tories,' Dave agreed at last, taking the proffered joint expertly, like a surgeon receiving a scalpel, as he too took a deep, satisfying lug.

'Do you always just agree, Dave? Is that how you go on: agreeing?'

'Oh, no,' replied Dave, a little put out.

'You're working-class, right?' he said, changing tack and retrieving the joint.

'Yeah,' said Dave, knowing he'd have to supply a bit more as Tom looked on expectantly. 'My old man used to work at the Albert Docks, before joining the production line at Ford's, Dagenham plant.'

'It's closed now, right?' Tom's tone was interrogational rather than friendly.

'Yeah,' answered Dave, aware that *yeah* wasn't enough.

'You're the first in your family to go to university then?'

'I am – and you?' he said, feeling brave.

'Oh, yeah: miner's son. None of the generation before me went. Only went and fought in bloody wars and dug coal for the bastards.'

'Yeah, the bastards.'

'You're repeating again, Dave,' Tom said, giving him a sharp dig with a biro pen he'd been turning between his fingers.

'Hey!'

'Come on, don't get upset, I'm only messing with yer,' he laughed, smoking some more and passing it over, which seemed to make up for the jab.

'Thanks,' said Dave, rubbing his arm and getting more paranoid by the second, his head turning to mush as the resin kicked in.

'So, do you have a lot of friends, Dave – I mean at uni?'

'Not really, mainly old friends.'

'Like you then – ordinary.'

'Yeah, I suppose.'

'Mum and dad, they must have found it strange; you know, mixing with intellectuals.' He laughed at this.

It was probably the drugs, but Dave appeared to have drifted off to some far corner of the globe.

'Hey!'

'Sorry . . . I was miles away,' he managed, rubbing his bleary eyes.

'You really need to keep up,' said Tom, checking his rear-view mirror. 'So, tell me, are you going on the Troops Out march at the weekend?'

'No . . . I have a deadline on Monday.'

'A deadline, Dave? As in an assignment – an essay?'

'Yeah, Monday.'

'Do you know what I do with deadlines, Dave? I tell them to fuck off! I tell them –' now prodding Dave with the pen – 'to –' prod –'fuck –' prod – 'off!' Tom said, eventually letting his serious tone and demeanour slip to a more amiable one as he burst out laughing.

'Fuck off, will yer!' shouted Dave, perturbed while at the same time making it appear like a bit of playground fun, which he wanted to put a stop to.

'Oh, Dave, I barely know you, but I can tell you're a funny one.' Now putting the pen behind his ear, Tom smiled broadly as he expertly started up the engine without a struggle or the wires being seen. 'I'd better get you home; it's getting late,' he began as Dave tried to say that he could still get the bus. 'Upton Park, isn't it?' he continued, ignoring his passenger as he reached across and clunk, clicked his seat belt.

'We want to get you home safely, now, don't we, petal,' he said, patting him on the knee. Dave flinched at the touch.

Chapter Six

'Pepperoni with no olives.'

    'No, with.'

'Sorry, Jake. We've got some in the kitchen,' Jack said, rising stiffly.

'Dad, don't bother, it's all right.'

'No, Jake, where there's pizza there has to be olives. Just a jiffy,' Jack said, making quick time to the adjacent kitchen.

'Well, OK then – if it's only a jiffy,' shouted Jake after him.

'Right,' he said, returning from the kitchen, sitting down and opening a big jar of black olives, placing them on the Moroccan coffee table, as Jake switched TV channels and a black–and–white movie flickered in the corner of their nicely cluttered front room. 'Ah, this is *Blackboard Jungle* with Glenn Ford. He teaches a class of delinquent teenagers in Brooklyn. Because his name is Mr Dadier they call him Daddy-O,' said Jack, opening his own pizza box and scooping up a slice of American Hot with extra garlic.

'Right,' Jake replied, kicking off his trainers and bringing his knees up to his chin. They were waiting for *Star Wars* to start.

'Sorry about yesterday, Jake,' Jack said as an afterthought, trying desperately to escape the memory of Dean Waters' detached eyeball.

'It was fine, Dad. Sergeant Evans was very nice. She used to be a model.'

'Did she now?' he said, raising an eyebrow as Glenn Ford wrestled a switchblade off one of his students.

'And she hasn't got a boyfriend.'

It was a noticeable pattern. More and more it seemed that when Jake met a single woman he wouldn't stop dropping hints to his dad. Jack reasoned that it was only natural that his son wanted a new mummy, although it still made him feel uneasy every time it happened. And then of course there was his age to consider: forty-five plus.

'Dad, it's Skuld,' said Jake excitedly as the key could be heard turning in the latch. Skuld was the main surrogate substitute that Jake had in mind and his father knew and fought it, despite his own feelings. Their Icelandic au pair was thirty. A little odd at times and quite old for her chosen profession, she could switch quickly from playfully happy to moody and stern. Stereo-typically Scandinavian with fair hair, a tiny turned-up nose, and rosy cheeks, she was an unwanted distraction for Jack, who felt guilty no matter which woman turned his head. It was the sexual tension in the house when Jake had gone to bed which troubled him most. The awkward moments of bumping into her on the landing at bedtime in her pyjamas; the odd glimpse of her in a towel in the bathroom mirror as he climbed the stairs, tired and emotional, to bed, and feeling like a dirty old man each time. And of course, there had been the times when she'd tended to him on the couch during his drunken stupors, placing a bowl beside his head, taking off his socks, and covering him with a blanket. She was very much a part of the emotional fabric of the house. Jake of course loved her.

Even back then, drunk, sad, and incoherent, the feel of her touch as she gently cradled his aching, spinning head had made an indelible print on his soul. He had traced her soothing smile through the haze of his helpless gaze. At times, pleading for clarity, to be free of the hold that drink had over him, he had wished himself younger, sober (naturally), and starting out on a new journey together with her.

'*Jack, it doesn't have to be like this. Maybe we have a way?*'

Whether Skuld had said it or not, he'd clung to what was either prophetic or a drunken slur of an apparition, dancing mockingly before him. And although he fought against it, he couldn't stop himself from not seeing her through a domestic viewfinder. Never comparing her to Mandy, he was nonetheless seeing her more than someone who cooked and cleaned, her attractiveness and charm were a light to his darkness. Her slow movement as she effortlessly swept through their home made him desire her more as he struggled to decipher what he perceived in her gaze, as if it were somehow tangled up in her expectant blue eyes. The silent awkwardness which at times was so deafening, sitting feet apart on a sofa, lost and yet found in seemingly mutual longing for one another, drove him to despair. It was as if the tension would somehow bring them together. And then there had been Jake's birthday . . .

'We all have to hold hands,' his son had declared as they stood around the lit cake. 'Like we used to with Mum.' It was the first time Jack had held Skuld's hand and he'd almost cried – yes, because of Mandy; because of his son's need for family moments; but more for the intimacy of a woman's touch. This woman's touch. It was only a glance, a smile, and maybe Skuld was playing along for Jake's sake, but he held on to it nonetheless, as an aging fool or as an honest man who realised he needed more than just the drink and a lifetime of policing.

Skuld was full of wise Icelandic sayings. 'Everyone wants to be a lord, but no one wants to carry the bag,' she would suddenly say, commenting on some news item on TV or life in general as Jake would throw his dad a playful look. One of her favourite sayings they particularly liked was, 'I took him to the bakery,' meaning 'I kicked his arse!'

'Skuld!' cried Jake as she burst into the room clutching an array of shopping bags.

'This is for you and this is for you,' she said, handing out two bags before slumping down on the sofa.

'Hats,' cried Jake, pulling on a woollen monkey hat with furry ears. 'Put yours on, Dad,' he insisted as his father reluctantly put on a brightly patterned dog cap with hanging flaps.

'Just like in Iceland,' she laughed.

'Thanks, Skuld, you shouldn't have.' Jack smiled as he asked her if she would like some pizza.

'No, I ate with Jelka.'

'So your friend's gone back then?'

'Yes.' She had returned to being affirmative Skuld. This happened intermittently and was partly due to their overuse of phrasal verbs. 'I have to change and then go bathe,' she said out of the blue, suddenly getting up and standing to attention.

'Right,' said Jack, blushing, then eyeing his son for a reaction. Jake was trying not to laugh.

'I have to go, bye.'

'Bye,' they both said.

Settling down to watch the beginning of the film, dad and son in stationary bliss, munching crisps and nuts, sat beside each other, bonded by the sense of doing nothing. Jake knew his father was off to the station at eight, so was milking every minute, asking if he could stay up late with Skuld to watch the rest of *Star Wars* if he got into his pyjamas early.

'I don't mind, but you'll have to ask Skuld first.'

'That's just brill,' said Jake, nuzzling into his father's shoulder, knowing that Skuld would happily let him stay up all night.

The cosy, safe TV and sofa time soon ebbed away, and before he knew it Jack was alone and heading back towards the city, driving with ease and strangely slowly for someone who was just beginning a new case. Still smarting from the goose chase of the previous day, Jack had reluctantly gone over the new ironed-out story of how Brian Edwards had beaten Bob Barnes' (not Barry, Steve, Martin, or Deano's) dog to a pulp. With Edwards no longer a suspect he was released on bail, having been charged with extreme animal cruelty and possession with intent to supply. A distraught Bob Barnes was receiving counselling and had been let off with a caution, having been found with a small amount of hash.

Although annoyed at the wasted time and resources, Jack was at least pleased it was behind him. Being in the game for so long had to a degree drained his enthusiasm and general interest in police procedure, which was pretty much the same whatever the case even the weird ones. That said, once started he was like a dog with a bone; he'd shake it and chew it until every piece was consumed. That was probably why he'd become such a slow starter. He'd seen and heard too much and had bored of the usual lines of enquiry.

As he drove, the evening appeared to hang heavy, its inky blackness covering the congested, huddled, hanging buildings as if submerged beneath the sea, each street symmetrical as if part of a runway leading to the centre of the city. The darkness on each side of the road was like a blackened smudge. The centre was littered with red rear lights, forming orderly queues, their exhaust pipes fuzzy in the dazzle and blanket of night. Opening his window wide, Jack sniffed the night air as he made the traffic lights before they glowed red. Watching an old lady pulling a trolley bag behind her, it was as if there were suddenly pockets of human activity the darkness had failed to blot out. Winding up his window, Jack turned on the radio and landed on Procol Harum's 'A Whiter Shade of Pale', which he floated on all the way to the station where he despondently parked up.

'Pencil, tell me something new? And no more bloody junkie dog-killers,' was Jack's request upon entering the operations room that evening, before flopping down at his desk. 'Any leads?' he said, sensing that Pencil, although a reasonably good detective, wasn't, to pardon the pun, always the sharpest tool in the box.

'Nothing that really stands out, sir.'

I'll let him have that one, thought Jack, noting his detective's hesitation at the end of the sentence as he'd glanced at him for approval or disapproval.

'Just tell me what you've got,' he said slowly, trying to hide his irritation. 'Anyone seen in the area?'

'Not in Langley Road, sir, but a yellow car was spotted by a man walking his dog in the street that runs parallel to it. Sabine Road.'

'But what links the car to the murder scene?'

'Sir?'

'To Langley Road.'

'Oh, sorry, sir; the alleyway – there's an alley that links both Sabine Road and Langley Road. The car was seen parked by the alley around the time of death. The man said the driver was a woman.'

'Anyone else in the car?'

'No, sir.'

'She could have been waiting for the suspect?'

'Yes, sir.'

He can't help it, thought Jack, wrestling with the *sir* situation again and coming to the conclusion that he'd probably just have to tolerate it.

'What else? What about Dean Waters; what do we know about him?'

'Twenty-two years old; student; attending London South Bank University; living at his gran's house while she lives five doors down with his parents.'

'So, the gran is being looked after by ...?'

'Her daughter; she can no longer look after herself.'

'While Dean gets his independence by living in his gran's house?'

'So it seems, sir.'

'Cheaper than finding student accommodation in South London.'

'His dad said he wanted to be around his family and friends.'

'Not your usual student then?'

'No, sir.'

'What about a girlfriend?'

'Nothing serious. According to his family he'd never really had a steady girlfriend.'

'In trouble before: drugs; anything?'

'No, sir: clean.'

'Anything more on the stamp?'

'No, sir.'

'So, all we really have so far is a girl in a yellow car: a possible accomplice or acquaintance, or just a coincidence. And a stay-at-home student.'

'Yes, sir.'

'Speak to some of his uni pals. See if they've noticed anything different of late: change of mood, acting strange, any new people on the scene – the usual.'

'Yes, guv.'

'Anything back from Forensics: hairs, fingerprints, saliva, fluids of any type?'

'No, sir.'

'He, and we're supposing it's a *he* because of the brutality and force of the assault, was wearing gloves.'

'Planned attack.'

'Very good, Pencil. Yes, a planned attack.' He smiled, thinking his own son could have easily come to the same conclusion, but pleased that he'd at least temporarily dispensed with the *yes, sirs*. 'And the twenty-pound note could mean anything or nothing; though I think we've eliminated drugs as there was nothing found at the scene or in his system, right?'

'Right.'

'Now, if I'm correct,' Jack said pensively, 'I don't think this is a one-off. The smudged stamp is inconclusive; he wanted to tell

59

us some kind of story and he failed. The murder, the ferocity of the assault, is somehow linked to that ink smudge.'

'There's a motive in the story.'

'Yes,' Jack sighed, because he could sense that Pencil was becoming a little bit flowery in his observations. He pondered a moment, biting a nail and then examining it. 'I want to talk to the parents myself. We'll go now – offer our condolences, that sort of thing.' Pencil eagerly nodded his head. 'Right, get your coat, we're going back to Bow,' Jack said, relieved that police procedure had at last exhausted itself and that some kind of action was taking place.

DS Sharpner was one of the best drivers on the Met. He had a maximum reflex stat of ninety-eight per cent, had never crashed a patrol car, and had won every car chase in his time without a single smash or fatality to his name. Even so . . .

'Slow down, Pencil, please,' growled Jack, who was feeling the effects of the American Hot with extra garlic bubbling up inside him.

'Sorry, guv, I get carried away sometimes,' he said proudly.

'And park in Sabine Road; I want to walk through the alley.'

'Yes, sir,' he replied, slowly turning right so as not to upset his boss. He managed to find a spot outside the launderette.

'Right, let's walk.'

Alleyways: sinister dark places. Nothing good happens in an alley, except rubbish bins being emptied, mused Jack as he stopped briefly with Pencil at his shoulder to examine an old boot he'd almost tripped over.

'The alley's already been checked, guv,' said Pencil, anticipating his boss's next question as Jack kicked the boot roughly to one side and gruffly mumbled, 'Good.'

There were definitely two Jacks: impatient Detective Chief Inspector Jack and caring, fun-loving, dad Jack. Now he was the warm convivial one of the two as the two detectives entered the solemn front room of the Waters' three-up, three-down red brick terrace.

'I'm so sorry,' said Jack, clutching with both hands those of the parents whose distant stares said it all, as he too fought with his own demons all over again. 'I know it's not an appropriate time and we can come back another day,' he continued, 'but we really want to catch who did this.'

'No, it's fine,' said Dean's dad. 'Do you want to stay, love?' he asked his wife, who had a twisted, startled expression across her face. She simply shook her head and shuffled out of the room. 'She's in bits; she'll never get over this.'

'I know,' said Jack, knowing that they'd both never be the same people they were twenty-four hours ago.

'Only twenty-two.' Jack let Mr Waters continue as they sat down. He wanted it to evolve naturally without too much interruption or probing on his part. 'The first in the family to go to university. We were so happy when he got in. I'm a brick-layer, you see; was so pleased that he wouldn't have to freeze his bollocks off on a site. Dead proud,' he added, grimacing at having said *dead* in the same breath as being *proud*.

'And he wanted to remain with his family when he went to college?' asked Jack softly.

'Oh, yes, he wanted to stay with his mates, said he couldn't relate to a lot of the other students.'

'What was he studying?'

'Psychology.'

The irony, thought Jack, stroking his chin and deciding that he didn't really want to press the honest man any further.

'He was a quiet lad – never any bother. You know, down to earth,' Dean's dad said as he glanced at a school photograph on the mantelpiece. 'Just normal.'

'I'm really sorry.'

'It's OK. It's the way of the world,' he replied solemnly, now staring lost at another photograph of what looked like a holiday snap of Dean taking part in a Donkey Derby.

'Mr Waters,' Jack said, rising, 'there's not much I can say about your son's murder at the moment, only that I promise you and your wife that I shall do all that I can to find who did this.'

Pencil reluctantly got to his feet, towering above everyone else, his head almost touching the low ceiling, a little bamboozled as to why Jack hadn't asked more questions.

'So sorry,' repeated Jack, again holding out his hand. 'I hope you get your son back soon,' he said. 'I'll find out what's happening,' he concluded, knowing that pathologists could be terribly meticulous and annoyingly slow. As they said their solemn goodbyes he glanced back down to the kitchen, where Mrs Waters stood motionless, cradling what looked like an old school jumper.

'I couldn't quiz the poor man too much,' admitted Jack, relieved to be outside in the cold night air. 'Sometimes you just have to know when to call it a day.' His colleague merely nodded. 'Pencil, I think I'm going to go straight home after you've dropped me off at the station,' he said as the sergeant closed the gate behind them and they headed back to the alley. 'I think we have enough for now; just follow up on the people in the area that he already knew.'

'And the girl.'

'Yes, and the girl,' replied Jack, scanning the now dark alley as they came to the car. 'Although I think we're only going to find out more when he strikes again.'

After leaving the station the drive home had been a surprisingly enjoyable ride. The light drizzle and sparkling streetlamps had made the Mile End Road appear magical, like a mini New York suburb (if that was possible). Of course, the jazz helped: Dexter Gordon's recording of 'Three O'Clock in the Morning' wafting warm and melancholic, a clear, dreamy saxophone to soothe the most hardened of bastards. Pulling into the same streets he'd grown up in, Jack felt a longing for his past surroundings and the simple life he now lived with his son and he'd have to say Skuld as well; although of course he found the feeling a difficult one. Two lives, he thought to himself, parking outside his house and turning off the ignition, observing the flashing TV through the chink in the curtains of his front room.

Luckily, apart from the tragedy with Chris, he never took his work home with him. Mandy always used to remark to other officers' wives, whose husbands would drink and become silent, how Jack simply switched off once he'd walked through the door. 'The perfect police husband,' she'd say.

'Skuld?'

She was fast asleep on the sofa, her knees pulled up tight to her chest, exposing her legs sprouting from her dressing-gown. Taking his coat off, he gently tucked it around her legs, more out of a need to protect his eyes than to keep her warm. Sitting down at the far end of the couch, he kicked off his shoes and took a handful of dry roasted nuts which were still left over from earlier. Reaching to the coffee table for his latest edition of *Boxing Monthly*, he turned to an article he'd been reading on new upcoming British boxers. It was a sport he loved; he was fascinated by the planning of a fight: when to up the pace, when to hold back, when to attack. Like birdwatching, it was a distraction.

'I was just dreaming,' said Skuld, suddenly stretching, her toe jabbing Jack's thigh. He nearly choked on a nut at the touch. 'Oh, I'm sorry,' she said, quickly retrieving her leg and sitting upright.

'It's OK' he replied, feeling a little embarrassed.

'Thank you for the lend of your coat,' she added, now folding it and draping it over the back of the sofa. 'Just like in Iceland,' she added now, pointing at his socks. 'Because of the ice, boots are always left outside.'

'Oh,' he laughed, at first wondering what she was on about.

'In Seyðisfjörður, the snow can be so high even a bear-man couldn't open the house door.'

Skuld didn't really talk about her homeland much. Jack knew only that her family had moved away from the north-east of the country to Reykjavik, to escape the desolate weather of Seyðisfjörður where they were originally from.

After several minutes of awkward conversation on his part, in which he'd managed to find out what time Jake had gone to bed and that they'd watched the rest of *Star Wars*, he and Skuld both settled down to saying very little, watching a wildlife programme, which was fine until a troop of baboons began mating with each other, at which point an embarrassed Jack slipped out to the kitchen and made himself a sandwich. Returning a while later he was relieved to see the apes fighting among themselves.

'It's OK, they've finished now,' announced Skuld, watching one of the monkeys push another one out of a tree. 'They're playing now,' she added as Jack blushed a deep purple, knowing he'd been found out.

He should have known. Why was a man in his forties, with a ten-year-old son and a responsible job, acting and feeling like a shy inexperienced teenager? He was so obviously attracted to her, his growing infatuation making him feel that a middle-aged man should know better, instead of seeing it for what it purely was: the need, the desire to be intimate again.

'Do you think you'll stay in England?'

Why did he ask that? he thought. He could have asked her if she liked David Bowie or something more mundane.

'Yes, I think,' she said, reaching for her white wine. 'Though I can't get skyr,' she added, giggling.

'Oh, yeah' said Jack, remembering a long drawn-out description by Skuld which determined that it was an Icelandic dairy product, thick and creamy, looking something like yogurt and cream cheese.

'Yes, I miss Iceland,' she said, her mind as if on a snowbound, windswept fjord.

'Didn't you have a boyfriend back home?' He really was losing the run of himself. For the time that Skuld had been with them, he'd never asked her about her private life and had certainly avoided this line of enquiry.

'No, I wanted to find an English man,' she said, her blue eyes a little wider than usual as if being accused of something.

'So, I guess you're staying put then?' he said, clumsily pulling loose his tie.

'Yes, staying put,' she laughed, aware that she was copying his speech patterns. 'And you, Jack, what will you do with your life?' she said earnestly as her cheeks flushed.

Some men get confused when around beautiful women. They no longer know who they are or what the right answer is when pressed for one. Jack was no different. What she had asked could have meant so many different things and yet he naturally bumbled and fell at the first hurdle. He knew he desperately needed companionship, but to actually say it coherently would be nigh impossible as he felt his vocal cords tighten and close.

'It's OK, Jack, don't say anything.' She was now turned completely around, cross-legged and leaning in towards him, tears in her eyes. 'I know the hard times you've had.'

At that moment he wanted to wrap her in his arms and press his mouth passionately on to hers. He needed to let go of all the hurt, the frustration; to release the neurosis which men like him carried around with them for most of their lives. He wanted to be free of the past.

'Jack, you all right?' she said, placing a hand on his shoulder. He'd frozen; he couldn't answer; he suddenly felt like a completely helpless, vulnerable child, as he thought of his ninth birthday, when his mother and father had given him his first ever watch; how many years later, after his dad's sudden diagnosis with cancer, his father had drifted away so quickly he could hardly count the time it took – seeing only a blur and then a big black hole. One day he was there and then he was gone – it was all he could remember.

'Jack? It is all right.'

They were the last words spoken for what seemed a lifetime as she moved closer, took his hand in hers, and kissed him. As the tears welled up in his eyes, she pulled him closer. Trembling, he let her guide him as she unbuttoned his shirt.

It had been quick, intense, grappled for, a chain reaction, an exchange of longing necessity which brought them both to the rushed only outcome, arrived at in an explosion of need. His head now resting on her chest, as she stroked his brow, Jack was temporarily free. He had yet to say a single word, wanted to savour the silence, the warmth, the intimacy, without interrupting its magic.

Skuld was the first to speak.

'Jack?'

'Skuld,' he said, glad to hear his own voice again.

'We have a saying in Iceland,' she began, 'would you like to hear it in English?'

'Of course,' he said, afraid to move in case she stopped playing with his hair.

'*He doesn't walk whole to the forest.*'

'You mean me?' he laughed.

'Well, yes,' she giggled, kissing his cheek, 'but now, you do walk whole to the forest.'

Chapter Seven

'Upton Park is that way,' pointed Dave, wriggling in his seat, his brow visibly streaked with beads of sweat.

'I know; I have to pick up some placards for the march at the weekend.'

'Oh.'

'The one you're not going to!' Tom spat with venom, before bursting out laughing again, which given the strength of the joint and the amount they had both consumed wasn't surprising or out of the ordinary. They headed out towards the Albert Docks, where Dave had said his father used to work. 'Your dad's old stomping ground,' he said with a hint of sarcasm, which Dave didn't notice or answer. 'Oi, I'm talking to yer!' he snarled, jabbing him with the pen which had made a sudden comeback.

'Hey! Cut it out, will yer! You fucking psycho.'

'That's not very nice, Dave,' he said, making light of the prodding, 'to call someone a psycho,' he added as if hurt. 'Here, light this up,' he ordered, throwing him another spliff. 'Good stuff, hey?' he said after a while. Dave lit it and inhaled hard, more out of desperation than anything else as he was forced to answer this time and delivered a quick 'yeah'.

'You don't mind smoking my blow, do you, Dave?'

Again, Dave replied instantly. 'Trippy,' he said, which Tom seemed pleased with as they drove in total silence, inhaling and exhaling in a rich Moroccan fog.

Abruptly pulling into a piece of wasteland dotted with derelict outbuildings, Tom brought the car skidding to a halt, as if performing an emergency stop on his driving test.

'Here we are, Dave,' he said, turning off the ignition and tapping Dave's knee with the ever-present biro. 'Give us a hand with the placards, will yer?' he said, putting on his leather gloves.

'Sure,' Dave said, stoned, staggering out of the Panda.

'This way,' he beckoned as they both walked and kind of floated towards the dark concrete ruins. Getting closer, Tom suddenly stopped and turned around as if randomly deciding to confront him. 'What yer call me?' he said coldly, taking a step forward.

'N-nothing,' stammered Dave.

'Yes, you did – called me a fucking psycho.'

'I was ...'

'No, hold on, Dave. I'm going to give you a chance here, not to speak in circles. Did you or didn't you call me a psycho?' he now asked calmly.

'Well ... yes,' he admitted, now shaking as a cold gust of wind suddenly blew.

'Do you want to fight me, Dave?' he continued, doing a little shuffle. 'Man to man – so to speak,' he laughed.

Feeling sick and scared by the suggestions, Dave just shook his head, taking two steps back.

'Come on, Dave,' Tom said, now moving forward, his fists raised like a gentleman boxer. 'Hit me – right here,' he motioned, jutting out his chin, 'free punch.'

Dave hesitated for a second, wondering what he should do next, the tension and weirdness of the situation driving him to tears. 'Please stop,' he blubbed. Tom mimicked his plea as he lightly slapped him across the cheek with the flat of his hand. The wind whistled and whirled around them.

'What would yer old man say, eh, Dave? "Let 'im 'ave it, son; hit 'im!" How about this, Dave?' Tom said, slapping him harder, this time on the other cheek. 'You like that – you like being beaten, don't you; you fucking love it,' he snarled, smacking him harder.

'Please don't,' quivered Dave as Tom hit him with more ferocity.

Stopping and lowering his fists, Tom gave the impression that maybe the nastiness was over. 'Say you love me, and I'll leave you alone,' he said suddenly.

Rooted to the ground, Dave considered his options. Like a trapped animal he thought of running; doing as he was asked or remaining silent.

The authority of God, thought Tom, excitedly awaiting the outcome of the conundrum, tossed like a bone to a whimpering dog as Dave trembled.

'So, you don't love me then?' he snapped, now using the pen again as he poked Dave hard in the stomach. He already knew the next words his victim would utter.

'I love you; I love you!' Dave screamed, cowering and covering his body as best he could as Tom let the pen spitefully dig a bit more.

70

The steady wind was now accompanied by a relentless spray which bounced off the banks of the Thames and was now falling in lashing sheets of rain all around them.

'What are you, queer or something, Dave – you want to fuck me?' he said mockingly, his wet quiff now completely covering his wild eyes.

'No,' was all he could manage.

'Yes, you are – say you're queer. No, let's correct that – not very PC, is it, Dave? People who attend university don't say words like that, do they? Say you're gay. Yeah, that's much better. Say you're gay!' The slapping had started again as Dave began to back-pedal on his heels. 'Say it!' (Slap) 'Say it!' (Slap)

'But I'm not!'

'Say it!' (Slap)

'OK, I'm gay!' Dave cried, falling to his knees, sobbing like a child and holding his head in his hands. 'I'm gay!'

Having his answer, Tom stood like Superman, hands on hips, waiting to pass down judgement on the head of the grovelling, broken, drenched young man before him. Lifting his foot and swinging it hard he kicked Dave flat in the face. The nose bone crunched, and snot and blood flew to one side like a paint splat on a Jackson Pollock canvas.

7.30 a.m. The alarm bell ringing in his head sounded from next door. Startled, Jack looked around him at the discarded clothes, the empty bottle of wine on the bedside table, and then lastly Skuld's naked hip protruding like a mound of fine white sand from the strewn duvet. 'Shit,' he said, stumbling out of the unfamiliar bed, and reaching for his pants, shirt, and trousers.

Closing the door quietly behind him, Jack looked in the direction of his son's ajar bedroom door. Hugging his teddy Alfie tight, Jake counted a few numbers out loud and turned over into his digit dream as Jack scurried on to his blue and grey en suite bathroom. Relieving himself and showering, he quickly shaved and put on some clean work clothes, which really amounted to his second grey suit, blue shirt, and brown tie. Tiptoeing downstairs he could hear Jake yawn loudly.

In the sanctuary of the kitchen, he made some coffee and got Jake's cereal ready. Catching his reflection in the glass frame of a photograph which captured a family trip to Legoland, he felt sad. Remembering the wonderful day they had and of course Mandy's smiling face, which gazed out at him, he wondered what she would have made of last night. Pouring the hot water into the cafetière, he smelt the heavenly aroma of French coffee. Stirring it, he was surprised that he didn't feel guilty; knew deep down that Mandy would have wanted him to move on with his life and have a normal relationship again. The sadness he felt was a strange, warm, melancholic feeling, one that wasn't unwelcome in any way; perhaps the kind of emotion you experience when you move on, he pondered, smiling to himself as the first positive thought of the morning entered his head.

'Jack, morning,' said Skuld neutrally, briefly kissing him on the cheek and squeezing his shoulder as she passed.

'Morning,' said Jack, as if he was addressing the postman.

'Don't be embarrassed,' she said suddenly turning to face him. 'A coward will never bed a pretty woman,' she added teasingly, 'it's an old Icelandic saying.'

'Come here, you,' he said, pulling her close as if returning to

72

the mould of her warm body where he'd just slept. 'I think you took me to the bakery last night,' he whispered as their mouths realigned, opening and closing once more together like clams in a simmering sauce.

'Dad! Skuld!'

'Jake,' said Jack, untangling himself and for some reason straightening his tie.

'Jakey,' repeated Skuld naturally, ruffling his blond hair and asking him if he'd like some toast as Jack, not for the first time, became hot, bothered, and speechless.

Together at the breakfast table father and son sat, the family picture on the wall above them even more poignant than before. Sipping his coffee, Jack looked from the frame to his son, to Skuld, and then back again to his wife, who smiled back from the frame.

'Dad, it's OK. I really like Skuld,' said Jake, beaming like it was his birthday and patting his father's forearm. 'It was always going to happen,' he added, holding out the palms of his hands and shrugging his shoulders, giving the impression he'd planned the whole thing.

'Jam, Jakey?' called out Skuld, retying the belt of her dressing-gown more securely.

'Yes, please,' he said, bouncing up and down in his chair, as if he'd just been asked to help himself to anything in a toy shop window. And as he did, a relieved Jack had a glimpse of the future and the fine young man Jake was becoming. His son's emotional stability astounded him. If people could be a little more like his son, they'd be happier, he thought.

Looking at the photograph in front of him one more time it felt as if they were all together again. As Skuld took her place at the table, it seemed as if a new family was being formed and the family in the picture had nodded its head in approval.

'Dad, did you hear the cuckoo this morning? I think he's set up camp in the garden.'

'No, I didn't; though it's a bit early for the cuckoo,' replied Jack as he grabbed a slice of toast and slid into his jacket.

Kissing domestic bliss goodbye, he left a happy man. Could the day get any better, he wondered as he closed the door to his happy home. Was it really that easy: a potential new relationship with the au pair (OK, it did sound a bit creepy) and a delighted son?

Sometimes things moved very fast, especially when the years were slipping by. At forty-five, Jack needed that side of his life to take off with some speed. He'd fought it tooth and nail up to now. The newly acknowledged chemistry between himself and Skuld was bound to collide and spiral out of control for better or worse. His son was right, he reasoned: '*it was always going to happen.*'

Contented, recharged, and with a smile that would take some wiping off, he drove to work with more purpose than the night before.

The Mile End Road was still covered with crisp, glistening frost, giving the impression of an untouched iced birthday cake. The busy whirling road sweepers were cleaning, creeping along the double yellow lines, their loud mechanical arms like electric toothbrushes excavating every spot of plaque. It was the time of the morning Jack loved most: the magic of a grimy city opening up for business. The smell of bus diesel, mixed with frying bacon being cremated beyond steamed-up café windows where hunched builders, road workers, dustmen, cabbies, and van drivers refuelled for the rest of the day, as the street lights slowly

74

dimmed before being extinguished completely. It was an odd habit, but Jack always tried to capture the moment when the day began, when a yellowing bulb, almost embarrassed, flickered and then went out. It was how he remembered his own father's death – holding his hand in the early hours and then *blimp!* The light within him gone as peace spread across his face like a shroud.

Reaching the Mile End Police Station he was acutely aware that he hadn't thought of the Bow case once since he'd taken Skuld in his arms. Getting out of the car, Jack subliminally gave himself a pinch and reminded himself that DCI Hogan had to up his game and nail some bastards, and that he might have to take Pencil to the bakery (though not like Skuld had taken him!) if he kept saying *sir* every time Jack asked him a simple question.

'Pencil, anything new?' asked Jack, draping his jacket over an office chair.

'Well, we have a sighting of the yellow Fiat Panda, no ID or registration number though.'

'Where?' said Jack, a little exasperated that his detective didn't give all the necessary info in one sitting.

'Oh, sorry, sir: turning on to the main road and heading towards Stratford – it was the old man and the dog again, said he'd had a memory lapse, but that he'd remembered it after reporting the original sighting.'

'It's something, I suppose. If he's reliable.'

'Yes, sir,' said Pencil, sticking a fresh photograph of Dean Waters' mutilated body on to the timeline being pieced together on the whiteboard behind him. 'Oh, and the body of Waters has been released by the pathologist. The injuries are in line with our findings.'

'The pinning down of the arms?'

'Yes, sir.'

'Oh, and Pencil – two sugars,' he smiled, sitting down at his desk.

'Sorry, guv. Coffee, is it?'

'Please, and the papers.'

'On your desk, sir.'

'Oh, yes,' he sighed, glancing at the headline which read *Student Found Murdered at Gran's*. 'At least they haven't got the gory details yet,' said Jack, scanning the rest of the page. 'We want to keep that part quiet for as long as we can, for the family's sake,' he continued, looking up briefly. 'Plus, we know these sickos thrive on seeing their crimes splattered across the front pages. Release only what we are legally bound to.'

'Of course, sir. Two sugars,' Pencil added, plopping the cubes from an annoying height into Jack's West Ham mug. Drops fell on the newspapers. 'Sorry, sir,' he said, wiping them quickly with his sleeve.

'Maybe just hand me the sugars next time?' said Jack, not bothering to look up.

'Guv?' It was Samantha Evans, the new detective sergeant who'd been appointed as back-up to Pencil, the one whom Jake said hadn't got a boyfriend.

'Evans?' answered Jack, startled at her sudden entrance and the urgency in her voice.

'We've got another DB. Wasteland near Albert Docks, an old couple out walking with their dog found it this morning. Quite traumatised apparently.'

Not another dog-walker, thought Jack, carefully processing the information before moving into action. 'Right, let's go,' he said at last, feeling the adrenalin pumping in his legs as he jumped to his feet. 'Do what you do best, Pencil,'

'What's that?' asked Pencil incredulously.

'Drive,' said Jack, winking at Evans, who gave him a knowing smile as they scrambled for the door.

Relieved to be going somewhere, they sped away into the morning traffic as they skirted into the bus lane and did what all the other drivers wished they could do.

'Used to come up here as a kid; my dad used to bring me and my sister up to see the big cargo ships coming in,' said Jack as Pencil expertly jumped two red lights and overtook a couple of pulled-in lorries. 'You OK, Evans?' he called out, glancing over his shoulder at the young detective who was clearly gripping the driver's seat in front of her. 'He can move when he wants to,' he laughed as she went visibly green and then ashen as Pencil took another turning without changing down the gears. 'All right, Pencil – we want to get there in one piece,' he said at last as the Albert Docks loomed into view. The old cranes were at different angles; probably left in the same position they were in when the last crate of tea was dropped at the feet of burly dockers. Now a ghost dock, it had a stately air to it: a reminder perhaps of better times.

'Here, guv,' said Evans from the back, her colour returning. 'That piece of ground there.'

'I remember it. Used to be a scaffolding yard,' said Jack as they drove into the cordoned-off crime scene.

The wasteland that lay before them resembled the last days of Stalingrad, with rubble and piping scattered all around; a desolate flatness which gave the impression that a tornado had airlifted the disappeared buildings to another continent.

'Where's the body?' Jack instantly asked the uniformed officer nearby as he got out of the car.

'Over here, sir,' said the officer, leading the way towards the dilapidated outbuildings.

'Shit!' said Jack, stepping in a very deep muddy puddle. 'Remind me to bring boots next time, will you, Pencil?' he said, a hint of irritation and blame in his voice. Pencil just nodded.

Nearing the concrete shed where the scaffolding boards used to be kept, they said very little, the uniformed officer commenting on the weather to which the others just shook their heads.

'It's not pretty, sir,' said the officer, pulling up the police tape for them to enter.

'Oh, my God . . .' said Jack.

After the initial shock, the sheer horror, the detectives' mindset quickly adjusted to the destruction and pummelling of the corpse, like a piece of meat. They had it all in one sickly catalogue of evidence: the body covered in blood and mud in the crucifix position; two biro pens used as daggers and plunged deep into both eye sockets; front teeth scattered around the radius of the head like small glistening pearls in the dirt; the victim's T-shirt strewn to one side; presumably ripped from his back in his struggle to get away; his nose split in two; inflicted by possible stamping or a heavy blow to the face; a discarded cherry red Doc Martens shoe nearby.

'Pencil, here,' said Jack crouching down, 'get me a tissue.'

'Here, sir,' said Pencil, retrieving one from his pocket.

'Look,' continued Jack, carefully wiping some blood and

liquid mud from the victim's head. 'We've got it,' he said excitedly, revealing a clear ink stamp. 'The bastard got it right this time,' he added as he tried to avoid the pen-eyes gazing up at him.

'What is it, sir?' said Pencil.

'A star with something in the middle,' said Evans, joining them in the crouching position.

'Well,' said Jack, dabbing the middle of the circle, 'if I'm not mistaken, it's a skull.'

'A skull within a star?' remarked Pencil, stating the obvious.

'Do you know what it is, guv?' asked Evans.

'Yes, it's Class War,' said Jack matter-of-factly, standing up as the others joined him.

'They're an anarchist group, aren't they, sir — want to start a class war?' stated Evans, almost as if she was now in competition with Pencil.

'Something like that. *The only just war is class war* — that's it, that's their slogan,' he said, repeating the slogan again.

'Pretty good slogan,' said Pencil as Jack gave him a stern look.

'They're a bit of a mixed bag all right,' continued Jack in answer to Evans's question. 'An extreme version of Militant Tendency who were big in the eighties. This group are hard to pin down; an unfathomable band of anarchists, Socialist Workers' Party members, and hard left groups; left-wing extremism with the added confusion of celebrated chaos.'

'So, is this political, sir?' asked Evans, pushing a loose curl behind her ear.

'Could be,' said Jack, scratching his head, 'although we can't be sure for certain until we get a profile on the DB.' He beckoned the waiting officer and asked him if anyone had checked the victim's pockets for ID.

'No, thought we'd wait, sir.'

'Good. Pencil, check his pockets. Put your gloves on, man!' Jack snapped as the detective moved in unprotected. 'So, what have we got here?' he said as Pencil produced a rolled-up piece of paper from the victim's trouser pocket and straightened it out.

'It says *fopdoodle*, sir.'

'Fopdoodle,' repeated Jack slowly, trying to get his tongue round it. 'Any guesses?' he asked, to which they both shook their heads. 'Judging by the blood and mud stains and the way it appears to have been forced into the pocket to be left hanging for us to see, I suspect that it's not the victim's. Looks like it was stuffed in after the struggle.'

'Like the note in the mouth of Dean Waters.'

'Good point, Pencil. Another message maybe? Check it out, Evans. Might be in some dictionary somewhere?'

'Yes, guv.'

'OK, we need a positive ID on this one. Before we can move on with the stamp, we need a profile. Was he a member of any political groups; what class did he fall into; is this a class-motivated attack?' he added for good measure, having seen a glazed expression spread across Pencil's face. 'The biros in the eyes: check the files, see if this has been done before. This is an unusual one, and if this is the second then it probably isn't the last. So, think,' he added, tapping his forehead. 'Is this nutter trying to send out a message?' he said as both his detectives vigorously shook their heads in unison.

Chapter Eight

'Sal, do you want me to get some more wine?' asked Pete, pulling up his boxer shorts and strolling across the room. 'What?'

'Go to the offie; get some drink,' repeated Pete, feeling he should change the message in case she hadn't understood the first.

'No, just come back to bed,' she yawned with a wry smile as he dashed back, taking off his shorts in mid-flow, before jumping on her.

'Stay here for a couple of days,' said Sally, flipping him on his back and climbing up his body.

'What, so you can take advantage of me when you feel like it?' he said, gripping her tightly.

'Yes, of course that,' she giggled, pushing her pink hair out of her eyes. 'No, I just feel a bit freaked at the moment – that Tom fella; he was a bit weird.'

'He didn't seem that bad,' said Pete, wriggling beneath her and trying to get comfortable.

'Oh, I know,' she said dismissively. 'Ah, losing my earring, the one my nan gave me; it's just thrown me a bit.'

'Don't worry, Sal,' he murmured, moving his hands up her back and then slowly lowering her shoulders towards him.

'You can watch me telly all day if you want,' she said, smiling.

'I think you've persuaded me,' he laughed as she slowly kissed him.

Quietly pulling up outside twenty-two Spencer Drive, Tom parked the car, one wheel on and one off the pavement, as best he could to replicate the precarious parking of earlier. Producing a tissue from his pocket he made a speedy sweep of the interior: wiping down the seats, handles, and last of all the steering wheel. He had all bases touched, even the petrol cap, which was luckily a screw-on replacement lid, allowed him to refill the car on the way back. Readjusting the driver's seat, he'd more or less got the vehicle back to its previous condition.

'Pete, that staying at home watching daytime TV really gives you a lot of energy,' Sally said, satisfied as she rolled off her giant boyfriend.

'Maybe move the TV into the bedroom then?' he laughed, pulling the duvet off them both and playfully pulling Sally by the ankle down the bed.

Go away, she demanded silently as a Union Jack beanbag threatened to gate-crash the party.

Pete didn't work. Not out of choice, only that there was nothing suitable for him to do. A Pure Maths graduate, he struggled to find employment. It was as if he was too intelligent for the world of work. A couple of universities had offered him

part-time lecturing, but he wasn't interested; was more motivated by doing nothing and just thinking, and that of course
involved a lot of TV-watching. It was his information pod.
How could anyone ever be bored when they had hours of old
films and documentaries to digest?

A quick scurry of tippy-toe activity and Tom was back crouching by the window. The scene before him hadn't changed that
much, apart from the action which was taking place a few yards
from him. Again, Sally's white skin and arched back were the
focus of his hard gaze. It could have been hours, though it was
only minutes before Tom surfaced from his reverie and averted
his longing eyes. Getting to his feet he brushed his wet knees
and then left the spot as quickly as he had arrived, not showing
any emotion or sign of annoyance as if he had quietly logged and
frozen the entire episode in his head for later recall.

After one final glance at the parked car, Tom was soon turning the corner of Spencer Drive. As if being struck by a stray
thought he ran across the street. Opening the door of the piss-
smelling phone box, he dialled and waited.

'Harriet, hi – it's Marcus. How are you? Yes, I know it's late.
Sorry I didn't call round yesterday. Yeah, very busy at the moment.
No, I'm not in Greenwich. Just in town, had a few drinks with
some friends. Hold on,' he said grappling with the receiver as
the pips went and he quickly forced two ten-pence pieces into
the slot. 'Can you hear me? Good. Shall I come over? OK, brilliant. Look forward to it. OK, see you then. I do too – bye.'

Feeling the tension in his tonsils loosen as he had effortlessly
fallen back into his own natural upper-middle-class vernacular,

he laughed loudly to himself. The intonation which at times could sound clipped, as if a bell had been cleanly rung, came each time he opened his privileged mouth.

The last tube to Notting Hill Gate had been like a ghost train. Apart from the odd drunk City worker, the carriage was empty. No social justice to be administered this time, he thought, looking around him. Glancing down at his muddy trousers, he cursed himself for not thinking of bringing a change of clothes.

Running up the escalator and jumping the unmanned barrier he climbed the steps to the street above. Pleased to see the white stucco town houses of Notting Hill and the warm glow of affluent, trendy flats and apartments, he moved briskly along the wet glistening pavements as he pushed his blood-stained T-shirt deep into his overcoat pocket.

'Marcus, you old bugger, come in,' said the tall, slender brunette wearing a pair of black satin pyjamas. 'Look at the state of you; is that the new fashion they're sporting in Greenwich these days?' she said, guiding him by the waist into the high-ceilinged glowing hallway.

'Got a bit pissed, fell over, celebrating with some uni pals,' he added, kissing her tenderly on the cheek.

'Well, at least your shirt's clean,' she said, returning the kiss as they both entered the lounge and collapsed on to the bright, heavily pillowed couch.

'Ciggie?' she said, lighting one herself and passing one to Marcus.

'Thanks.'

'So, how's college going?'

'Good, I've changed one of my courses. I'm now doing Seventeenth-Century Literature instead of Holocaust Literature.'

'Sounds interesting,' she said taking a deep satisfied draw on her cigarette while turning her head to one side then lazily exhaling all the smoke.

'I've hardly seen you these last few weeks – I was getting worried.'

'Work to do, a lot of things to complete; deadlines, so to speak,' he added, swishing the fringe off his face.

'Still getting the cheque from Daddy, I hope?'

'Of course,' he replied incredulously, holding out his arms. 'I am the only heir.' He laughed.

'Some day a well-off one – primogeniture and all that.'

'And you have to share with sister and two brothers.'

'That's why I'm Daddy's favourite.'

'Cute, I wouldn't expect anything else.'

Harriet Thompson-Dickinson was an ex-girlfriend, or more to the point, an on-off one. They met, socialised with each other's friends, and slept together. All done in a non-committed kind of way; in a posh Notting Hill manner.

'Hey, why don't I run you a bath and then we can both hop into bed,' she said, stroking his knee.

Rising from the dirty water Marcus thought of the past twenty-four hours. Could it get any better? he thought, hooking the chain of the plug with his toe and pulling it. He was in a hurry; he wanted (no, he desired) to complete the sequence swirling around his mind. Feeling the excitement of it, he quickly dried off and walked naked into the bedroom where Harriet waited for him, sprawled across her luxurious king-sized bed wearing nothing but a decadent smile.

'Marcus. You're very worked up,' she said breathlessly as he gently stroked her arched back.

Focusing on her spine, Marcus fingered the tiny delicate bones popping out of her skin every time she moved. Falling on to the mattress beside her, his hands slid from her hips across to the curve of her spine where they fell and rested, feeling the shape of her backbone. Holding the sensation and now the total recall of Sally's body as she had done the same to Pete, he marvelled at the scene; at the picture he'd managed to frame and bring back to life, all the time keeping the image for as long as he could until Harriet rolled off him and reached for the fags.

What a brilliant day, he thought as he closed his eyes and took a lustful drag of the cigarette Harriet had tenderly lit for him and popped in his mouth. She now lay with her head on his chest, her smooth legs wrapped around his side as she let out a heavenly sigh.

Chapter Nine

The whole Skuld episode had been an unusual development in Jack's life. Even after the initial consummation, it was still a little awkward. He was more than happy with what had occurred, but there was no getting over the suddenness of it all. Arriving home late having followed up on a few leads, Jack found himself in exactly the same situation as the previous night: Jake safely in bed and Skuld curled up on the sofa waiting for him (well, in his mind anyway). Would it be like this every time, he wondered as he appeared to be entering another groundhog evening.

'Jack,' said Skuld, staring robotically at the TV, 'you don't have to sit down there,' as Jack went to throw himself down in his usual spot at the end of the couch.

'No, I suppose not.' He followed her cue and plopped down beside her.

'Bad day?' she said, still watching the *Channel Four News*.

'Not bad,' he said, stretching out and placing his arm over the back of the sofa and touching her shoulder like a teenage boy on a first date at the cinema.

'Do you want to talk first?' she asked suddenly, turning and giving him a quick peck on the cheek.

'First?' said Jack enquiringly as an image from the night before flashed before him.

'Yes, before you eat.'

Do women's minds work the same as men's? Are we ever in sync with one another? thought Jack, who had assumed she was talking about going to bed together again.

'Oh, let's talk,' he said sheepishly, wondering what was on the agenda.

'Are you ever on the news, Jack?' she said, hugging his arm.

'Not really.'

The last time he was on the news it had been the Wanstead incident. It was as if he'd been caught in a time loop. Seeing himself on TV the next day: dazed, haunted, and withdrawn; just going through the motions. Seeing himself so damaged and vulnerable, he had tended to shy away from interviews with the press and had lately used Pencil, briefing him thoroughly before pushing him in front of the camera. This Pencil took in his stride, though he did need a lot of coaching. He was naturally a better driver than communicator, though a dab hand at hard facts, repetitive statements, *no comments*, and *the police are following every line of enquiry* cop-speak.

'So, Jack, you like me – yes?'

'Of course,' he said, realising that some housekeeping was obviously on the agenda.

'I'm your girlfriend now?' She was back to staring at the TV.

Luckily, Jack was used to Skuld's directness. If anything, it was something he loved about her: the ability to say it as it is. Maybe it was being in the force for so long, but he preferred straight-talking logic as opposed to pussy-footing around the houses, pontification. Yes, and double yes, he wanted her to be his girlfriend; he also knew that Jake would want the same, so he was more than happy to be guided by this beautifully strange woman as he simply replied, 'Yes.'

'Good,' she said, turning and kissing him on the lips. 'As we say in Iceland: the burnt child fears the fire.'

'Right,' he said, not really being able to figure it out. Not that it mattered.

'So, still separate rooms?'

'Yes, I think so; if that's all right with you?'

'Yes, I think separate is good. You will visit me from time to time?' she said, placing her hand on his knee as they briefly kissed and then sat in blissful silence as *Panorama* started.

''Ere we go, 'ere we go, 'ere we go — 'ere we go!' chanted Marcus, clapping in time to the mindless song, smashing and circling the walls of the rounded tunnel like a skateboard speeding through a tube as it resounded like thunder from Island Gardens to Greenwich on the other side. 'Wah! Wah! Ewah!' he began, screeching like a flock of seagulls, loving the pounding echo. 'Wah! Ewah!' With his long black overcoat splaying out behind him, he ran like a demented crow with outstretched wings towards his nest on the other side of the river.

'It's OK, luv, I've 'ad me breakfast,' he said to the startled woman who'd got halfway down the tunnel before the din had started. Cowering to one side she let him pass as he continued his 'Ewah!' noises and dashed for the exit. Slowing as he reached the lifts and the spiral steps, he turned up his collar, preparing to take the steps to the cold early-morning air, when someone moved out of the shadows and approached him.

'Got any money, mate?' said the young man in the black hoodie, holding out a begging hand.

'Breakfast time again,' said Marcus, stopping abruptly in his tracks.

'Cash; got any money?' said the boy menacingly, taking a step forward as Marcus automatically held out his hand, stopping him in his tracks.

'Mugger or beggar? Come on, it's easy!' he added, reading the confused expression on the pale face of the evolving mind in front of him. 'Easy,' he continued slowly, prodding him in the shoulder. 'Are. You. A. Mugger. Or. A. Fucking. Scrounger?' he spat.

Grabbing Marcus by the scruff of his collar, the young man made his move as he brought his head back, ready to butt. Recognising the action, Marcus instantly craned his neck and positioned the top of his head for total impact.

'Fuck!' cried the boy, blood dripping from the deep cut to his forehead as he staggered backwards, having taken the full force of his mistimed head butt.

'Not too bright, are you, luv?' Marcus said, putting his arm around his shoulder. 'Not the full shilling,' he added, moving his hand to the back of the boy's neck and grabbing it tightly as if he were a ventriloquist. 'Think that you deserve a living for doing nothing – like a parasite? *Abschaum!*' he shouted suddenly, smashing the young man's face up against the white-tiled tunnel wall. '*Abschaum!*' he screamed as blood smeared down the wall each time he dragged his face across it.

Slumped on the ground, the mugger looked up as if awaiting further retribution and closed his eyes, fearing the worst.

'Open your eyes,' Marcus said gently, kicking him in the side as he obliged and waited. 'You're a lucky one, do you know that?' he began softly, regaining his breath. 'And it's because you know what you are that you are a lucky boy,' he stressed, 'you know who you are – don't you?'

The boy nodded frantically as if sensing a way out.

'And because you know you are shit. I'm going to let you wallow in it. You see, you're honest; you tried to mug me. If you survive today, you'll rob someone else, you'll do nothing with your life, just grab, drink and screw. You'll go unnoticed, you'll never bother voting; you'll just take the crumbs the State throws you and you'll produce kids, loads of the buggers, just like yourself, all living on handouts and robbing.'

A little confused as to the outcome the young man began to cry, stammering a 'Sorry, mate' in between sobs.

'Fucking beautiful,' laughed Marcus, 'you really are fucking beautiful,' he repeated, kneeling down at his side as if he were about to administer the last rites as he kissed him on the forehead. 'Beautiful,' he said again, rising and standing over the young man, feet apart like some gunslinger. Reaching into his pocket, he produced a shiny pound coin.

'Heads or tails?'

The boy said nothing.

'Look, this is how it is: you win; you live. I win; you die. Oh, look at the fear,' he continued mockingly. 'Your expression – oh, bless!'

'Heads,' whimpered the boy.

'Are you sure? I think it's going to be tails; like the one between your legs,' he said, holding up the coin between his finger and thumb.

'OK, tails,' he spluttered, spitting blood on to the ground.

'But it might be heads; I am sometimes wrong,' he said, toying with the young man.

'Heads then!' he whined in desperation.

'And that's your final call?' Marcus teased.

'Yes!'

'OK, let's play live or die.'

Flipping the coin, he let it fall on the boy's chest.

Back in the kitchen the next morning, Jack had to take a second just to make sure it was all really happening again. The dynamics had changed so utterly. Luckily, Skuld's effortless, natural charm had eased his nerves and made the short transition an easy one. Looking around him at both his son and Skuld, it was as if they'd always been a family, warts and all. And by the expression on Jake's face it was the warts that were at the breakfast table.

'Jake, everything all right at school?' he asked, taking a long sip of coffee and straightening his tie.

'Yeah.'

'You're quiet this morning, Jakey,' called out Skuld, unloading the dishwasher.

'You're still all right about me and Skuld — aren't you?' whispered Jack, leaning forward over the kitchen table.

'Of course,' said his son, not his beaming self.

It's school, thought Jack, reclining back on his chair. 'I'll drop you off this morning.'

'No, Dad, it's fine; I'll go with Skuld,' he replied anxiously.

It's definitely school, Jack asserted, taking a bite of toast and thinking of the numerous scenarios that could be interfering with his son's otherwise happy life.

'Jakey, I've got your PE top,' said Skuld, holding up the freshly laundered navy-blue sweatshirt. 'Take the old one off and I'll wash it,' she said, standing behind him and holding up the sleeves.

'No, I'll do it,' he said irritably, as the top came off in her hands to reveal purple bruising to his upper arms.

'Jake, what are these?' asked his concerned dad, taking his son's elbow and examining the marks. 'And don't say *nothing*,' he added softly, holding his hand.

'Some of the other boys ...' he began, before stopping and bursting out crying as Jack felt his blood rise.

'Some boys what, Jakey?' asked Skuld, now protectively standing over him and encasing his crying head in her hands.

'It's OK,' mouthed Jack, 'I've got this. What did they do, Jake?' Jack said softly as his son felt as if he were being wrapped up by the warm layers of his father's words.

'They said all cops are pigs and that I was a son of a pig,' he said quietly, looking up for a reaction.

'Ahh, don't listen to them, Jake,' began Jack calmly, 'they're just stupid. People call us pigs all the time; it goes with the job and after all, it is just a word,' he added, putting his arm around his son's shoulders.

'I know,' smiled his son, wiping his red eyes.

'Jack, we will go find them,' announced Skuld, fetching her coat and appearing a foot taller than usual.

'No, Skuld,' he said, almost laughing and at the same time loving her total loyalty. 'I'll sort it,' he said simply before returning his attention to his son. 'What about the bruises, Jake; how did you get them?'

'They just punched my arms,' he replied, omitting the part that one of them had held him, while another spat repeatedly in his face.

Stepping out into the cold, early-morning wind, Marcus sniffed the air as the rigging of the *Cutty Sark* shook and braced itself for another gust blowing up across the Thames. Greenwich was like a ghost town. It was only seven thirty and people were only just making for the tunnel and Island Gardens on the other side, hurrying mechanically to work like suited penguins.

Deep underground, Mark Cox opened his eyes and picked the coin up off his chest. 'Heads,' he said to himself, examining the coin as he squinted through sticky blood-soaked eyelashes. 'Heads!' he cried again, letting out a loud cackle as commuters quickly side-stepped him, avoiding eye contact as they scurried along the tunnel, oblivious to what appeared to be another annoying drunk who'd taken an alcohol-fuelled tumble.

Letting himself into his lair above the Blue Thunder chip shop, Tom draped his overcoat over the solitary armchair and threw his bloodstained T-shirt in the corner with the rest of his laundry, as he began to strip, folding each item of clothing and placing them neatly on the chair. Picking up a black marker pen from the coffee table he entered his tiny box-bedroom, crouched down, and knelt at the foot of the bed as if in prayer. Taking the lid off the pen he began to sketch on the wall a picture of Sally in the exact pose he'd captured before she entered the bath: her long slender porcelain back, her mane of hair and stately air, as she'd lifted her locks off her angular shoulders. He had it all. Finishing, he roughly circled the figure as if caging it and wrote underneath: *to be continued* as he clasped the silver earring tightly in his hand and fell back on to his single bed. Staring at the ceiling he let the events of the past forty-eight hours gently wash over him. Each tide and ripple a warm reminder of his power. Every memory now a sacrament to be honoured and knelt before. His hands resting on his beating heart, he closed his eyes and felt a surge of life run through his fingers.

Chapter Ten

Nine a.m. and no Pencil. Unusual, thought Jack, thumbing through the young detective's in-tray. Slumping back in his chair and reclining as far as he could, he thought of his son, and what he'd like to do to the little fuckers who were destroying his innocence. Maybe he should go direct to the headmaster? That he knew would be a dead-end street. From his own experience in the Force, he knew that trouble sometimes had to be dealt with by the same means, and that often meant facing it head on and dealing with it in a forceful way. Taking out his Filofax, he quickly located the 'M's, and searched out *Brendan Maloney*.

'Brendan, Jack Hogan. How are you? Didn't get you up? Good. Yeah, I'm still with the Force. You still on the pool team? I must get down the Crown sometime, give you a game. Look, listen, I've got a problem, something you may be able to help me with ...'

Brendan Maloney was an old schoolfriend and, like Jack, second generation London Irish. He ran his own building company and in his younger years had been respected as a hardman with a big heart. Married with six children, he'd got into a bit of financial trouble in the late eighties and had borrowed a large amount of money from some small-time North London Irish gangster, who was unfairly putting up the interest hourly, bragging about how he was going to break Brendan's legs. Helping his friend out, Jack, having friends at the Highbury station, had managed to put the squeeze on the guy, who was running a couple of not-totally-kosher businesses. He was told to drop the threat and write off the debt, unless he wanted his enterprises raided every day. This he quickly agreed to and was never heard of again.

'Your sons, Kieran and Enda; they still go to Jake's school, right?'

They did, and at a year older than Jake, they were the lads on the block. Like their father, they were respected, well-liked, and a little bit feared.

'Thanks, Brendan. Give my love to Mary. Cheers, mate. Bye,' Jack said, having relayed the finer details of the problem. Sorted, he thought, replacing the receiver on the handset. A little scare, a warning to lay off his son. Wouldn't any father do the same? If you weren't a hardnut, then you had to have a few tough friends to help you out now and again. To survive in an East London school, you had to have back-up.

Job done, Jack happened to briefly glance out of the side window which backed on to the stairwell, beyond which was the custody suite, only to see Pencil's side profile, half hidden by a large industrial bin, as he stepped back into the light. Detective Sergeant Samantha Evans followed, kissing him on the lips before straightening her suit and heading off briskly towards the compound and newly washed patrol cars. Nearly falling off his chair, Jack readjusted his tie as Pencil entered the office. The whole readjustment of the tie thing was becoming a nervous tic of sorts.

'Guv,' said Pencil, his towering presence filling the room. 'Coffee, sir?' he said casually and with what appeared a more confident swagger than usual.

'Yes, but I'll do the sugar,' Jack said dryly. Wondering if he should go into the whole discretion–at–work ethical bullshit, he thought of Skuld's sleeping expression and the contented smile she had when he'd awoken that morning. Deciding that his sergeant also deserved a bit of happiness, he concluded that he'd have to overlook the indiscretion with Evans for now. 'So, what've we got on the Albert Docks case?'

'Well, we have an ID on the DB,' he began, flipping the pages of his notebook. 'A David Wilkins, known as Dave, aged twenty-two, student at East London University, Stratford.'

'Profile?'

'Well, young man on his own, vicious beating, could be gang-related?'

'Could be, perhaps check out local gang activity in the area.'

'Yes, sir.'

'Any indication of this being a homophobic attack. Do we know if the victim was gay?'

'There have always been attacks in the area, though nothing as serious as this. So far there's no indication of him being gay.'

'See when the most recent attack was and check it out.'

'Yes, sir.'

Pencil it seemed had come to a full stop as Jack drummed his fingers impatiently on the table.

'Anything else?'

'You mean the class thing?'

'Yes, the class thing,' said Jack irritably. Pencil always brought out the worst in him.

'Same as Dean Waters, sir.'

'What, first to go to university, working-class background and all that?'

'Yes, sir, father was a docker at the Albert Docks until just before it closed down. Was also on the production line at Ford's. Died two years ago from a blood clot on the brain.'

'Mother?'

'Lives in East Ham.'

'And Dave, where did he live?'

'Upton Park, sir.'

'Only a few miles apart.'

'Yes, sir.'

'And the biro pens – anything in the files?'

'No, sir, only a pupil at Waltham College poking another student's eye out in a prank gone wrong.'

'Accident?' enquired Jack, wondering why he bothered sometimes.

'Oh, yeah, of course, nothing in it.'

Why'd you bother saying it, thought Jack, briefly staring out the window as he considered giving his detective another dressing down and then quickly deciding not to.

'Right, and what about the piece of paper: *fopdoodle*?'

'Ah, yes, sir, I've got it here somewhere,' said Pencil, riffling through his pockets. 'Here it is,' he continued, unrolling the crumpled piece of paper. '*Fopdoodle*: an old English word meaning an insignificant or foolish person.'

'So, we have a working-class, insignificant person. Sounds like class hatred reversed.'

99

'Sir, I don't get it.'

Jack knew by the glazed puzzlement cemented in Pencil's frown that he'd some explaining to do. 'It's the normal class warfare reversed: we have the stamp – the-only-just-war-is-class-war stuff, meaning the prevalence and ultimate supremacy of the working class over the privileged – and then we have two working-class murder victims, both nearly identical backgrounds, both stamped in the same way, each receiving an old-fashioned bully's beating. The person we are looking for isn't necessarily who we think he should be. The stamp indicates a working-class freedom fighter, but we may be looking for a hater of the working classes.'

'And what about the university connection, sir?' asked Pencil who'd miraculously managed to keep up.

'Good point; it's the crucial thing they have in common: they're the first in their family to go. Look here,' he continued, pointing to the newspaper unfolded on his desk. 'It says that since 1991, for the first time there has been an upsurge in students from working-class families taking up full-time university places. Don't you see?' said Jack excitedly stabbing the page with his finger, 'this is a significant rise – it's noticeable. It's not like when I went to the polytechnic. It means you can now go to any university in the country and you'll find the sons and daughters of dockers and bricklayers,' he concluded, picking up a red marker pen and scribbling, *Thinks that working-class people shouldn't go to university* on the whiteboard and underlining it roughly.

'He wants to keep them down.'

'Yes, maybe,' Jack said, pensively rubbing his chin before continuing. 'And the pens? Knowledge: perhaps turning the knowledge they've gained on themselves. The same as with the first murder; trying to physically pull the brain from their head, to get rid of what they have – or should I say shouldn't have – learnt, to dispose of it all.'

'Wow,' said Pencil a little stunned at the intensity of the lesson in criminal psychology.

'It may be just all baloney, of course,' added Jack with a wry smile, 'but sometimes we have to go with the wacky stuff,' he said, sipping his coffee.

Pencil was now busy adding evidence to the timeline on the whiteboard, which due to his height was higher than Jack's scribble.

'And the yellow car; what have we got on that?' asked Jack, watching him carefully write *knowlege* on the board. 'There's a "d" in *knowledge*,' he sighed.

'Sorry, sir,' said Pencil, fixing the mistake before answering Jack's initial question. 'Samantha, I mean DS Evans, has the car data,' he said, blushing deeply at the error.

Jack thought again about having the discretion talk but decided on protocol instead. 'They did tell you to use surnames only at the Police Academy – didn't they?' he asked, enjoying watching Pencil squirm a bit more as Evans suddenly entered the room.

'Sir, we've got a number of leads on the car,' she announced in a flurry, a little flushed and ever so obviously avoiding eye contact with Pencil, who was now trying to hide at his desk.

She's good, thought Jack, she's going to play it cool with her new boyfriend, ice cold, until the shift is done when she'll probably dive on him. 'What have we got?' he asked.

'Well, we're now sure it's the Panda; it was spotted around the time of Dean Waters' murder. We also have the same car leaving the Albert Docks at the time of the second murder; spotted by a security guard on the adjacent site who took down the reg number because the driver was acting suspiciously, turning off the lights as he left the area before heading West. Oh,' she added, catching her breath, 'and the tyre tracks at the docks are those of a Fiat Panda, so it's definitely the car.'

'Good work, Evans. So, we have a number plate?'

'Yes, sir, we have registration ID; not stolen; licence owner is a female, Ms Sally Drayton, a student, address is twenty-two Spencer Drive, Hackney.'

'Could be the girl waiting in the car by the alley in Bow?' said Jack, standing and pacing up and down with his hands in his pockets.

'An accomplice?' asked Pencil, who had remained rather quiet since 'Samantha's' arrival.

'Well, let's not get too carried away. We don't want to alarm her.'

'Bring her in, sir?' asked Evans, still yet to acknowledge Pencil's existence.

'No, just a chat. We'll interview her at the flat to begin with.'

'Right,' said Pencil, standing and getting his coat.

'I think Evans and I will do the tag work on this one,' Jack began, registering the disappointment on Pencil's face. 'We need a female involved,' he added gently, 'and we don't want to crowd her out.'

'Yes, sir,' he said dejectedly, taking off his coat and sitting back down.

'What are you doing?' Jack said. 'You're driving!' He laughed, giving Evans a knowing look. Evans blushed deeply.

Chapter Eleven

'Bloody hell, Pete, you've tidied up,' said Sally, throwing her rucksack on the floor.

'Yeah, the telly's broken,' he said sadly as if a piece of him had just died. 'So I had nothing to do.'

'Was it the fuzzy thing – you know, the snowy, jumpy stuff?'

'Yeah, but more snowy, with wiggly lines, than jumpy.'

'Oh, well, you have to hit it,' she said as if it were the most obvious thing to do.

'Hit it?' said Pete, stirred into action and heading with purpose towards the TV.

'Yeah; turn it on first and then hit it about three times,' she said as Pete did as he was instructed.

'There, see – nothing,' said Pete, nodding at the small, blinking portable TV set.

'You're doing it wrong; hit it on the left. Yeah, about there,' she said as he pointed to the spot, 'about three times and hard.'

Doing as he was told, images suddenly appeared on the screen, as if the first picture being beamed from the Moon had arrived.

'You're bloody brilliant, you are,' said Pete, scooping her up in his arms, his mood now considerably improved since his life-line had been restored.

'You've cooked as well,' she said, taking off her parka and smiling broadly. She was a bit teary too because no one ever cooked for her, not even her mum when she went back home during the holidays. It had been something she had missed out on during her childhood. Her mother, who suffered with anxiety and depression, hadn't cooked since Sally was six, when her recently redundant father Ian had reluctantly taken over operations.

'Just a curry,' replied Pete modestly – he'd been able to remember a chickpea vegetable curry recipe, word for word and measure for measure, from his previous day's viewing.

'So, so love you,' she said, crawling up his body and kissing him squarely on the forehead, 'and bloody love curry too,' she added excitedly, sliding back down to the floor.

'How's uni?' he asked, ushering her towards the small kitchen from where the heavenly smell of fresh coriander and garlic was wafting.

'Not bad, I think I like the sculpture now; it's more me,' she said, running her fingers through her pink hair which was now streaked with stone dust.

'Looks like you've been in the thick of it all right,' he said, dusting her head with a washing-up cloth he'd just picked off the kitchen counter.

'Oh, yeah, it's a gusto a go-go, with me,' she laughed, sitting down at the laid table. 'And look at all this,' she cried, looking at the place for two. 'Perhaps I shouldn't have told you about the telly?'

'But,' said Pete, dramatically slow and sounding very much like Michael Caine, 'without the medium of TV, I wouldn't have known how to make the bloody curry in the first place.'

'Shall I just sit here then and let you dish up?'

'Yeah, just sit there,' he smiled.

As if a nagging doubt had just been remembered, she began, 'Pete?'

'What?'

'There was a funny thing: I was sure I could smell dope in the car.'

'Right,' said Pete, draining the balti rice as he became temporarily invisible by the thick steam.

'And not only that, there seemed to be more petrol in it than the last time I checked.'

Although not a good driver, Sally, who had broken down a number of times due to not having any petrol in the tank, was now near-obsessive about checking it and had made a mental note that when she'd returned from Sarah's, she'd had exactly half a tank left. Now it was definitely three-quarters full.

'Don't you think that's odd, Pete?' she asked as he appeared through the evaporating mist.

'Well, yes.'

'What do you think then?' she pressed him.

'I guess it's a mystery, but at least you have more petrol than when you started!'

'I think I'll just leave it,' she said simply, turning her attention to the plate of curry now in front of her.

'Maybe it was a ghostly joint-loving philanthropist?' said Pete all of a sudden, sensing that a joke was probably needed to make her feel better.

'Yeah, that's more likely the explanation,' she smiled when, as if by pure comic timing, there was a loud knock on the front door.

'Shit!' she said, rising just as she was going to tuck in, 'who the hell's that?'

'Sally Drayton?' said Evans.

'Yes?'

'Police; can we come in?'

'Well, I suppose so,' she said cautiously as Jack and Evans entered.

'Sal, what's up?' Pete said, looming at the kitchen door frame holding a wooden spoon. For some reason Jack wanted to make a quip for him to put the weapon down, but decided against it.

'It's OK –' he felt like saying *sonny* – 'just a few questions,' said Jack firmly, holding up his ID. 'DCI Hogan and this is DS Evans.'

'Serious stuff?' said Pete, now feeling increasingly protective.

'Look, it might be better if we get DS Sharpner in here as well,' said Jack to Evans, who took a second to register that he meant Pencil.

'What is it?' asked Sally, slowly becoming alarmed as Pencil entered the hallway, banging his head off the paper ball-shaped lampshade.

'Sally,' began Evans, 'we can either do it here or down at the station – I think here is better?' she added gently, guiding her by the arm into the living room.

'DS Sharpner, perhaps you might take this young man's details and movements of the last few days; maybe in the kitchen?'

'Yes, sir.'

'Good. Right, now everybody's happy,' said Jack, turning towards Pete, 'and I'd say you can put that spoon down now!' He smiled as he turned and entered the living room.

'You OK?' said Jack, sitting down directly opposite Sally, who was accompanied by Evans on the tiny sofa.

'Not really,' she said, anxiously glancing at Evans who smiled sympathetically.

'Look. I'll cut to the chase,' began Jack. 'There was a murder in Bow two days ago and we believe that your car was parked nearby and that you may have been present in the car at the time ...'

Jack stopped there, noticing the colour drain from Sally's already pale face.

'The alley,' she said tearfully, 'you mean when I parked at the alley.'

'Yes, the alley,' repeated Jack, glancing at Evans.

'I was waiting there.'

'For who?'

'That weirdo, Tom,' she began now, a little irritated.

'Tom who?' interjected Evans.

'Don't know his surname; I was just dropping him home.'

'Where?' said Jack, as Evans took out her notepad and pen.

'Stratford.'

'Address?'

'He just got me to leave him at the shopping centre.'

'And when you stopped in Bow, what did he say?'

'That he had to see a friend; to lend him some money.'

'Did you notice anything strange after that?'

'No, he just seemed the same. Talked about the crows a lot.'

'The crows?'

'Oh, just the ones making a noise in the alley, that's all.'

'Right, so you dropped him off at the bus station, by the shopping centre?'

'Yeah, I watched him for a while, he was acting weird, with his arms outstretched like a bird. Then thinking he'd seen me watching him, I pulled away.'

Retracing the events of the day, Sally, now a little more relaxed, recalled the journey: starting with picking him up as a favour to a friend from the night before's party; the drive up the Mile End Road, and how she really knew very little about him, only that he had a Yorkshire accent and studied English and History somewhere in London; which university she didn't know.

'Did your friend from the party know him?' asked Jack.

'God, no. He'd passed out on her floor. Nobody knew him. My friend Jean rang me the next day to ask if I'd drop him off – she knew I was heading that way, to my friend Sarah's,' she added breathlessly.

'And after leaving your friend Sarah's?'

'I drove home.'

'And then what?'

'Stayed in.'

'All night?'

'Yeah, until it was time for uni the next morning.' Jack looked at Evans who read his expression instantly.

'Did anyone borrow your car?' said Evans.

'No.'

'Anyone here with you?' asked Jack.

'Yeah, Pete – the guy next door, my boyfriend,' she said, innocently blushing.

'All night?' interrupted Evans.

'Yes, all night,' she replied, reddening some more.

'You see, Sally, after the first murder that morning there was a second one that night and we believe your car was also at that scene,' began Jack, shifting in his seat and then leaning forward.

'Christ! This is turning into a nightmare,' she stammered as Evans clasped her shaking hand.

'We're only making enquiries. Just need to piece together where you were.'

'The car!' she cried suddenly. 'I was only just saying to Pete about the smell of dope in the car, and there was definitely more petrol in it than when I last drove – I always check it religiously.'

'Could have been moved?' said Evans to Jack.

'Does this Tom know your address?' asked Jack.

'God, I hope not,' she said, managing a nervous smile.

'Sally,' he said, starting to wind up the questioning and trying to make it sound as unthreatening as he could. 'This is how it works: I'm going to ask you to come down to the station to make a full statement. Your car is going to be taken away for forensic examination. We'll get a statement off your boyfriend as well,' he concluded, making it sound as if it was the most natural thing in the world to be doing.

'What, now?' she said anxiously.

'You'll be back in an hour,' said Evans, patting her hand, 'your boyfriend can wait for you.'

'Oh, just out of interest, Sally,' Jack added, his hands pressed on the arm rests ready to get up, 'did he say anything about the working class?'

'The working class?' she repeated.

'Yes.'

'Well, he said he was working class and that's why he studied History and English, "*to see what the bastards did and wrote about us*," I think were his words.'

'Thanks, Sally, you've been most helpful,' said Jack, getting to his feet as Evans followed suit. 'We'll drive you down to the station. We won't keep you long,' he said, pleased he'd used his intuition and questioned her before she'd made a statement. He went to find Pencil.

'Detective Sergeant Sharpner! What are you doing?' cried Jack, peering inside the kitchen only to see his sergeant sitting down and tucking into a bowl of curry.

'Sorry, sir, it smelt so good. Pete here got it off the telly.'

Jack glanced at Evans, who'd blushed purple. 'Well, when you've finished your dinner, ask your new friend Pete to accompany you down to the station to make a statement,' he said, shaking his head and turning around quickly to hide his growing smile as he followed Evans and Sally out of the door.

Chapter Twelve

'*What do we want? Tories out! When do we want it? Now!*'
The small crowd of demonstrators had soon risen to
two hundred, as the hardcore SWP members were now joined
by young trendy students, many of whom were still a little
worse for wear having downed cheap beer at the Students'
Union the night before. A few anarchists, dressed in black, who
were a bit more scary and serious-looking than the hippy-dippy
students, shouted their own slogans. Predictably, '*The only just
war is class war*' was the most popular of the chants. In the din
of chaos most of the jumbled-up noise was drowned out by the
more organised loudhailers of the SWP.

'Kill the rich! Kill the rich!' shouted Marcus on his own,
somewhere between the SWP and the anarchists. Holding a
Tories Out placard, he pumped it up and down in time to the
chants and the beating of a drum by a grungy, dreadlocked class
warrior. In their own minds they were all warriors of sorts;
some more willing than others to break the law and get a criminal record. The anarchists, who were now shouting 'Kill the

pigs!' were certainly that brigade, veterans of the Poll Tax riots and the Can't Pay Won't Pay, prepared to go to jail fringe.

'Tom!' cried one of the demonstrators, coming up behind him and leading him onwards towards the throng of SWP supporters at the front. 'You're now officially a member,' said the stocky, small man who bore an uncanny resemblance to Bob Hoskins. Like many of the demonstrators, he was clearly a guilty middle-class type who was no doubt angry because he couldn't be anything else. 'Here,' he said, handing over the official badge.

'Thanks, Jim,' said Marcus, barely looking at it and plonking it in his pocket.

'Hey, we're having a drink afterwards, in memory of that Dave fella who was murdered.'

'Oh, yeah, Dave – nice bloke,' answered Marcus sadly. 'Hope they get who did it soon,' he added coldly.

'Yeah, one of our own – really,' pointed out Jim, sounding more Tony Blair than Bob Hoskins.

Nothing like you, thought Tom, who nonetheless agreed wholeheartedly. 'Where are you meeting?' he asked, fancying an afternoon's drinking.

'The Globe, Mile End Road. Do you know it?'

'Kind of,' replied Marcus, knowing it very well.

'That was close earlier,' said Pencil, climbing out of his jacket and throwing it hurriedly on the bed.

'We didn't do anything,' Evans said simply unbuttoning her blouse, 'well, not yet anyway.'

'I know, but I'm sure he saw us.'

'Ahh, Jack Hogan's just a pussycat.'

'Not with me, he's not,' said Pencil, now down to his underpants.

'He probably thinks we're together: boyfriend and girlfriend. If he only knew the truth,' she said, now totally naked as the bedroom door opened and a semi-clothed, red-headed woman walked in.

'You know Erika?' said Evans, placing her hand around her girlfriend's waist and pulling her in like a hooked fish, then kissing her on the lips.

'Erika,' nodded Pencil as if he were being introduced at a party.

'Alan hasn't done this kind of thing before,' continued Evans, taking him by the hand.

'Haven't you, Alan?' said the redhead. 'So, you've got the storyline?' she continued.

'Yes, we finished the middle part today at work – didn't we, Alan?' interrupted Evans, now placing Pencil's hand on Erika's hip, as they all huddled together in one bacchanalian embrace.

It had all begun at an after-work drinks party for retiring Sergeant Mike Bailey, when a tipsy Pencil had made a play for Evans, who, also a bit worse for wear, had reciprocated. After a passionate fumble in the pub car park, Evans, now sobered by the cold night air, had confessed that although she was bisexual, she was more lesbian than heterosexual and had a girlfriend named Erika. After the initial shock, Pencil had, after a brief adjustment period, returned, if a little awkwardly, to his prior relationship with his colleague. Evans on the other hand had been encouraged and excited by the prospect of perhaps introducing Pencil to Erika and maybe adding a bit more spice to their already active sex life. With Erika readily agreeing, a fantasy was put together, whereby Alan would relentlessly pursue her at work, which after a few risky liaisons would lead to him being enticed back to their flat where he would be introduced to Erika.

Pencil naturally was more than willing and as he'd had very little success in that department for some time, it was an opportunity that couldn't be overlooked.

The Globe, Mile End Road: a student pub for more mature students who'd grown out of the Students' Union bar at Queen Mary and Westfield College. A good place to head when afternoon lectures were over and you wanted to drink, talk shop, and impress; regurgitating what you'd just consumed. Marcus naturally felt more at home here among some of his own kind than with what he considered the unhealthy culture mix of classes in the student bar. More relaxed with the likes of Jim and now Sam Richards, he bought his pint and joined the small group of SWP students huddled around the long, sticky, beer-soaked table.

'Tom! Welcome to the Socialist Workers' Party,' announced Sam, who like Jim was radicalised and middle-class and trying his hardest to look like Noel Gallagher. Clearly the leader of the group, Sam slapped him on the back and tried to be as laddish as was possible for someone who'd grown up in a detached house and attended a respected grammar school.

'Thanks,' said Marcus, almost feeling as if he were among friends.

'To Dave!' toasted someone at the end of the table, to which everyone else did the same.

'You knew Dave, didn't you, Tom?' said Sam, taking a sip of his pint.

'Vaguely,' said Marcus, knowing that vaguely would be vague enough.

Just then, out the corner of his eye he spotted the joined-at-the-hip couple from the Stratford campus, who'd just walked in and sat with the young man at the end of the table who'd been doing the toasting.

'Excuse me a second,' said Marcus, as he rose with his pint and made his way to the end of the table.

'You two again?' he said playfully, sitting down as they temporarily froze as if they'd seen a ghost. 'Poor Dave, eh?' he continued, taking a long gulp of Guinness.

'A real shock,' replied Lucy with tears in her eyes. 'We'd only known him a couple of months.'

'He was always on his own,' added Luke. 'We just joined him one night.'

'I know – he was a quiet bloke,' said Marcus sympathetically.

'And to think it was that night when we were all having a drink,' said the girl as if it was all slowly coming back to her.

'I told him not to get the bus, and that I'd give him a lift, but he was having none of it, said something about going round a mate's house and maybe crashing there.'

'Yeah, said he had a few mates locally,' she said.

'If only he'd taken the lift,' said Marcus dramatically for good effect, 'he might be sitting here today!'

'True,' said Luke, losing interest and eyeing Marcus's pint and then looking at his lack of one.

Reading the signal immediately, sensing the potential of maybe becoming that good bloke who buys drinks for poor students again, Marcus took his cue. 'Pint?'

'You sure?'

'Yeah, drink to Dave,' he said as the annoying young man who'd made the toast before, on hearing the name, did so again as everyone else followed suit again: '*To Dave!*'

Having taken the orders of the couple and the toast master, whose name happened to be the same as his own, he made his way to the bar. Convinced that he'd done enough to dampen any suspicions they may have had about that night, he dismissed the idea of having to deal with them. Although he welcomed the idea, it would have been complicated, he reasoned as he paid the barman.

'All right, mate?' said the Cockney lad next to him who'd sidled up to the bar.

'Yeah, not bad,' replied Marcus, putting his change in his pocket. 'Do I know you?' he asked because he'd be annoyed with himself if he hadn't remembered a face.

'Charlie Harper,' said the lad in a bubbly sort of way. 'And no, you don't know me.'

Good, he thought. 'And?'

'I'm in my first year doing Computer Science.'

'Are you, Charlie?' he said, now a little interested. 'Why aren't you down the Students' Union bar with the rest of the freshers?'

'Ahh, a lot of them are fucking twats.'

'True,' said Tom. 'Come and join us,' he added, sensing an opportunity as he led him to the table.

★

'Are you sure you're all right with this?' said Evans, pulling up her navy trousers.

'I was OK, wasn't I?' replied Pencil, buttoning up his shirt, 'it's like nothing really happened.'

'You were brilliant, and Erika likes you too – I can tell,' she said warmly, pulling on her jacket. 'Are you not fazed by the weirdness of it all, though?' she added, now fully dressed. 'I mean, it's not what you'd expect to find behind everybody's bedroom door.'

'Yeah, it's odd,' began Pencil, who could easily have been talking to Jack now that he was fully clothed. 'I mean, I feel strange, but now we're both dressed, I feel normal again.'

'So, you're not going to fall for me or anything like that, are you?' she now said, hands on hips and legs apart. 'You know that could never be right?'

'No, of course not; we're just colleagues,' he said unconvincingly.

'Good,' she said, squeezing his hand, 'I don't want things to be strange at work.'

'Too busy for that,' he said, trying to make light of things, which for Pencil was a tricky manoeuvre.

'Oh, and Alan,' she said finally, opening the bedroom door, 'don't let Jack push you around so much, or rather don't give him a cause to, you know what I mean?'

'You're a gas, man,' laughed Marcus as Charlie delivered another punchline to a joke.

'Here, Tom, what about this one?' he started sounding even more Cockney. 'Why didn't the cement mixer marry the shovel?'

'Don't know,' said Tom, trying to sound remotely interested.

'It wasn't cement to be!' he rasped loudly, laughing at his own joke.

'So, are you the first in your family to go to university?' interrupted Marcus as the laughter ceased, pinching his wrist tightly beneath the table because he was sure that he knew the answer.

'Well, me and my sister. Jill went first and then me second. Me mum and dad were so proud. Particularly Mum: she still works as a cleaner, so you can imagine the party for Jill's graduation: a good, old-fashioned Cockney knees up.'

Marcus managed not to wince at that '*Cockney knees up*' and continued to smile broadly, showing his white teeth.

'Here, listen,' beckoned Charlie, moving in closer. 'Do you like Scalextric Formula One?'

Slightly bemused by the question, but sensing that this could be leading somewhere he'd like it to go, Marcus said that he did.

'Well, there's this huge apartment, down at Canary Wharf, that me mum cleans; owned by a rich Russian fella. On one floor he's got this gigantic track set up. Un-fucking-believable. Anyway, when he goes away, he leaves the keys with my mum, who lets me go down there and try it out.'

'Wow!'

'Sometimes I play all night.'

'Sounds my kind of thing.'

'Look, you must come down one night – it's well good.'

Nearly grimacing at the grammar, Marcus said he'd love to. 'That sounds right up my street!'

'Give us your number,' Charlie said, nudging his knee, 'and I'll give you a bell – I think he may be away next week.'

This couldn't get any better, he thought as he quickly scribbled his number on a beer mat. Now they're coming to me – the poor bastards.

'To Dave!' the toaster, Marcus, hollered again.

'To Dave!' they all echoed, as if he'd just got a promotion rather than having been brutally murdered by the man only a couple of feet away.

Chapter Thirteen

The snow was getting heavier and thicker by the second, and it was becoming harder to manoeuvre along the slushy main road. The newly purchased Stan Getz CD oozed in sweet time to the delicate falling snowflakes now brightening the otherwise drab surroundings of Stratford. Deciding to go it alone on some information that Dave Wilkins had regularly frequented the student bar at the University of East London, Jack had decided to pop in and being that it was on his way home, he'd made it his last call of the day.

Four o'clock; not bad, he thought, eyeing his watch as he parked the car. At least there wouldn't be too many students there yet. How wrong he was; the place was bursting. Entering, 'Freak Like Me' grated his eardrums and made him feel old as he winced at the noise. Strolling up to the bar he was more conscious than usual that he looked like a copper. Pushing past a few students wearing retro England shirts he found a space.

'Bitter lemon, please,' said Jack, gathering some change from his pocket and examining it.

'I'll have to see your student card if you want the student

price,' came the smart reply of the barman with numerous studs and rings in his ears and nose.

'Don't get smart, sonny – save it for the classroom,' said Jack, throwing him a deadly stare and producing his ID. 'I want to see the manager.'

'I am the manager,' replied the grinning smart-arse.

'Just a minute of your time, then,' he said, changing tack, as the manager nodded and his piercings jangled. 'You've heard about the murder of one of your regulars, Dave Wilkins?' Jack said, holding up a photograph.

'Yeah, didn't know him personally or anything, but yeah, he was here most nights. Used to sit on his own a lot – over there,' he gestured, pointing towards the small round table by the walled jukebox which was now blaring out 'Wonderwall', as two students to his left temporarily joined in on the first verse, only to stop dead because they didn't know the rest of the words.

'So, always on his own?'

'Well, no,' he countered, fiddling with one of his nose rings. 'There's a couple he sometimes sat with.'

'Boyfriend and girlfriend?' Jack interrupted, wanting to get the facts straight.

'Yeah, that's right, they come in here most nights; they started sitting with him.'

'Are they on campus?'

'I'd say so. In fact, they're right over there.' He nodded towards the opposite end of the bar, by the gents' toilet.

Christ, they look like children, thought Jack, noticing that they were glued to each other and holding hands as if one of them was hanging on for dear life on the edge of a mountain.

'Thanks,' said Jack, picking up his bitter lemon. 'Oh, and sorry about the "sonny" bit, I get a bit 1970s sometimes.'

'That's all right, guv,' the barman cheekily mimicked, 'my grandad used to say the same things.'

Jack smiled and wandered slowly over to the unsuspecting couple, who appeared to be sharing a pint of cider between them.

'I'm DCI Jack Hogan,' he began, showing them his badge as he sat down. 'And you are?'

Startled, they both looked up.

'Oh, I'm Luke and this is Lucy.'

'And I understand that you knew Dave Wilkins?'

'Yes,' Luke said.

'Knew him quite well?'

'No, not really, just felt sorry for him – sitting on his own all the time.'

'And what about the last time you saw him?'

'It was the night he was murdered,' said Lucy, as if everybody knew that.

Bingo, thought Jack, taking a sip of bitter lemon. 'Anything strange about him that night?'

'No,' said Lucy.

'A friend was with him, though; came in late in the evening,' said the boy.

'Name?'

'Tom.'

Double bingo. 'Do you know his surname?'

'No.'

'Know anything about him; what he said – anything?' continued Jack, sensing a hat-trick.

122

'Only that he was going on the march at the weekend.'

'The SWP thing,' added Lucy. 'We actually saw him on the same day as the march, in the Globe pub.'

'Mile End Road?'

'Yeah, that's it,' replied the girl.

'Did he say anything about the night in the bar?'

'Yes,' began Luke, 'he told us that Dave said he was going to crash at a friend's that night.'

'Why did he say that?'

'Well, Tom was going to give him a lift home.'

'And he said he didn't want one; that he was going to get the bus,' said the girl.

'Yeah, that's right,' agreed Luke.

So maybe he had the yellow Panda with him, thought Jack, slowly piecing it all together. 'Anything else?'

'Well,' said the girl timidly, and hesitating for a second, 'there was something else . . .' She began throwing her boyfriend nervous glances; he appeared to give her the nod to carry on. 'He said he had a couple of joints.'

'Asked us to join him for a smoke in the car,' said Luke.

'But we didn't,' announced Lucy innocently.

Sally Drayton was spot on, pondered Jack — the smell in the car; it all made sense.

Feeling that a good chunk of the nut had been cracked, Jack decided to wind things up. 'Look, write your details down here,' he said handing them a piece of paper and his pen, 'and if you see this Tom guy again, give me a call or contact one of my detectives, their names are on the back,' he added, taking their details off them and pressing his card into the girl's pale freckled hand as he got to his feet. 'I'd just like to have a chat with him,' he concluded for good measure, finding it difficult to wipe off the smile which was fast appearing on his face.

'Yes!' rasped Jack, clenching his fists as he walked away from the Union bar with a swagger in his step. Approaching his car, he felt great job satisfaction. It was the thing he loved about police work: the acting on a hunch, the coincidences like the couple in the bar who just happened to be there that afternoon, and then them being in The Globe on the same day of the march and of course, the smell of dope in the car that linked it all together.

'Shit!' It was his police radio, just as he was to rejoin Stan Getz and drive jazzily, leisurely, home.

'PC Smith calling, sir. You're to phone home – just received the call.'

Damn it! he thought, realising he'd left his mobile at the station. Remembering the payphone just inside the entrance of the students' bar, Jack backtracked as an ominous shiver ran down his spine.

'Skuld, what is it?' he said, instantly knowing something was wrong.

'It's Jake.' At the mere mention of his son's name his blood ran cold. 'He hasn't come home from school,' she said, clearly upset. 'I went up there to look – no Jake. Called his friend Mark's mum – not there either. Don't know what to do; it'll be getting dark soon. Jack, what shall I do?'

'Skuld, just wait there by the phone and don't leave the house. I'll drive around, I'm just leaving Stratford.'

'Oh, Jack, find him!' she said tearfully, hanging up.

Quickly contacting the station, he managed to get a patrol car which was already in the area to accompany him to Leytonstone. Back in the car and following the flashing light in front, he rapidly sped through red lights and down bus lanes. For some reason Mandy's sudden death began to plague his mind again as he tried to weigh up all the possibilities as to why Jake had disappeared.

They reached Leytonstone in minutes. The patrol car driver gave a casual wave, before rapidly heading off in the opposite direction, probably having received an emergency call.

Circling the tube station, Jack tried his hardest to immerse himself in being Policeman Jack as he returned to the High Street for the second time, crawling up towards the school and surrounding streets. Where would Jake go? he thought, despising the darkness which was now total.

'Jake, where are you?' he cried, losing his nerve for the first time and almost mislaying it completely. 'Think! Think, Jack!' he cursed, banging the steering wheel as he neared his own street. Suddenly accelerating, he performed a quick gear change and sped towards Epping Forest. There was a chance, he thought. It was their place, their father and son world. He might be there.

Instead of parking up he slowly mounted the pavement and drove on to the snow-layered grass flats. Putting his headlights on full beam, he drove until he reached the beginning of the forest. Stopping the car and leaving the engine running, he began to frantically beep the horn. Getting out, he surveyed the crisp snow. It will at least show signs of footprints, he thought, moving towards the trees. As if by chance (and it was chance) he spotted a number of broken lines in the snow. Further on, with the help of the lights from the car, he could just make out footprints, small enough to be his son's, leading into the forest. It was then that he spotted Jake's blue school bag left beside the upturned root of a tree.

'Jake! Jake! Jake!' he yelled, stepping into the forest as the sound of desperation echoed and ricocheted among the ominous trees. Finding himself further into the forest than he realised he instinctively stopped still and listened as the odd snowflake fell on his head in the silence. As if lost in a fairy story, he stood cold, scared, and lost. The whole forest now appeared gloomy as the shadows shifted and danced, each oak and birch tree closed, tight, and unforgiving as it defiantly impeded his vision. He'd never felt so helpless in his entire life, as he felt the urge to drop to his knees and pray. Then, through the darkness he could just make out the flicker of a bonfire and the mutter of distant voices. The Romany camp, he thought, now running through the dense forest towards the clearing, small branches scratching his face as he went. Reaching the perimeter of the camp Jack now slowed his pace. Flushed, leathery faces peered up from the fire, as he entered the quiet picture of the place, half hidden in the snow, beside a huge, downed oak. The gypsies looked on as if the stranger entering their abode was merely a rabbit or a squirrel. And there he was: Jake, sitting on a log with a couple of children, smiling, as if he was one of them.

'Jake!' Jack cried, tears in his eyes, 'you're safe!' He wrapped his arms around him as he smelt the warm, burnt, rustic odour of cinders in his son's hair and the Romanies nodded their heads in approval.

'What are you doing here, son?' he asked, sitting down next to him, 'we've been worried sick.'

'Dad, I'm all right.' The way he said it and looked deep into his father's eyes, Jack knew that nothing bad had happened.

Holding his son's hand tightly, Jake told him his story: that after school he'd decided to go to the forest to collect some leaves for a project they were doing in class. Seeing the smoke above the trees like before, he thought he'd seek it out and take a peep at the camp. It was then that the snow had got heavier and the further he'd got into the forest the more disorientated he'd become, until he was completely lost. Luckily two gypsy women (probably the ones they'd seen the week before) who were on their way back to the camp spotted him and asked him if he was OK. When he replied that he was lost, they kindly brought him back, made him a cup of tea, and waited for one of their husbands to return. As the men had failed to appear, the women were concerned about him leaving on his own and suggested he wait a little longer and that if they couldn't get to a phone box to phone Jack or Skuld, they'd bring him back themselves when their husbands returned.

'So, this had nothing to do with those boys at school?' asked Jack.

'Oh, no,' he replied brightly. 'I've got two new mates now: Enda and Kieran. They said that I'd never be bothered again and that if I was, I should just mention their names and that it would be sorted. So, no, Dad,' he concluded in his usual way, 'it was just the project, and I'm really sorry that I scared everyone.'

'Jake, I was petrified. Never again; OK?' he said firmly, placing a protective arm around his beautiful son as they said their thanks and farewells.

'You know what, Dad?' said his son, gazing up at him as the moonlight caught his large blue eyes.

'What?' he asked, wanting to hold his son's hand for ever and never let go.

'I'm sorry I took you to the bakery.'

'Don't worry, I've been doing a lot of that myself lately,' he smiled, ruffling Jake's blond mop as the beam of car headlamps lit up their rosy, relieved faces.

Chapter Fourteen

'So, Jake, you are all right now? No more forest walks – yes?'
'No, but I'm thinking of taking up karate, yes?' he replied with enough boyish cheek for Skuld to mutter that 'the cheeky boy never got the biscuit.'

'What about the cheeky girl?' asked Jack, perhaps a little too flirty for the breakfast table.

'Ah, the cheeky girl never needs the biscuit,' she said, giving Jack one of those looks that he was happily getting used to.

'Karate, hey, Jake?' said Jack, who'd never missed a trick in his life.

'Yeah, Enda and Kieran go.'

'Right,' reasoned Jack, 'good to be able to protect yourself,' he began slowly, 'as long as it's only used in defence.'

'Of course, Dad. You didn't have me down as a hooligan, did you?'

'Hooligan; what is a hooligan?' asked Skuld with a confused face.

'A bad boy,' replied Jack, taking a side wink at his smiling son, who added 'yobbo' to the evolving thesaurus.

'Oh,' began Jake, remembering something and almost holding up his hand, 'Enda and Kieran said that I'm Irish, like them.'

Jack was like a lot of children of Irish immigrants: they either embraced their parents' Irishness or fought against it and saw themselves as English. Jack followed his father's measured line that he should be an individual first and follow no flag but his own. With the bombing campaign in Britain intensifying it was best to just blend in than stand out. In hindsight it was why his mother had been insistent that her son have a more neutral and perhaps English name.

'Well, your grandparents are Irish, so you'd be able to play football for Ireland – though West Ham first,' laughed Jack.

His son wasn't letting him off that easily. 'So, what am I?'

'A Londoner first, and I'd say a very inquisitive one,' replied Jack, deciding that he'd use his father's *follow no flag but his own* advice at a later date.

'That will do,' answered Jake, cheekily stealing a piece of toast from his dad's plate.

'Well, Jack,' announced Skuld suddenly, pouring him and Jake some tea. 'Tonight – yes?'

Tonight, thought Jack, racking his brain and coming up with zero. He merely and perhaps unwisely shrugged his shoulders.

'My date, Jack,' she said playfully, punching him on the arm. 'Our dinner date.'

'Oh, that date; yeah, of course,' he lied, realising that he'd forgotten to book a table.

The date was to be the next important stage for him and Skuld in their growing relationship. A must-have occasion; a chance for Jack to show her how much he cared. As she'd reminded him, 'In Iceland, the first date is the first meeting of the faces.' Translated: the first time the eyes speak, and two people really see each other. The whole symbolism had affected Jack greatly as he began to realise more and more what a special woman she was, and how much he was falling in love with her.

'Dad, I did it,' whispered Jake, placing his hand on his father's as Skuld turned to retrieve the milk from the fridge. 'I've booked it.'

'How?' asked Jack in a hushed voice and a little concerned.

'I got Mark's mum to ring up,' replied his son. 'I just wanted to make sure you got it right,' he added innocently, but with the maturity of a growing diplomat.

'You have not forgotten, Jack?' said Skuld, returning with the milk.

'God, no,' he said, looking at Jake and knowing how important it was for him and how special it was for the woman he'd yet to tell he loved.

'What time?' asked Skuld, still a bit suspicious, as Jake splayed his four fingers and one thumb with one hand on the table, while laying three from the other hand beside them. Instantly reading the signal, Jack replied 'Eight,' as Skuld looked between them for any monkey business which may have been afoot.

'OK. Wear your new shirt and tie.'

Date secured, there was now the question of a little under-cover work to attend to at the East London University, where the SWP were to be handing out leaflets protesting at proposed Tory cuts to social security benefits. With a view to infiltrating the activists, it had been agreed that Jack would meet Pencil and Evans at Stratford Leisure Centre, from where they'd use one car before taking the short hike down to the university.

'Don't be late, Jack,' were Skuld's final words on the matter as she kissed and hugged him as if her life depended on it.

'Don't be late, Jack,' mimicked his son as Jack high-fived him and called him a little yobbo.

I like this new life, he thought as both Jake and Skuld waved enthusiastically from the doorstep as he pulled away. Who'd have thought that he had his own self-contained family under the same roof all along? If anything, he was pleased at the age difference between himself and Skuld. In his line of work, death could be waiting just around the corner and given his approaching fifties, if the unthinkable did happen, Jake would at least, maybe, have a young enough mother to guide him through his life.

Like Skuld, Mandy had been quite a bit younger than Jack. Surprisingly for them both children hadn't arrived straight away. After numerous IVF attempts, they'd given up on having children. Ironically, as soon as they did, Jake was miraculously conceived.

Spotting Pencil and Evans sitting patiently waiting for him outside the leisure centre, Jack wondered if they were heading in the same direction as himself and Skuld. Thinking of inviting them to a dinner party or maybe going on a couples' night out, he quickly put himself in check when he realised that it was Pencil he was thinking about and that work and pleasure didn't fit.

'Guv,' said Evans, instantly getting out of the front seat and revealing that she'd certainly done her homework: she was wearing black leggings, cherry-red Doc Martens, a tartan skirt, and a green duffel coat.

'You look the part,' said Jack, focusing on the black and white CND badge on her lapel.

'Thanks,' she replied, climbing into the back as Jack got in the front.

'Morning, Pencil.'

'Morning, sir.'

'Right,' began Jack, rubbing his hands. 'So, Evans, you're at Bristol University. You're down here staying with a friend, you're not in the SWP but you're involved in student politics and the left wing of the Labour Party.'

'Yes, sir.'

'You were a family friend of Dave Wilkins, went to school with his sister Sue. If you get a response or any flicker of recognition on Dave, then enquire about his friend—'

'Tom,' interrupted Evans, a bit restless and wanting to get going.

'Yes, see how far you can get – improvise, but ultimately: surname, possible contact details and university. As much as you can gather,' concluded Jack, aware that Evans was getting a little impatient, having already rehearsed everything the previous day.

'Yes, sir.'

'And if you do come face to face with this Tom guy, just say that Dave often spoke of him – the usual. He won't buy it, but a bit of paranoia wouldn't go amiss.'

'Yes, sir.'

'Me and Pencil here will do some surveillance, looking for any signs and changes in behaviour of the protestors you come into contact with.'

'Psychological surveillance,' piped in Pencil, trying a little bit harder than he needed to.

'Yeah, something like that,' said Jack dismissively. 'Right; ready?' he asked Evans, briefly turning his head.

'Yes, sir, ready.'

'OK, you start walking. We'll give you about fifteen minutes; just enough time for me and Detective Sergeant Sharpner here to get some coffees,' he said comically, with a heavy hint of sarcasm at the use of Pencil's official title. 'Oh,' he continued in the same light-hearted way, 'and let's be careful out there,' he smiled, using the old roll call catch phrase from *Hill Street Blues* as he winked at Evans in the mirror. She opened the car door and left.

Could Stratford get any more grim than it already was? thought Jack, spying a small dried-up puddle of blood by the smashed-up bus stop. Probably the leftovers of a street mugging or a drunken stumble, he pondered, as the car slowly moved along.

Parking up, Pencil went to fetch the takeaway coffees. Alone, Jack turned up the radio and listened to a phone-in from a woman who was posing the question: should older women date younger men? Trying not to think of himself and Skuld in the reverse of that enquiry, he instead turned the dial to a chirpy little song which he recognised as 'Alright' by Supergrass, harping on about the joys of being young.

'Guv, here; mind, it's hot,' Pencil said, passing him the paper cup and clambering in like an overgrown comedy partner to a slapstick joke.

'Lovely,' said Jack, smelling the rich aroma of coffee as he turned the radio down.

'There she is, sir.'

'Right, she's starting to mingle,' said Jack as Evans moved among the small, milling crowd of students.

Watching from the safety of their parking spot across the road, Jack was constantly having to make a peep hole in the steamed–up passenger-side window, an annoying part of surveillance from a car.

'No police, sir?'

'No, it's not classified as a demonstration; they're only leafleting – see, no placards,' he added, nodding in the direction of the university entrance. 'There's only about twenty people max.'

'I see,' replied Pencil, unusually anxious and glancing nervously in Evans's direction.

Maybe it's time to have that discussion, thought Jack, recognising the danger signs.

'You and Detective Evans – is it going all right?' Best to get it out there. Jack took a long sip of coffee and waited cagily in the silence that followed.

'Sorry, sir; what do you mean?'

He should have known that with Sharpner (to pardon the pun) he would have to be blunt if he wanted to get his message across. 'You two: you're an item, right? I saw you in the compound the other day.'

Blushing, Pencil rigorously shook his head and replied, 'No, no, sir.'

'It's OK, Pencil; really. I'm just making sure that it doesn't interfere with your judgements at work, that's all,' began Jack. 'I could see the anxiety on your face when Evans entered the group. I just don't want you to fall into that trap.'

'Sir, we're not an item,' Pencil said, gazing guiltily into his now empty cup.

'Just a fling then?' said Jack, knowing that Pencil was a natural spiller of the truth.

'Well, no, sir; you see . . . she already has a girlfriend,' he began timidly as Jack gasped '*Fucking hell*,' and spilled some of his coffee down his shirt. 'I just . . . join them sometimes – you know?'

'Wow,' said Jack, adding it all together and coming up with three.

'You won't say anything?' That was Pencil's last blushing word on the matter.

'Of course not,' Jack reassured him, 'whatever you do in your own time is your business as long as it doesn't break the law or interfere with work.'

After a few awkward minutes, they were at last relieved to be back on the job as Evans began talking to a short, thin man in a navy-blue windcheater.

'She's in,' said Jack, now back to viewing Evans as a colleague rather than part of a progressive love trio.

'Haven't met you before,' said the bespectacled Noel Gallagher wannabe.

'No, I'm not SWP – though I'm into student politics,' Evans whispered, making a joke of the fact they might be being listened to.

'Never can be too careful,' he said smiling. 'MI5 have a dossier on every member of the SWP, Militant Tendency, Communist Party – the lot,' he concluded, almost out of breath.

That she did know. There had been an unprecedented level of paranoia and unnecessary information-gathering since the miners' strike.

'Are you at London University then?' he asked, his eyes narrowing as if trying to place her face.

'No, Bristol.' The interrogation really had begun.

'You must know Bob . . .'

'Chapman,' she said immediately, knowing that he was bound to know the Students' Union presidents of most UK universities and throw a few names at her. 'He's SWP,' she concluded proudly.

A little more relaxed, he made another joke about having mistaken the singer and activist Billy Bragg for the right-wing Conservative member for Bromley South and telling him to fuck off at a miners' benefit in the late eighties, before being mortifyingly informed that it was the great man himself, who'd organised the event and was playing at the gig.

'Good with faces, then?' she quipped, recognising an opportunity.

'I suppose,' he said coyly, his attraction to her becoming increasingly obvious as he fidgeted with the woggle on his coat.

'I'm actually down visiting a friend,' she began, 'and of course I'm attending Dave Wilkins' funeral,' she said unexpectedly.

She didn't have to wait long for a shimmer of interest as he returned her forearm with a volley. 'Dave, yeah. Not a member, but used to tag along a lot. Really nice bloke.'

'I went to school with his sister Sue.'

'Really, wow – small world,' he said, realising that *wow* probably wasn't one of his better lines.

'The last time I saw Dave,' she began, now halfway through her previously prepared speech, 'he'd said that he'd made a good friend on a demonstration: Tom, I think his name was; came from up north somewhere,' she added, knowing he was about to cave in.

'Oh, yeah, that would be Tom Gray from Cortonwood, Barnsley; he's a student; just became a member.'

Trying to hide her excitement, she attempted to extract as much information as possible without arousing suspicion.

'Where does he study?'

'Do you know what? I don't know,' he answered, baffled, as if realising he'd been told very little by his new comrade.

'You probably don't even know where he lives?' She really was pushing her luck.

'Well, that wouldn't be appropriate,' he said, now more serious than before as he pushed his glasses up the bridge of his nose and his eyes narrowed once again.

I'm being rumbled, she thought, aware that she had perhaps got a little too carried away. 'So, do you want me to hand out any leaflets or anything?' she smiled, changing tack, but realising by his now pained expression that the game may be up.

'You're police – aren't you?' he said contemptuously.

'Of course not,' she laughed nervously.

'Piss off!' he said sternly, loud enough for the others to hear as they turned accusingly towards her.

Act, she thought, knowing she'd been found out and that Jack and Pencil were only across the street.

'Listen!' she said, suddenly snapping as she grabbed his arm, 'you're right, I'm police, and if you don't give me the fucking address, you're going in for questioning and for withholding information – understand?'

'Bullshit!' he shouted back in her face. 'Fucking pigs!' he raged as a small crowd gathered round him.

'OK, break it up,' growled Jack, ID in hand and shouldering the biggest guy in the group out of the way as Pencil placed his hand menacingly around the man's arm.

'I think we need to bring this one in for questioning, sir,' said Evans, her face still flushed and eyes wide.

'Right, come on, Castro; let's go,' said Jack, adding a little TV cop as they bundled him away.

'OK, you lot disperse!' shouted Pencil as they pushed their way back through the mainly student activists who booed and gave as much abuse as was possible without facing arrest.

'Right, Castro,' said Jack, climbing in beside him in the back of the car.

'That isn't funny,' replied the man indignantly.

'It is when you look nothing like a revolutionary,' said Jack, before sighing and continuing, 'Look, I don't care about the bloody SWP, the Communist Party, or the bloody Boys' Brigade, I just want you to answer my colleague's questions.'

'Police state!' the man protested.

'Really?' replied Jack dismissively as he turned to Evans, telling her to, 'Carry on.'

'Tom Gray's a new member, sir, and this individual is withholding information as to his whereabouts.'

'Is that so?' said Jack, raising a serious eyebrow, 'and why would you do that?'

The man didn't say anything, but remained silent, no doubt considering his options in the face of Fascist Police Oppression.

'Look,' began Jack, showing his exasperation, 'you can either give us what we need now and by the way, we haven't even asked you your name, or we can go down the station and interrogate you completely in relation to why you might be withholding information about a person we may be investigating. Or you can give us the address now and you can get back to handing out your leaflets – which by the way, I fully agree with.'

Remembering the long overdue unpaid traffic fine and his involvement in the Poll Tax riots, where he'd seen himself on TV the next day, throwing a scaffolding pole at a police car, the man knew that self-preservation rather than socialism was the necessary pill to be swallowed. Reaching into his army surplus bag he pulled out his Filofax, fingering it nervously until he got to the 'G's. 'Tom Gray: Flat One, fifty-two Orwell Gardens, Stratford.'

'Telephone number?' pressed Evans.

'He said he didn't have one.'

'Description?' chipped in Pencil, who'd been throwing him the odd evil glare.

'Make sure you don't make it up – we'll find you, Sam Richards,' stated Jack, who'd instantly spied his name as Sam had mistakenly gone to the first page of his Filofax where his own details lay.

'OK, very good, you saw my details,' Sam said, defeated.

'Force of habit, son; too many years of police work – now, the description.'

'About six foot two, dark wavy hair, usually in a fringe over his eyes, skinny, wears a long navy overcoat – that's about all I know about him.'

'DS Evans, anything else you want to ask Sam here?'

'No, sir,' she said, though deep down wanting to give the protester a piece of her mind.

'Well, Sam, that was easy – not so complicated after all,' said Jack.

'Yeah,' he managed limply.

'Let him out, DS Sharpner.'

'Yes, sir.'

'Oh, and just before you go – if you know anything you think we should know, I strongly advise you to contact us. Right, now go and do some protesting,' said Jack as Sam despondently got out of the car.

'Well done, Evans,' congratulated Jack as Pencil did the same.

'Ah, no, sir, I blew it,' she replied, flustered, as she watched Sam Richards slowly slump back towards his comrades.

'How?'

'He fancied me. I could have got his number and joined his group of friends, which would have led to Tom Gray.'

'It doesn't matter,' said Jack warmly, 'if necessary, we'll put a tail on him, but in the meantime, we'll get a warrant and scarper down to Orwell Gardens. Radio through and get that sorted now, Pencil,' concluded Jack, as Evans mouthed 'I'm all right,' to a relieved DS Sharpner.

Chapter Fifteen

'Number one?'
 'Yeah, all over.'
'Skinhead?'
'Kind of – just want a change,' said Marcus, staring at his reflection as the barber did as instructed and dramatically bulldozed the clippers down the centre of his scalp.

'You're not from round here then?' said the barber, who resembled and sounded like the actor Ray Winstone.

'North Yorkshire.'

'You down for West Ham versus Leeds?' he asked, now matching the sides with the top as Tom began to resemble a Royal Marine.

'No, just at college.'

'Oh,' said the barber, as if the whole idea was a waste of time and that the conversation wasn't worth taking further now that the football chat was off the agenda.

'Nice sheepskin, son,' he finally said, admiring his customer's new purchase from Camden Market. 'Used to 'ave one in the seventies when I was a suedehead. Making a comeback, are they?'

Marcus just shrugged. In truth, it was a new look: Fred Perry shirt, Levis, Gola trainers, and of course the sheepskin and now the haircut. Everybody it seemed wanted to mix and match the sixties, seventies, and eighties into one nineties Britpop image, of which there were many different uniforms and styles.

'How's that, me old cocker?' asked the barber, getting the hand mirror and showing him the back of his scalped head in the bigger one.

'Fantastic; thanks,' said Marcus without showing that he felt the opposite.

'Good, nice to 'ave the chat,' lied the barber, shaking his head and throwing his gaze to one of his waiting regulars as the young man paid and left without saying a word.

How a new haircut and a change of clothes can change the look of a person completely, Marcus thought as he put on his new Ray-Ban sunglasses and waited on the corner of Spencer Drive. Like all hunters he'd acted upon instinct and the sense of smell that led him back to his prey. It was almost like clockwork. His own inner time told him that she'd soon be venturing out on to the open plain.

'Sal, have you got everything?' asked Pete, picking up her already over-packed rucksack and throwing it over his large rounded shoulder.

Since the first visit by the police, the on-going investigation, and confiscation of her car, plus the distinct possibility that the murderer may know where she lived, Sally had decided that Pete's was the safest place to be.

'Pete, you don't think he knows where you live as well, do you?' whispered Sally, who clearly hadn't been sleeping since the investigation had begun; the deep black rings under her eyes giving her a ghoulish, haunted look which strangely enhanced the beauty beneath her vulnerability as she hung on tight to the arm of her protector.

'Sal, it hasn't been proved he knows where you live – let alone me.' Pete's practical words on the matter were enough to give her the peace of mind she was longing for. Being that Pete very rarely ventured out, it was by deduction the safest safe house to be holed up in.

'I guess,' said Sally, slightly more satisfied than before as she marvelled at her boyfriend's six foot three height and the security his huge frame generated. 'I can always hide behind you, I suppose,' she added as the gory details of Dean Waters and Dave Wilkins' murders, which she'd promised herself she wouldn't read in the papers, but had, flashed before her cloudy eyes and she visibly shivered.

Slamming the door behind her and checking the locks, she was relieved to be leaving. Even Grunge the cat was coming, being picked up and dropped off later by Pete's mate Andy who lived in the next street. As they now walked together on the sunny side of the street she strangely felt as if she was stepping into a new chapter in her life. There was going to be no more *Betrayal of Pete* and no bloody weirdo Tom.

'Morning,' said a young man adjusting his shades and pulling up the collar of his sheepskin coat as he lowered his head.

'Morning.'

'Who's that?' said Sally, holding Pete's hand tightly as they struggled along with her belongings.

'No idea,' replied Pete, as Marcus cupped his hands and lit a cigarette while giving the impression he was waiting to meet a friend.

Remaining still until they turned the corner at the end of the road, Marcus slowly began to move, catching up, then pulling back when he was within a safe distance of the couple as they strode hand in hand through the red-brick estate. They soon made it on to the main road which led down to Hackney tube station. Crossing the road and looking around them, they quickly arrived at Clifton Road. Giving the street one more nervous glance, Sally followed Pete into the first-floor flat of the dilapidated townhouse next to a grim-looking café called The Full English.

'Phew! Do you think anyone saw us come in?' asked Sally.

'Seriously,' smiled Pete, 'we're not in a spy thriller.'

'I know,' she said, trying her hardest to remain upbeat when all she really wanted to do was cry. Nestling her head into his chest they both hung on tight as they leaned back against the now closed front door.

Outside beyond the entrance stood Marcus, feet apart, staring straight at the frosted-glass panelling; his gaze steady, like an X-ray machine scanning every inch of their entwined bodies. Taking off his dark glasses he remained quite still for some time, mapping out the property, imagining its interior, while putting together numerous scenarios which could be played out in the not-too-distant future. Focusing on their silhouette, he now visualised himself there with Sally as she looked dreamily into his eyes and kissed him tenderly.

As if completing the sequence and then turning off the lights in his head, he put his glasses back on and swaggered away back down the street from which he'd flown.

Chapter Sixteen

'So, Jack; our first date?'

She looked like a Nordic angel, wearing a strapless white fifties pleated dress and matching flat ballet shoes, her blonde locks tied back into an Athenian bun.

'You look amazing.'

'You like my look, then?' she said, holding his hand across the table, her blue eyes sparkling, lit by the burning candle in a red jar.

There was so much he wanted to say, much of it forbidden so early into a relationship. He was in love with her, had only kidded himself that it was merely desire and awkwardness on his part. It was the line of adoration which usually popped up its head months down the line, when you would consciously practise the words over and over, as you nervously waited for the right moment. And now he felt the urge so strong that he couldn't keep it in any longer. 'Skuld?'

'Yes, Jack?' she answered, the edge of the table digging into her ribs as she bent across the divide.

'I want you to know now, right now, that I really love you,' said the old romantic, kissing her tenderly on the lips and sliding a thin black box across the table. 'And this is for you.' Jack was old-fashioned; he also understood how important the night was for Skuld and he wanted to pull out all the stops.

'Oh, Jack,' she said, tears welling up in her eyes, 'no one has ever been so kind.' She squeezed his hand. 'It's beautiful,' she cried, taking out the elegant pearl bracelet and putting it on. 'You know, Jack, ever since I walked through your door, I loved you too.'

Stop the music. Was life really that good?

'Oi, Alfonso, two more beers over 'ere now, pronto!'

Jack had clocked them as soon as they'd walked in: a little tipsy and certainly not on a dinner date themselves, the two lads were only interested in quickly refuelling and getting some more beers down their necks before heading for a nightclub to track down some unfortunate girls for a night of no-strings-attached sex.

'Fuck it!' shouted the bigger of the two, spilling his lager down the front of his trousers as the short, stocky, tattooed bulldog one belched and called him a 'stupid cunt'.

They were a type he knew well: extremely dangerous in a pack; difficult in pairs. To stop them you had to pick them off one by one and you had to be pretty clever and ardent in your approach – there could be no pleasantries or reasoning with these two.

'Thank you,' said Jack as the starters arrived.

'Thank you,' copied Skuld, attempting her poshest English accent as the bruschetta landed in front of her, red, gloriously oily and glossy.

'You're welcome,' said the pretty, petite brunette with the Sophia Loren smile and looks.

'You're welcome 'ere anytime, luv,' remarked the bulldog,

patting his chunky thigh as the other specimen cackled and added another vile derogatory comment as she passed.

'Jack,' pleaded Skuld, obviously upset and a little afraid. 'What are you going to do?' she asked, glancing nervously in their direction as the atmosphere thickened and the temperature plummeted.

The same question had been swimming around his own mind as the comments were beginning to get closer to home. Act now and he could have a full-blown bar brawl on his hands with no back-up. Say nothing and it was only a matter of time before the remarks started flying Skuld's way. He'd already heard one of them attempting her accent when telling a loud joke about an Eskimo who wanted to marry a fish.

Hard stares were definitely out the window, as was firmly asking them to keep it down. As for the worried-looking manager pretending that nothing was happening? No, he was definitely alone on the muscle front.

'Fucking foreigners,' muttered the bigger one with the gold tooth.

That may have been directed at them; hopefully at the Italian drinks waiter instead, prayed Jack, a bead of sweat forming on his brow as his heart began to thump like a big bass drum.

'Jack, I need to go to the toilet,' said Skuld, going to get up.

Worst case scenario, thought Jack, now worried as he grabbed her hand to stop her.

'Wait,' he whispered. 'Trust me, just hold on for a second,' he said, looking around him at the other customers who were clearly pretending they were somewhere else, avoiding his eyes as they stared as if actors in a play at their plates.

'But, Jack . . .'

'But, Jack,' came the echo from the louts' table.

Maybe the bar-room brawl was the only option, thought Jack, contemplating pushing Skuld under the table, grabbing the half-empty bottle of wine, and smashing it on the table.

'Just going for a piss,' announced the bulldog, his primal shape rising from the table like steam from cloudy urine.

Not quite perfect, but better, pondered Jack, giving Skuld a reassuring smile as he excused himself in a more refined way.

'Jack, be careful,' said Skuld.

'Stay put,' he said as he squeezed her hand and rose from his seat.

Walking past the sole remaining knuckle-dragger, Jack heard him suck his teeth and felt the *I am a hard-bastard* stare on his back, stabbing him all the way to the bar.

'You the manager?' Jack asked the immaculately dressed young man who could easily be mistaken for an estate manager or a professional footballer.

'Yes, sir. How may I help you?'

'Look, I want you to do me a favour,' he said, pulling him to one side. 'I'm going to the gents and I might be some time. I want you to go up there and have a conversation with my girl-friend; she's from Iceland. Got it?'

'Yes, sir,' he answered, confused at the request.

'While I sort this problem out for you,' he added, nodding towards the gents as the penny finally dropped in the young man's slot.

Strolling towards the bathroom to confront whatever waited for him beyond the door, Jack felt the same dreaded sensations he always experienced when he anticipated violence; the

149

frantic, accelerated heartbeat and the sickness in the pit of the stomach, which was only released when aggression had been unleashed with free abandon.

Clenching his fist, Jack slowly pushed open the door of the gents and entered, instinctively looking to the empty urinal, in which water was now cascading down the stainless steel wall like a waterfall. Must be in the middle cubicle, thought Jack, surveying the other two open doors, before tip-toeing in and dropping the latch of the door behind him.

A rustle of paper and a long hard sniff from the cubicle. Jack knew he had the bastard, had him just where he wanted him: compromised and isolated within the dingy crapper box where he belonged.

The short sniffs were a giveaway. More likely speed than cocaine, thought Jack. Cocaine was still the chosen drug of the well-heeled while speed and heroin were for the less well-off, the class divide which neatly pigeon-holed the criminal poor and desperate into one murky, seedy, media pissed-in, overflow-ing pot.

Two raps on the door and the obligatory 'Piss off' came. Because of Skuld and her special night, Jack had it all thought out, instantly had a strategy within his sights – a no-nonsense, no-fuss solution to a grubby episode – if it all went according to plan.

'I thought I told you to piss off!' spat the tattooed ape, open-ing the door, his head and neck as if one melting into an over-sculpted pair of meaty shoulders, a dab of white powder hovering beneath his left nostril.

'Not a very nice welcome,' said Jack, hands now casually confident in his trouser pockets.

'Are you fucking mad! Do you know who I am?' said the wide-eyed maniac, pupils dilated.

'No, but do tell me; I'd be interested to know.'

'Mad Freddy Hubbard,' he said menacingly, moving towards him.

'Mad Freddy?' laughed Jack. 'Never heard of yer, son,' he said, stopping him in his tracks and producing his ID. 'DCI Jack Hogan, never off fucking duty,' he said, grabbing Freddy suddenly by the throat and forcing him backwards into the cubicle, bringing his shaven head down hard on to the top of the cistern. 'Do you know, I've been nicking prats like you for years! With the same stupid fucking nicknames! Mad this, crazy that –' he started pressing the man's face across the white ceramic – 'and they all speak the same shit and make the same threats, as they spend their entire worthless lives ruining others', shitting on everything that they come into contact with. Is that who you are; mad, stupid Freddy Hubbard?'

He stopped right there, his anger near getting out of control as he contemplated smashing Freddy's face against the white-tiled wall.

'So, what've we got here?' began Jack, composing himself and reaching into Freddy's back pocket to produce a small cling-film wrap of white powder. 'Speed? Not much, but enough,' he added, plonking it down in front of Freddy's eyes. 'Bit quiet, Freddy. Don't want to get nicked, is that it? A bit too much form this year? Yeah, thought so,' said Jack, releasing his grip as Freddy got to his feet. 'So, what's the story, Freddy, where's all the bravado gone – the big man stuff?' he added, noting the confused look on his ignorant face.

'My girlfriend's pregnant.'

'Don't give me that! I wasn't born yesterday,' snarled Jack, roughly grabbing his chin and pushing his head back against the wall of the cubicle.

'All right! I can't go back to prison,' he capitulated, 'can't go this time,' he pleaded.

'Oh, I get it,' said Jack, letting him go again. 'Someone inside you don't want to meet, someone you've pissed off. And I thought you were Mad Freddy Hubbard?'

Knowing he'd been rumbled, Freddy said nothing.

'Well, Freddy,' said Jack, straightening his new shirt and tie, 'this is what's going to happen,' he began, picking up the small ball of speed and spinning it between his fingers. 'First, you're going to walk back into the restaurant with me, you're going to quietly tell that piece of shit you're with you've been nabbed and that you have to leave, then you're going to turn and apologise to my girlfriend and then you're going to scarper,' he concluded, plopping the ball of speed into the toilet and flushing. '*Comprende?*'

Agreeing, Freddy lowered his eyes in defeat.

'And just remember, Freddy: I know you now, just like I probably know the nutter who wants to slash your face with a blade melted into a toothbrush courtesy of B Landing at the Scrubs.'

Returning from the gents minutes later, Jack followed by a dejected, not so mad any more Freddy, it appeared as if the two of them just had a friendly chat about the football as they made their way back to their tables. Doing as instructed and muttering a few grunts in his mate's ear, his friend quickly split and left Freddy alone to make his apologies to a stone-faced Skuld, who merely stared through him in an indifferent, yet mildly amused kind of way given the seriousness of the situation.

'Jack, what did you say — did you tell him that you are a policeman and that you have a gun?' asked Skuld after Freddy had left.

'Something like that,' he replied, now seated and feeling a little jaded now that the adrenalin rush had subsided and relative normality had returned as the other diners smiled politely in their direction, relieved that their evenings had been saved.

You're never off-duty even in restaurants, there's always something out of place or someone not acting as they should and playing the bollocks, he thought as the manager arrived with a complimentary bottle of champagne and the news that the rest of the evening was on the house.

'Champagne, Jack? Just like kings and queens in the parlour,' she said excitedly.

It was just another thing he loved about her: the way she could switch from what could have been for some a disaster to girlish wonder the next, pragmatic and seamless in her zeal for the good things in life.

With the evening back on course, you would have had to pinch yourself to remember that it could have been so different had those gorillas ruled supreme in the jungle. Was all life like police work, wondered Jack as he poured more champagne: piecing everything together and hoping that all the shit in the world could somehow be flushed away. Then there was the mess that couldn't be cleaned up: the dead ends that brought you down with a bang, the ones that couldn't be power-hosed away, that turned around and kicked you in the face as you hit the last wall, all the time knowing that all your hard work had led to nothing, where you had no choice but to just sit and wait for your luck to change, always the most crushing feeling for any detective.

And that was certainly the case three hours previously at Tom Gray's last known address.

'Evans, you take the back.'

'Yes, sir,' she said, immediately springing into action and running towards the rear of the building.

'Give her a few seconds,' began Jack. 'Right now,' he said, 'give a good loud rap on the door,' he instructed, touching the handle of his gun beneath his coat.

'No answer, sir,' said Pencil, stating the obvious.

'Right, kick it in.'

Like his driving, Pencil's door-breaking was legendary. It was rumoured he wore size-fourteen boots and that one crack at a door was usually enough to split the thickest of frames.

'It was definitely Orwell Gardens, wasn't it?' asked Jack hesitantly as Pencil took three steps back for his run-up.

'Affirmative, sir.'

'"Affirmative": what are you, DS bloody Spock Sharpner all of a sudden?'

'No, sir,' he said, eyeing up the size and thickness of the job in hand.

'Kick it!'

Jack had seen him do it so many times before: Pencil merely appeared to stroll through the door as the sound of splintering wood rung in their ears as the frame creaked and broke on impact.

'Nice work.'

'Thanks, sir.'

Instantly spying the solitary letter on the mat surrounded by junk mail, Jack knew it was a no-go as he picked up the envelope

addressed to Tom Gray and opened it up to the SWP membership contents inside. They didn't have to venture any further
because three feet into the hall was a deep cavernous hole where
the distant sound of flowing water could be heard, beyond
which a derelict staircase led to nowhere – the whole place had
been gutted for renovation and no doubt abandoned when the
money ran out. Gray was using an unfinished building site as
a decoy. The perfect invisible pseudo-abode for a man who
wanted to be the hunter rather than the hunted.

'Sir, there's no back to the house,' said Evans breathlessly,
appearing at Pencil's shoulder. 'It's being held up by steel beams;
it's a ruin.'

'I know,' replied Jack, staring into the deep cavity as if hoping
to see a light which led to another chamber.

'Jack?'

In the time he'd known Skuld, he knew from the tone of
enquiry that she had something important to say.

'Yes, Skuld,' he said, topping up her glass.

'If you had something to say and you really wanted to say it,
no matter what outcome, would you say it?'

'Like I did earlier?'

'Yes.'

She was still kind of smiling, so it couldn't have been that
bad, nothing like any of the wrecking balls doing the rounds in
Jack's head.

'Well,' said Jack, shifting nervously in his seat. 'I suppose I
would,' he added as she stopped smiling.

'I had an abortion many years ago,' she began, lowering her

155

eyes as if she'd committed a terrible crime. 'I was very young; stupid – Jack.'

'That's all right, Skuld,' he reassured her, 'you were young – things happen.'

'Yes, I was a teen— what is the word, Jack?' she said, exasperated because she wanted to say it right.

'Teenager.'

'Yes, teenager – seventeen, me and this boy, we couldn't do it. He wanted to travel and so did I. So . . .' she faltered, 'we got rid of the baby,' she said sadly, tears welling in her eyes as Jack held her hand. 'It was hard, Jack, but there was more. Doctor told me my womb was thin; you know, not strong.'

'Oh,' he replied, puzzled, trying to keep up with the changing story.

'Said it would be harder to have a baby, the older I got. And now I'm thirty.'

'Right,' he said, sensing what may or may not be coming next.

'Well, now I want to,' she said simply, her stare steady as if looking deep into his soul for an answer.

'A baby?' he replied, shocked, but slowly putting it all together the way he would in the interrogation room.

'Yes, a baby; I'll understand if you don't,' she concluded in a way that suggested she'd given it a lot of thought and the outcome of their way forward together rested on this not so strange, yet life-changing request.

Well, there he had it: seas parting, planetary collision, alien invasion and Jesus making a comeback. He reasoned with himself. How could he argue with a young woman's desire to have a child? OK, he wasn't going to be around for as long as Skuld, but their family, his and Skuld's, would have grown by then.

And the benefits of Jake having a brother or sister, and a young mother, outweighed any selfish feelings he may have had about quietly retiring and taking up birdwatching on a more full-time basis. When you got to Jack's age, you didn't ponder so much when hit by a bombshell.

What an end to a beautifully odd and very human evening, he thought, as he said 'Yes' to what would be a lifetime of nappies, playdates, school pick-ups, and long arduous school holidays followed by sleepless nights waiting for a teenager to arrive home from the disco.

Uncrossing her fingers, Skuld said a silent prayer. *He's the one*, she told herself, wishing his body had a door to it which she could open and climb into and shut behind her for ever.

'We'll start tonight, Jack, yes?' she said, standing, her dreams answered.

'Why not,' said Jack, still in a state of possible fatherhood, as he grabbed his coat and guided her by the waist towards the door.

'Goodnight,' said the manager, opening the door and thanking Jack again for the one-man expulsion exercise of earlier.

'He showed him his gun,' laughed Skuld. The manager smiled nervously at the notion as he ushered them out into the deep inky darkness.

Many of the streetlights were either broken or barely on as they strolled the short distance to their home. The moon, big and bright, shone down on them, with the crisp frost and the echo of their footsteps magically accompanying them home.

Like Christmas Eves years ago, thought Jack, remembering long, staggering walks home from the local pub to his mum and dad's as the distant celebrations and sounds of inebriation became duller until you were left with that drink-induced whisper: that cold, glittering stillness, that real winter Noel, that optimism, that drunken, spiritual feeling when you just want to lose your clothes and cry pure tears of unexplained happiness.

'Well, Jack, you made me very happy tonight,' Skuld said as Jack put the key in the latch. 'I think it's written in the sky,' she announced, pointing at the shooting stars which had decided to join the party, quietly exploding above their heads.

Chapter Seventeen

Funny how they don't build terraced houses any more, thought Jack, remembering how they used to be council estates before high rises arrived, tearing up communities as they were re-housed beyond the trees. The streets of his childhood were unchanged, though there seemed to be more litter back then, when people used to casually toss rubbish out of passing cars and empty the contents of their pockets out on to the pavements. The grimy yellow brick terraces were exactly the same. 'Good bricks, those,' his father would always remark, making the point that they only had red ones back in Ireland, and that he'd helped lay most of them as a young man before taking the boat to England where he discovered the yellow ones for the first time.

Jack noted the original green front doors as he passed, and, sadly, the growing number of anaemic new PVC ones standing to attention like white sheets. Avoiding a patch of staggered dog shit, which gave the impression it was evenly placed like land mines awaiting a casualty, Jack smiled to himself as he remembered how when he was a boy his dad had told him to adopt a healthy mixture of looking at his feet and staring straight ahead when walking, with the likelihood you would step in less muck if you did.

Jack had been lucky, his dad had had the knack for making enough money to keep his family well-clothed and fed, unlike many of his peers who often went to school with no socks (just Woolworths shoes), a grimy parka, and dirty, snot-strewn faces. They were by no means privileged, but they were the only family in the street that had had a full bookcase, and there was an old piano in the front room which his father had lifted out of a skip. His mother, Aileen, a great singer and self-taught musician, and his father, Michael, a prolific reader, said that it was because they were from the land of poets, scholars, and musicians. It was why Jack was naturally pushed towards college while the rest of his friends blindly accepted their lot and headed to the army, building sites, and factories.

Standing outside 46 Ashmere Gardens, Jack reached into his pocket and pulled out his mum and dad's wedding picture: his mother, proud, upright, her expression full of love and admiration for the handsome man by her side, with his Brylcreemed quiff, no doubt combed back meticulously a dozen times that sunny morning, as his new wife linked her arm in his for all eternity.

Jack rapped at the door a third time. His mother seemed to take a little longer each time he called. It was his weekly visit, and one which he always tried to keep no matter how busy things were at work.

'Jack,' she said on opening the door, as she always did, as if he'd just returned from a very long maritime voyage. 'You're looking so thin.' She always said this too, ever since his dad had passed away from his short battle with lung cancer, which had left him looking like a waxy version of his previous self. 'I've got some boxty from the Irish Centre shop,' she added, proudly holding out the pre-packed potato breads as if they were an exotic gift. 'I'll fry up some rashers with them.'

Jack had stopped pleading with her years ago, knowing that her insistence would always win through and overtake any notions he had of having a healthy diet. She headed for the electric cooker which she always wished was a range like the one they used to have back home in Galway.

The ticking of the clock, the stillness that you only experience in old buildings, was still there, that sacred silence that could only be interrupted by a screaming kettle or the turning of the dial on the radio for the midday news. On the shelves of the dresser sat the breakfast set consisting of egg cups, saucers, bowls and tea plates with *Littlehampton* inscribed across a sunny beach scene, which made him smile as he remembered how he and his sister Helen used to moan about their annual camping holiday in West Sussex, which they called the gypsy trek.

'Ahh, you don't know you're living,' their father would call back from the driver's seat of their mauve Morris Minor as he'd tell a tale about hard living and poverty back in Ireland.

'Only priests and misery,' his mother would add as she'd wink at her husband, who would be trying his hardest to remain serious and not laugh.

'The egg cups,' he said suddenly as his mum turned the boxty in the pan, 'we really loved Littlehampton, you know.'

'You always were both little tykes,' replied his mum, reminding him that it was his dad who'd won the breakfast set in a talent contest at the campsite, doing his best Elvis Presley.

Sitting at the small Formica table, Jack looked up as he always did at the signed photograph of Robert Mitchum his father had got from a friend when the star was filming *Ryan's Daughter*. He didn't know why exactly, but the American reminded him of his father's stoicism and natural ability to just get on with things, which brought him to why he was there that morning.

'Here,' said his mum, placing the fry-up before him. 'You need feeding up.'

'Mum?'

'Yes, Jack?'

'Me and Skuld . . . you remember Skuld?'

'Of course I do, I'm not completely gone in the head, you know.'

He loved her smile and turn of phrase, the way she just took everything in her stride like his dad.

'We're together now, and it's getting serious – you know . . . It's good for Jake.' He was bumbling now, like an unsure child.

'Jack, Jack, Jack,' she said as if the words were descending notes, 'it's fine – I'm not that old-fashioned,' she said, placing her veiny hand on his shoulder. 'You need to move on – Mandy would have wanted you to,' she added carefully with all the wisdom of a mother.

His mum was one in a million, she always said the right things and particularly when he needed a gentle prod in the right direction. From Mandy to his mum, he couldn't explain it exactly; maybe *he* was just plain old-fashioned, but he needed their approval.

'Mandy was a wonderful wife and mother, she'd be upset if you didn't move on with your life.'

'And Dad?' he asked, because he needed that too.

'What do you think – wasn't he always telling you to be your own man?' She had her arm draped lovingly across his shoulders now. 'Do it for yourself, and for Jake, and that pretty woman from Iceland.'

He felt like crying as he embraced his mother like he always had, and because he could, unlike a lot of his generation.

'Love you, Mum,' he said as she tenderly leaned over him and kissed him on the forehead.

'Your dad was always fiercely proud of you, Jack.'

Chapter Eighteen

Alan Sharpner understood the desperation of loneliness. Living alone after his girlfriend Pam had left him for a swimming coach named Giorgio, he had been looking for a miracle in the love department. Although not the brightest bobby on the beat, he had realised after reading Pam's lengthy list of criticisms in her Dear John (Dear Alan!) letter that he had to radically up his game.

The Ideal Partners Dating Agency had struggled to find him a decent match, politely informing him that it was an increasingly selective market. The nearest he'd got to compatibility was with a divorced chiropodist named Gill who'd discovered that after years of fixing feet she'd developed OCD and could no longer work happily. They'd gone on a few dates, but Pencil's obviously very large shoe size had added to her phobia. She'd also left a letter, saying it was her and not him, when really it was a large annoying chunk of him.

When Evans had appeared, a vision of bleached hair and bright red lipstick with a dangerously seductive proposal, he believed he'd found his niche, empowered by the fantasy that the two women both desired him. It was surprising what a bit of encouragement and praise could do to boost the ego of an otherwise very ordinary guy ...

Evans breathed heavily, the gear stick digging into her thigh as they became more entangled in each other. 'Yes!' she shouted, abruptly grabbing Pencil's hand and making him stop. At the same time Pencil began worrying about the widening wet stain now evident on his trousers.

'Wow!' She was laughing now, pulling her other leg back over to the passenger side and straightening her clothes. 'We really need to be a lot more careful, Alan. I mean, I know it's a deserted compound, but anyone could see us,' she added, re-applying the lipstick which Pencil had snogged off her.

Pencil nodded and tried to appear engaged, although his mind had been elsewhere – in fact, thinking about his mother (God knows how he had managed to get the wet patch!).

The first time Pencil had met him, his mum's new man, Mick, had placed his hand high up on her thigh and brought it casually down to her aging knee. Smiling as if nothing had happened, Pencil had tucked back into his vindaloo as his mother blushed and squeezed Mick's leg in reciprocation as she beamed like a teenager on a first date.

'And that's another thing, Alan,' she'd said, noticing that he'd drifted away from the heart to heart they were having a few days later. 'Mick said you keep staring at him funny – almost intimidating him, I think were his words.'

'No, I don't,' he managed, fiddling with a loose button on his shirt and avoiding his mother's stare. 'Mum, what do you see in him? I mean, he's nothing like Dad was.'

'Alan, you're a man of the world now. You know about needs and things.'

'Mum, please!' he pleaded, blushing brightly and wishing he hadn't worn the red shirt.

'Oh, come on, Alan; I'm allowed a bit of fun now and again! It's not as if I said I was going to join a nunnery when your dad died . . .'

'Alan, are you listening to me?' said Evans, staring at him in disbelief.

'Just as well I'm going straight home,' he said, refocusing and examining his groin.

'Jack was in a hurry tonight,' she said, ignoring the comment and adjusting her hair in the mirror. 'I reckon he had a date; have you noticed how happy he is lately?'

'Not really,' replied Pencil, who was now using a lighter to dry his trousers.

'Don't do that; you haven't got to get out of the car,' she said dismissively.

'I suppose,' he answered, putting the lighter back on the dashboard.

'Did you know the detective you replaced? Christine?'

'Chris? Yeah. The guv was very fond of her; it was rumoured they were an item,' he added, guiltily remembering his admission to Jack about his own relationship with Evans.

'He never got over what happened then?'

'As far as I know he never mentioned it. The lads say her face literally came off . . . When they covered her up, it was the skull in a grey suit that they remembered, not the fresh-faced young detective.'

'Christ, poor Jack!'

'Thankfully, he's never been in the same situation again.'

'The one we all dread?'

Pencil didn't answer, just nodded as they both sat within the concrete silence of the compound.

Chapter Nineteen

Jack couldn't sleep. Information overload had kept him awake most of the night. The visit to his mum's had done him the world of good, but the case was plaguing him, as he came to the realisation that Tom Gray was the front runner and that he himself would be doing most of the chasing.

Giving up on sleep, he decided to get to the station early. Not bothering to wake Skuld or Jake, he enjoyed a leisurely drive and landed at his desk at eight with a takeaway coffee and toasted bacon sandwich.

'Morning, sir.' It was newly promoted Detective Constable Mike Gallagher holding a blue file (always a good sign). 'Evans asked me to follow up on the Tom Gray Barnsley connection, sir.'

'Thanks,' said Jack, taking a sip of coffee and then wiping the grease off his fingers with a paper towel before taking the file. 'Congratulations on your rise to stardom, by the way,' he quipped, turning the first page of a two-sheet report.

'Thanks, sir, it feels strange not wearing a uniform any more.'

'That's about as good as it gets,' said Jack, not bothering to look up.

'Right,' said Gallagher, a bit puzzled.

'No, really,' began Jack, 'it's all downhill from here on.' Sensing Gallagher's lack of humour, he quickly closed the conversation, telling him that he was only joking and congratulating him again.

Now alone he had the strange feeling that what lay before him was maybe a turning point of sorts.

'So,' began Jack, working through the report, 'what do we have? One family of Grays in the Cortonwood area of Barnsley.' Makes life a lot easier, he thought. 'Colliery town. Father: Tom Gray senior; miner, naturally; married to Jane Pilkington. Three children: Tom, Mary, and Debra. So, Tom Gray is our psycho man.' Reading on in silence, he intermittently made a few comments. 'Pit closed down in 1985.' One of many on Thatcher's death list during the miners' strike, he mused. 'Hold on, dad dies 1992 – poor sod – and Tom junior goes missing in 1993.' Something else caught his attention. 'Oh,' he said suddenly, now distracted and picking up a newspaper cutting from the file. The nineteen-year-old Tom Gray smiled back at him, his black curly hair and missing front tooth giving him a roguish kind of David Essex look. On another sheet of paper, the same black-and-white image peered up at him, this time plastered on to a Metropolitan Police missing advertisement dated 1993 – *believed to be in the London area*, it read.

Well, they all are, thought Jack, placing it beside the news cutting. Standing and moving to the whiteboard behind him, Jack started scribbling much of the information in the columns that Pencil had previously drawn. *Probable/Improbable* he wrote. Probable: that their man was this Tom Gray, being that his family were the only Grays in the Cortonwood area. Improbable:

that a missing person could lay low for so long, get an education, attend university, and wage a hate-fuelled class war against his own people. Striking a line under his handiwork and aggressively throwing the blue marker on to the desk, he sat back down. At least they had a photo, age, and full name, he reasoned, though there had to be more. He tore apart his bacon sandwich and washed it down with the remainder of the lukewarm coffee.

Whistling the tune of a David Essex song, he fingered the corner of the photograph of the young man. The boy's lost expression and dead eyes revealed that this was not a confident individual gazing up at him. Cheeky, perhaps, in a boyish way, but it was all he could read and gather from the image. *Who are you, Tom Gray, who are you?*

Gazing out the window, he thought of the miners' strike: the hatred, the police being used as political battering rams to break the strikers, bitter times. Luckily, Jack had been promoted by then and had missed out on being transferred to other parts of the country to baton charge the picket lines. A bad time to be a copper: the whole country hated you and the job became a little bit harder all because a grocer's daughter wanted to smash working-class solidarity and break good community relations that went back generations.

'Morning, sir.'

'Sir.'

It was Evans and Pencil, stumbling in as if returning from a nightclub. Trying to hide their embarrassment they looked intently at Jack's board work behind him.

Pencil was first to speak. 'You've been busy, sir.'

'Yes, thought I'd get in early,' he replied, finishing off his now cold sandwich and wondering if his two detectives had been three in a bed earlier.

'What have we got, sir?' Evans said, almost standing to attention and poised for business.

'Well, Gallagher has been most productive,' he started, glancing at Pencil who for some reason blushed. 'Pulled out some important intel.'

Going over the finer details of the information gathered, Jack let the new leads filter through and digest.

'This is how I see it,' he continued, 'although the info fits, this Tom Gray is not our man – it's very unlikely. Our Tom Gray is someone else.'

'An imposter.'

'Yes, Pencil; a bit strong perhaps,' he laughed, 'maybe too Sherlock Holmes, but yes, it's not him. Somehow, he's got hold of this young man's profile and is doing the rounds claiming to be him, or a version of him. Probably to cover his own tracks.'

'So, do we continue to look for him?' asked Evans.

'Of course. We remain as before. The only change is that the man who's claiming to be Tom Gray is not him.'

'Someone else,' said Pencil.

Maybe he was just feeling his age, but were the new breed of detective not as quick on the uptake? He was sure he'd never repeated the obvious as much as Pencil did, even when he was just starting out.

'Have either of you compiled a list of the universities which have relevant English modules on their courses?'

'In London there's six, sir,' said Evans, coming to the rescue.

'What about the East London area?'

'Just one: Queen Mary and Westfield College.'

'How many students?'

'Well, it's a half module, so there's only about twenty on the course.'

'We'll start there. Contact the college and arrange a meeting for this afternoon.'

After a morning of redrawing the timeline and criss-crossing the evidence at their disposal, and following up on a few loose leads – mainly people possibly involved in the vacuous Class War group – they had pretty much exhausted the line of enquiry. Forensics from the car had only produced a few hairs from Sally Drayton and Pete Brown, the fingerprints of Dave Wilkins, and some mud from the Albert Docks, but little else.

Queen Mary and Westfield College sat on a smelly corner of the East End, a cultural think tank stuck like a sterile plaster on the bald head of a chanting Intercity skinhead. Heavy traffic and fumes were what you first noticed about the place when you got out of your parents' car, and then eventually, after a few weeks, came the feeling that if you ventured out of the confines of learning you'd probably be stabbed or worse still – never seen again.

'Harold Pinter; isn't he a playwright?' asked Jack as they read the plaque above the door of the English Department.

'Wasn't my subject at school,' replied Evans as Pencil looked at his boots.

'So, look,' said Jack, hands in pockets, 'you two, interview together, OK?'

'Girls as well?' interrupted Evans.

'Yes, find out if they've heard of Gray.'

Notably, Tom Gray's name wasn't on the list, nor was it in any other London university database. In theory he wasn't a student anywhere in the capital. Not to be deterred, they agreed to question students attending relevant English courses in London and follow their instincts (the main reason he'd decided to pair Evans with Pencil rather than leaving him to his own initiative).

'Inspector Hogan?'

'Yes.'

'Mathew Rose-Smith,' said the young man who looked more like a student than a lecturer.

I hate all these new double-barrelled names, thought Jack as he introduced Pencil and Evans.

'Any oddballs?' he asked.

'No,' replied Rose-Smith.

'Have you got the thumbscrews?' he asked Pencil, who had to agree with Evans, that Jack appeared to be in a good mood of late.

'Oh, thumbscrews!' chuffed Rose-Smith, slowly grasping what non-academic humour was like.

'I'm in here, am I?' asked Jack, not waiting for a reply and entering room R12 anyway.

'You're in here,' said Rose-Smith showing the other two into R14. Jack felt like saying no funny business but held on to his loose tongue.

After the first eight interviews Jack was getting nowhere. Did this new species of student only say 'no/yes/don't know'? Whatever happened to *University Challenge*?

'Name?' asked Jack despondently.

'Marcus Bennett-Woods,' came the crisp, no-nonsense reply.

More like *University Challenge* now, thought Jack, a bit more interested than before. Although he had been fooled by the tight crop when the young man had first entered the room, he was at least a lot different to anything that had gone before.

'So, Marcus.'

'Yes?' came the cutting response, delivered in an almost antagonistic way, ripping into Jack's flow and knocking him off balance.

Noting the young man's obvious lack of benevolence, he continued. 'Heard of Tom Gray?'

'Is he a Romantic poet?' asked Marcus, his white teeth and square jaw more prominent under the seminar room spotlights.

Play it cool, thought Jack.

'No,' he said, 'we believe he's a student, one with an unhealthy appetite for murder.'

'A hungry killer, then?'

'Something like that,' he replied, wanting to fly across the table and run the smug posh git's face up the wall. 'Why did you choose English, Marcus?'

'Because I'm proud of our literary heritage and I love words.'

'And you're a History student as well?'

'Yes.'

'You want to know what the bastards did to the working class?' stated Jack, cleverly having learnt segments of Sally's statement.

'Perhaps Eric Hopkins' *A Social History of the English Working Class* would be a good source of reference to begin with?' replied Marcus pompously.

Looking right through him, Jack saw the mutilated faces of

Dean and Dave and tried to merge them all together into the face of the young, confident man in front of him who didn't flinch or crack but continued smiling politely.

'Into student politics, Marcus?'

'If you call being a Young Conservative student politics, then yes.'

'So, not in the SWP then?' Jack was really relishing the possibility of unsettling the person before him.

'Hardly.'

It's not him, he's just a privileged smart-arsed toff who's enjoying a bit of jousting.

'Why this period of English; why not Latin?' asked Jack, knowing that Latin was an option on the course.

'It's our language . . .'

'Oh,' said Jack, flipping a biro pen between his fingers, which he could see Marcus tried not to show an interest in. 'Know a bit of old English myself,' announced Jack, breaking the sudden silence. 'Do tell if I'm not pronouncing it right: *fopdoodle.*'

There was a spark, but you'd have had to be mega-quick to catch it. Jack couldn't be sure now: there might have been something, but he couldn't conclusively say there was.

'Very good,' replied Marcus. 'You're a natural,' he added, not batting an eyelid.

'Live nearby?' continued Jack, disliking the man across from him more every time he opened his mouth.

'You're not asking me my address, are you, officer?' came the smart reply, presumably knowing that he could only be asked that if he was a suspect or witness to a crime.

Jack visibly winced at the 'officer' jibe and had to desperately fight the urge to retaliate.

'Greenwich, actually,' announced Marcus to the original question. 'Backside of the Empire, they used to call it.'

'Really,' said Jack, not bothering to look up.

A knock on the door and Rose-Wood popped his head around it. 'Sorry, Detective Chief Inspector, these students have a lecture in ten minutes,' he apologised.

'I'm just finishing,' answered Jack, rising menacingly, 'just give me a second.' Rose-Wood apologised again and disappeared. '*Fopdoodle*,' he continued after a few seconds, giving Marcus his most penetrating stare. 'Forgot to ask you what it means,' he said, wanting to hear it for himself.

'Fopdoodle: why fopdoodle, officer? Sorry, *Detective Chief Inspector*. I know how the police like to get their facts right.'

'So, what does it mean?' he repeated, ignoring the asides.

'Fopdoodle is a word to describe an insignificant, foolish man or woman. You could also say "raggabrash", meaning a grubby type of person, if you really wanted to be mean.'

'Is that what you are, Marcus, *mean*?'

Marcus didn't reply but kept grinning.

'Do you think working-class people are insignificant?' Jack asked, his eyes narrowing as he moved closer.

'Why would I say that, Detective Chief Inspector?' he asked calmly, folding his arms as Jack leaned over him.

'You don't think that then?'

'Is this turning into an interrogation? Maybe I should get Mathew,' he mocked.

It's exactly what he thinks, thought Jack, though unsure if it really had any bearing on finding their man or whether it was because he'd taken an instant dislike to the young man and his elitist stuck-up manner. Choosing the latter, he decided to bring it to an end.

'Oh, just one thing before you leave . . .' began Jack as Marcus made for the door. 'Remember,' he started slowly, 'the only just war is class war.'

Why he said it, he didn't know, but it seemed an appropriate conclusion to what had been a frustrating interview. Not bothering to reply, Marcus stuck out his chin, smirked, and left without saying a word.

Chapter Twenty

'Marcus, why are you so early?' asked an immaculate Harriet Thompson-Dickinson, opening the door to what she thought were her party guests.

She was surprised, he was never on time.

'Sorry, had an irritating encounter with a nauseating little man called Hogan,' he said, clearly not himself and looking as if he'd started his own party already. He swayed uneasily on the doorstep.

The so-called irritating encounter had led to a drunken one after a late-afternoon drinking bout in the Globe. Leaving the pub and deciding to get a bite to eat he'd stumbled into the nearby chip shop, where the Chinese owner had temporarily run out of batter and been busy at the back preparing some more. Annoyed at having to wait, Marcus had reached over the counter (thinking no one had seen him) and had grabbed a chicken wing from the hot counter. Seen by the owner's two sons, they'd easily bundled him out on to the pavement where he fell unceremoniously into the gutter. He'd lain there for some time before being helped to his feet by an old bag lady.

Brushing himself down, he'd headed for the tube station where he drunkenly made his way to Notting Hill Gate sooner than he had anticipated.

'Are you hammered already?'

'A bit,' he smiled as he casually swished past her. 'And I've had a haircut as well,' he added, slurring his words.

Although she didn't like the cropped hair, she said, 'It suits you,' as she let him in and closed the door.

'Can I help?' he asked, looking around him in amazement at the assortment of twinkly party lights, baubles, and coloured candles littering the huge open–plan main room.

'There's no need; I got caterers in – why do it yourself, when you can buy it all and just wait for it to turn up?'

Makes sense, thought Marcus, taking the customary already lit cigarette from between Harriet's outstretched fingers.

'What's the party for?' he asked, inhaling deeply, standing legs apart with the roaring open fire behind him.

'For my employees, and a few friends of course,' she said as if he should know.

'Employees,' he quipped, 'what employees?'

'The people I employ in my interior design company: Amanda, Charlotte, and Bob.'

Antenna up, he responded immediately, 'Bob? What does Bob do?'

'He takes care of the painters; makes sure they're doing as instructed.'

A foreman on a building site, he thought. He instantly took a dislike to the person he'd never met before.

'You already met Charlotte, at my birthday. You couldn't take your eyes off her arse.'

Charlotte: he remembered her well, in that figure-hugging Armani dress.

'So, who's this Hogan person?' she continued, knowing that Marcus was probably mentally undressing Charlotte as she brought the conversation back full circle.

'Ah, he's a no one,' he replied dismissively and annoyed at being brought back round to his initial remark.

But DCI Jack Hogan wasn't a no one. Marcus had been shaken by the encounter and reluctantly impressed by his cunning and sarcasm; the mind games performed effortlessly by a seasoned pro who understood the dark arts and intricacies of the mind. Although he knew he'd passed the test and managed to grin his way through Jack's hard stares, he also realised that the present impasse was only temporary and that a future meeting between the two would most certainly take place. When he'd left R12 he was torn between the desire to rip Jack's head off and to politely tell him that it had been a pleasure and that he looked forward to meeting him again when the whole episode would be put to rest.

'Do you want to freshen up before the guests arrive, Marcus? I'll run you a bath.'

Why was she so good to him; always wanting to please him? he wondered as Charlotte's figure and Sally's curved back merged into one, settling in his mind what he really wanted to do before the partygoers arrived.

'Not again, Marcus,' she laughed as he suddenly lifted her up on to the black Venetian desk beside the drinks cabinet and frantically pulled at her dress.

Like before, when he'd been denied by the looming Pete as Sally waited for him, and now his scrape with DCI Hogan, it had released an urge to put things right, to exorcise himself and get back on track. As he rushed with an addictive urgency, he realised that Harriet was fulfilling that need, that role, more and more, and that each time they had sex he felt stronger and strangely superior to everyone around him. It was a topping-up of his ego. He needed her, not only to live out his fantasies, but also to ultimately die by them one day. Each time they went to bed, it was because he was either angry or needing to put a story board into play, orchestrated by his muse, who strengthened his natural bond with the strong and those who should rule for ever.

'You seem really turned on lately,' she said as they both dressed.

'You'd be complaining if I wasn't,' he laughed, now pouring himself a large Scotch (really a full glass measure) from the nearby drinks cabinet.

'You won't get too drunk, will you?' Harriet said, concerned and aware that the first guests would soon be arriving.

Saying it would be his one and only drink of the evening, he assured her (although she wasn't totally convinced) that he was OK and not completely pissed. Omitting the word *yet*. 'I'll just go and freshen up.'

In the bathroom, he dimmed the spotlights as he listened to the soothing pouring of water from the tap. Plunging his face into the basin of cold water, he emerged to the quiet, airless tranquillity. Standing in the silence it was as if he were in a Japanese water garden. He listened intently to the distant voices of guests arriving, like clanking wind charms. One man and a woman, he thought, quickly retrieving the data from the next room. Not Charlotte, her voice was more high-pitched and distinctive. No, these two must be Amanda and Bob. Yes, that's definitely Bob, he mused with a whole heap of hatred, pushing the door slightly open, instantly locating the nasal whine of a smart-arsed middle-class, pseudo-working-class lad.

Bob was doing his finest John Lydon impersonation as he sneered at some comment from Amanda about not knowing what to wear to a party she'd recently attended at the Ritz. Gathering as much of a profile as was possible, he was soon dressed and in the hallway, creeping down towards the open-plan area and the drone of the man he just had to dislike.

'Don't you feel you're being fooled?' whined Bob, a chippy fashionista dressed in a green tartan suit and a button-down blue check shirt fastened at the top, his hair gelled back and spiked at the front.

'But I think everyone should buy shares,' continued Amanda, who from what Marcus could remember looked very much like Charlotte.

'I thought Johnny Rotten was in the room?' announced Marcus, slowly walking into view as if from the side of a stage and staring straight at Bob, who visibly winced at the jibe. It was obviously closer to the bone than Marcus had realised.

'Sorry?' enquired Bob, who would have been wiser to ignore the comment than to ask for an explanation of it.

'John Lydon. Johnny Rotten,' Marcus repeated slowly as if spelling out the words to a simpleton, 'ex-vocalist of the Sex Pistols, formed Public Image,' he added with a bit more spite as he took a suave sip of his scotch.

'Bob, Amanda, this is Marcus,' intervened Harriet, as if pushing aside any unpleasantness that had stumbled into the room.

'Oh, the boyfriend!' whined Bob, giving back as good as he got as he smiled, *touché*.

'Amanda's moving to Notting Hill,' said Harriet, giving Marcus a warning stare which told him to lay off and bottle it.

'And Marcus, where do you live?' said Bob with a sneer, not ready to give up his attack strategy.

Looking him up and down, Marcus had his measure: his reach, weight, likes and dislikes in one swoop. Searching deeper he saw the man's insecurities, the armour he was using (so far to good effect) and the feeling, the real doubt, which would leap into his mind if he were to hit him with the sharpest and cruellest of quips.

So, he took his hunch and threw it at him, square in the face. And it was a good guess: puerile and ignorant, but wasn't that the best way to get at people?

'Sorry, I'm not gay, Bob,' he announced sarcastically, 'didn't you just say I was Harriet's boyfriend?'

There he had him. The Lydon whine was stuffed back down his throat, the confidence drained from his face, his cheeks red-dening as if being rammed up against a striking miner with a riot shield. *You're not out yet, are you?* he thought, reading the sweaty expression and helplessness in his grimace.

Reading the signs that things were quickly turning nasty, Harriet and Amanda swiftly hijacked the conversation, reeling a blushing Bob back in, as they talked shop and made comical observations about a notorious client.

'Greenwich, actually,' Marcus said suddenly in answer to Bob's aborted attack. 'A lot of your lot there,' he laughed, before taking another large gulp of scotch.

'Marcus, stop!' pleaded Harriet sternly, pulling him away from the others as the doorbell rang and Bob looked at his shiny brown shoes.

'Sorry!' he shouted loudly as he volunteered to get the door.

'Emma, Jeremy, Pattie, and whatever your name is?' he said to the last person who entered as he enthusiastically kissed them on each side of the cheek, as Harriet, who hadn't got to the door before him, did the same. 'Come in!' he roared raucously, 'we're a real mix of company tonight; all different persuasions – eh, Bob?'

'Shhh! Just cut it out,' hissed Harriet through gritted teeth as she welcomed them in. 'You're spoiling my evening,' she said, like a ventriloquist drinking a glass of water as she spoke.

'Maybe I'll go and get some fags? Oops! Sorry, Bob!' he giggled to himself as he staggered out the still open door.

'Maybe you shouldn't come back till you've sobered up!' snapped Harriet on the doorstep, throwing him his sheepskin jacket. 'Perhaps you'd be better off at a football match or with some oiks down at the dog track!' she snarled, slamming the door with a bang.

'Maybe I will!' he shouted at the closed door as he stumbled on a few yards before falling against a tall swaying garden hedge. Reclining back, as if into a large comfy green cushion, he let the bush take his full weight. Lying with the hedge beneath him he gazed up at the sparkly stars. Closing his eyes, he soon fell into a deep, cosmic, drunken stupor.

'Marcus, your mother and I need to talk to you.' Sebastian Bennett-Woods, a tall, dark, elegant-looking man with steely greyish eyes, a strong jaw, and military moustache, surveyed his son sternly. Even in the early-evening blue hue of his drawing room, his father emerged as a formidable presence, all six foot three of him, the officious, no-nonsense British diplomat he was proud to be. His mother, sitting quietly at an un-played grand piano, gazed into the distance, looking remarkably like a 1970s heiress, sporting a beige jumpsuit, brown headscarf, and an array of sparkling rings and bangles, appearing as if she was totally alone in the room. 'The commissioner, Lord Daniels, is being relieved of his duties. We are all going to have to leave, I'm afraid. The African holiday is over; we're moving back to London.'

Sebastian should have made it to commissioner. It was meant to be, but it didn't happen, and he instead remained a diplomat with the Home Office. When the family arrived back in London from Zambia, their only child and son had to temporarily attend a state school until a suitable public school could be found. It was only for a couple of weeks – it wasn't as if he'd have to mingle for very long. Anyway, it would do him good to see how the other half lived, were his father's sentiments. Not his mother's though, who detested the idea and who constantly longed for the heat and exotic surroundings of their spacious residence in Africa and the privileged education her son would have received if they'd stayed . . .

'What!' cried Marcus, turning suddenly and rolling off the hedge on to a flower bed in a front garden, the side of his face and hair falling unceremoniously into a waiting muddy puddle. 'Fuck,' he said before scrunching up into the foetal position and closing his eyes again . . .

'What's your name, then?' came the cruel South London accent, blown in on a fag-stinking gust of menace.

'Marcus.'

'Oi, Tony, fucking posh kid 'ere.'

Tony Gulliver, Chelsea fan, full-time bully and bigot, biggest boy in the school, lifted his acned, bulbous, Dickensian head and snarled 'Wanker,' in Marcus's direction as he swaggered over, cupping his hands as he lit a cigarette as he went. 'What's ya second name?' growled Gulliver.

'Bennett-Woods,' stammered Marcus as he did up the top button of his shirt beneath his immaculate uniform.

'Bennett-Woods,' chimed in the other boy, pushing his face into Marcus's, 'what a fucking name, eh?'

'Yeah,' said Gulliver, blowing smoke and bad breath into Marcus's face. 'Needs a bit of that name washed away, I fink, don't you, Del?' he added, smirking in his friend's direction. 'Bogs, I fink?'

They were just outside the toilets. It was only a brief struggle as they frog-marched Marcus into the piss-smelling urinal.

'What about this one?' said Del, kicking open the cubicle door, 'been blocked for weeks – pretty shitty now; had one myself, this morning.' He laughed as Gulliver joined in, roughly grabbing the back of Marcus's neck.

'Right, Bennett-fucking-Woods, welcome to Bolingbroke Comprehensive,' Gulliver said, as he forced Marcus's head under, into the abyss of piss, gob, and shit, before pulling the chain.

'No, no!' cried Marcus, and then licked his dry, thirsty lips as some late party-goers laughed and joked their way past the front garden where he shabbily lay. His eyes flickering and threatening to open, he lay still as he went back under again.

★

'Are you lost?'

'No, just walking around.'

'You look lost.'

'Fine, really.'

Marcus had recognised him instantly from the numerous missing ads littered around the capital. It was his eyes that gave him away, not the now strewn locks which made him look younger and more vulnerable than his mugshot already implied.

'Do you smoke? Here,' he said as Tom Gray nodded. 'Take one,' he gestured.

'Thanks.'

Putting a friendly arm around his shoulder, they walked away as Tom hesitated for a second, peered back, and wondered if he should have kept walking.

'We'll be fine,' Marcus kept repeating, as he steadied his grip and they made for the bright lights of the City.

Opening his eyes to a starry sky and the realisation that he'd been dreaming, Marcus slowly got to his feet and stood awhile, letting the blood circulate down his legs to his toes. Remembering the last part of his reverie, he saw himself again walking away with Tom Gray, who was smiling as if his life had suddenly begun. Slowly wiping the mud from his face with his sleeve, he wondered why he wasn't at the party and instead climbing back through a hedge. Approaching voices rounding the corner instantly made him want to dive back into the front garden, as what were late party guests got closer. Straightening himself, he pulled up the collar of his jacket and reached for his last cigarette and lit it, cupping his hands like Gulliver. As the two women and one man got closer, he turned his cheek away to hide the mud on the other.

'Marcus, isn't it?' said Charlotte, briefly stopping as the group passed.

'No, it's Tom, actually,' he replied standoffishly as he turned on his heels and went in the opposite direction. 'Tom Gray!' he shouted back at them, 'The name's Tom fucking Gray!'

Chapter Twenty-one

'Is it a pond or lake? I'm not sure,' enquired Skuld, adjusting her hood to give her more protection from the north wind which was just gently beginning to blow in rising gusts across the flats.

'Lake,' said Jake proudly before his father could open his mouth. It was his new thing: either finishing off people's sentences or correcting them.

'In fact, there are eighty lakes and ponds in Epping Forest alone,' announced Jack, pulling a knot in his scarf as they walked in the crisp morning-dewy grass. 'This is an ancient woodland and a former Royal Park,' he concluded.

'And you just watch birds?' asked Skuld, who'd just joined their father/son hobby of logging the names of birds.

'You use this book here, Skuld,' said Jake, offering her his. 'You locate the bird, say, a crested grebe –' he was showing off! – 'and you write it in your notepad, with the time, date, and location,' he added, squiggling his finger in mid-air.

'You look through the glasses first, yes?'

'They're binoculars—' began Jake.

'OK, Jake, Skuld knows what they are.'

'No, I don't,' she said innocently, shaking her head as it moved independently within the hood of her purple anorak.

'Look, you see there?' instructed Jake, sounding very much like his father and pointing towards the left of the lake where it dipped magically as if into the forest. 'That's a heron; that's your first bird, Skuld, see?' he continued excitedly. 'You can write it down in the book; your first catch!'

It was Skuld's day off, although the whole idea of Skuld's free time had changed now. Her days off had become family days out, which Jake tended to dictate in terms of activity.

Ever since the baby revelation during their dinner date, Jack had been uncannily calm. Why he'd not been shocked that night, or even a little worried, was still baffling. As he looked at Skuld now, obediently (for Jake's sake) scribbling her first find in the book, he realised that time had come to represent very little for him now. From Mandy's death to Skuld, he could see it all in hours rather than years. Like the birds in the trees, he was probably falling into the natural rhythm of life. What they all had were days, long, beautiful days within a too-short time span.

'Here, Jake,' said Jack, picking a rusty-looking pin out of the ground and handing it to him. 'Do you know what this is?'

'A pin for nets?'

Jake was always surprising his father. If it wasn't his amazing empathy with the adult world, then it was his penchant for analysing something in a split second and giving a quick, reasoned response.

'That's right, for clap nets; bird catchers used to use them.'

'I know, you told me.'

'Did I?'

'Yes.'

'And I bet you can tell me the time and date?'

'Of course,' smiled his son as Skuld surveyed the trees with her binoculars.

'Bird! Bird!' she shouted suddenly, pointing frantically. 'Bird!'

'Hold on,' said Jack, following her gaze. 'Oh, yes, look, Jake, a red kite,' he said, handing over his eyeglasses.

'Wow! Skuld, that's a great catch, hey, Dad?'

'Sure is,' he replied, tears starting in his eyes as he smiled at the amazing woman across from him who did a little victory dance.

'Eh, this birdwatching, it's easy for me,' she said. 'As we say in Iceland: he who catches the bird, eats the pie also,' she concluded proudly. Jake gave his father a playful smile as they both tried not to laugh.

'Pint, dad?' said Jake, never one to miss the familiar sequence which always led to the Hitchcock Hotel.

'Bit early, but, yeah, why not? It's brass monkeys out here,' he said, loudly clapping his hands and rubbing them together as if some imaginary fire was before him.

'Brass monkeys, Jack?'

'Cold; it means very cold,' related Jake, looking at his father, aware that he'd been answering for him most of that morning.

'First I have two monkeys of my own to check up on,' said Jack, glancing at his watch, knowing that both Pencil and Evans would probably be having a cup of tea. 'I'll catch you two up in a minute,' he said, taking out his new mobile phone which at times felt like a hindrance, 'if I can get a good connection,' he added, still not totally at home with the new technology.

'Is that you, Pencil? Not a great reception up here on Wanstead Flats. What? No, not the council estate – Epping Forest. Right, have you got anything for me?'

The previous day had been a dull one. Not just the weather, which was wet and grey, but also in terms of routine police work. They had decided to order a new print run of Tom Gray's missing-person poster, to give the impression the police were still searching for him and perhaps unnerve the person who was pretending to be him. As far as missing people went, it had worked in the past. One's memory tended to catch up in time. By mid-afternoon much of the West and East Ends had been plastered with Tom Gray's never-aging image, with the added caption of *Believed to still be in the London area* tagged to it. While Evans took care of the logistics of it all, Jack had decided that he and Pencil would tail Sam Richards for the afternoon and see if any new faces showed up on another leafleting campaign of London campuses, this one to stop British occupation of Northern Ireland.

'What do students care about Northern Ireland?' Pencil had asked as he sat back down in the car, passing Jack his takeout coffee.

'You'd be surprised what they care about,' answered Jack, pouring in two sachets of brown sugar and stirring it furiously. 'You went to college, didn't you?' he enquired, staring out at the few students who'd begun milling around a *Troops Out* placard and handing out leaflets.

'Edmonton College of Further Education.'

'You never got involved in student politics then?'

'Well, a bit of CND,' he replied modestly.

'Christ, you'll have MI5 and MI6 on you if they find that out!' Jack laughed, taking a satisfying sip of coffee.

'Do you think so?' Pencil asked timidly.

'Probably.'

'Oh,' he said simply, looking slightly worried.

'How did you get into that?' Jack was enjoying himself as he continued. 'Don't tell me,' he said, holding up his hand. 'It was a girl.'

'Yeah . . . how did you guess?'

'Profiling.'

'Yeah, of course,' said Pencil, aware of what the police did but oblivious to the fact that it seemed ludicrous to think he had a political conscience.

'I was in the Labour Party at polytechnic – definitely on the list,' added Jack as if in a TV interview. 'Only for one year; wanted to see a fairer society. Like a lot of young people, I was a socialist for a week.'

'Did you go straight into the force after college?'

'No, I wanted to go into the Merchant Navy – to see the world; had all the information from career guidance. And then one day I was mugged walking back to my college digs. Three blokes jumped me. Gave me a pasting and took my wallet. Managed to dig one of them a few times. Well, anyway, the police officers were so good to me; made me understand that these things can happen to anyone. I'd never thought about that before, you know, being a victim of crime. And there I was: a statistic. It was then that I decided I wanted to become a copper.'

'I always wanted to be in the police,' said Pencil eagerly, 'used to watch *The Sweeney* as a kid.'

'So, who were you: George Carter or Jack Regan?'

'Oh, Carter, sir; he got all the women,' said Pencil, going to say *birds*, but remembering that he shouldn't.

'True,' said Jack, thinking of saying the same thing that Pencil had stopped himself from saying.

'You're a bit like Regan, sir, sometimes,' he added, not sure if he should have.

'Shut it!' shouted Jack, doing his best John Thaw impersonation as they both laughed.

'The TV's not what it used to be these days,' said Pencil, as he eyed a couple of students laughing excitedly, apparently exchanging phone numbers.

'How's your mum these days – is she getting on OK?'

Pencil reddened as he thought of the vindaloo incident and of how he'd done a background check on Mick Ashby.

'She still misses Dad,' Pencil said, fiddling with the collar of his shirt.

'How long has he been . . . ?'

'Eight years – died on my birthday,' he muttered as his head temporarily dropped.

You poor bugger, thought Jack, gazing over at his sergeant whose lower lip quivered, like a child preparing to cry. 'She must be lonely?' he said, thinking of his own long, arduous and tormented grief.

'She's got herself a fella . . . this Mick Ashby . . .' He was going to ask if Jack had heard of him, like he would if they were talking shop about a nonce.

Jack didn't need to say anything, he knew straight away what Pencil was implying – hadn't he done enough of his own checks on people he wasn't quite sure about? 'Well, it's good she's found someone,' he said at last.

'I suppose,' said Pencil, who was gradually beginning to realise that even his aging mum had needs – even sexual ones.

'Banana?' asked Jack, producing two from a brown paper bag on the dashboard, 'or an apple?' he said, springing the fruit from the same bag.

'Oh; apple.'

'Here,' said Jack, playfully tossing it over, 'they always come down!' Pencil surprisingly got the joke as he expertly caught it like he was fielding for England.

'Hey, guv, there's Richards – looks like he's got himself a girlfriend,' he said uncharacteristically nudging his boss and taking a large bite of his apple.

'She's young. Must be a fresher – probably just discovered Karl Marx,' said Jack, wiping the passenger window with his hand to get a better look.

'Is he a friend of Richards?'

'No, he's the father of Communism – are you sure you went to college?'

'Sir?'

'Never mind,' replied Jack, suddenly becoming gloomy. He'd been on so many stakeouts before and they were often fruitless operations. He knew the signs: the aimless chit-chat, endless cups of coffee, and watching people do nothing.

'Do you think he'll show?' asked Pencil as if reading his mind.

'If it's where he finds his victims, he might.'

'Sir, do you think the real Tom Gray is dead?' said Pencil as he annoyingly placed his apple core in the unused ashtray.

'In all honesty, yes,' said Jack flatly, briefly staring at the apple core.

'Murdered?'

'Probably.'

Jack never committed himself fully at this stage, but he was pretty sure that the man who had slaughtered Dean and Dave would most certainly have done the same to Tom Gray.

'Hey, have you got one of those posters?'

Jack didn't know why he hadn't thought of it before, as Pencil reached on to the back seat.

'Here, sir.'

He knew Tom Gray wasn't their man, but that he could be used provocatively to get a reaction in their search for his imposter.

'Any drawing pins?'

'Drawing pins, sir,' repeated Pencil, handing Jack the box as if he were a surgeon asking for a scalpel.

'You stay here and watch the crowd.'

'Yes, sir.'

Time for a bit of psychology, Jack thought as he left the car and crossed the road to the East London Campus.

'Morning,' he said brightly, brushing past Sam Richards and his female friend as he took the steps of the Students' Union. 'Is this the student notice board?' he enquired as Sam and his group looked on incredulously. Eventually someone grudgingly replied, 'Yes.'

'Thanks,' said Jack, turning to the board and pinning up Tom Gray's missing poster and then retracing his steps. 'Tom Gray: missing person – anyone seen him?' he asked, now at Sam's shoulder.

'Police intimidation again?' said Sam, bravely attempting to appear tough in front of his friends.

'No, Sam, just routine police work. Missing people all over London; ordinary, working-class people,' he added.

'You know that's not Tom Gray – you're just playing games.'

'Am I, Sam? I hope you're not playing games,' he said, turning the comment back on him, 'and if you are, you might just stop and recall the little matter of the Poll Tax riots.'

He knew Sam had no knowledge of his intel, but he'd done his homework and had seen the footage for himself. 'Throwing scaffolding poles is a bit dangerous, Sam,' he continued, enjoying the changing expression on Sam's face, which had gone from cocky to downturned. 'Particularly when aimed at police officers,' he smiled. Sam's unsteady stare hit the ground. Inside knowledge always hurts those outside of the loop; hurts even more when you hurl it at them, thought Jack as Sam's dejected look said it all.

'If you do see your friend Tom again, you will let me know – won't you, Sam?'

'Oh, Inspector Hogan,' a far-off voice purred quietly, 'you're good; you're really good!'

Marcus, who'd almost stumbled into Jack's path, pulling back just in time as he side-stepped and leapt into the entrance of the old library a hundred yards from the Students' Union, looked on.

'That will worry him,' Jack announced, getting back in the car. 'No harm throwing the odd grenade into the mix now and again.'

'Sir?'

'Never mind, Pencil, let's just get back to the station,' he said with a growing smile on his face.

Marcus watched them pulling away slowly in the dull drizzle. Sniffing the air as the car unsuspectingly passed him, he let out a loud 'Wah! Wah!' as he quickly turned on his heel and headed east, away from the canvassing Marxists and easily led students.

'What's that?' shouted Jack, shaking his mobile as an icy wind blew in across the flats. 'Good; yeah, and get Evans to put together an identity-kit with those two students in Stratford; see if we can get a likeness. Then we'll show it to that smug git Richards. Oh, and Pencil: there's a re-run of *The Sweeney* tonight on BBC Two!' he shouted, not sure if he was being drowned out by the blustering wind. 'You might pick up some tips,' he laughed, hanging up quickly and heading up the steps of the Hitchcock Hotel and the source of his newfound happiness.

'Jack, were you watching birds again?' asked Skuld as he entered the warm, snug, glowing bar.

'If only,' he replied, trying to contain his laughter.

Chapter Twenty-two

Canary Wharf, South Quay, February 1996: a windy sky-scape of straight lines, space-age glass oblongs, blues, greys, and metallic shades; an architectural playground walled by suc-cess, greed and profit. To the left: Tower Hamlets, council estates, daubed spray paint walls and degradation.

Closing his eyes briefly as the driverless DLR train trundled on, Marcus blocked out the squalor of the passing tower blocks of the poor, instead focusing on the end of the line where wealth and prestige oozed into the silver glistening sky like an urban Disneyland. Alighting at South Quay, he walked the three hundred yards to Coal Harbour Lane and turned as instructed on to Drum Lane, where he came to Bell Tower Apartments: a large old warehouse which had been renovated and turned into spacious luxury flats. Pressing the intercom of apartment six, he waited.

The previous morning, Marcus had slept in. Not bothering to shower the night before, his hair still matted with dry mud, and with a hangover from hell, which clanged and tolled like a church bell, he tried to summon the will to begin another day. Staring bleary-eyed at his handiwork at the foot of his bed, he mentally traced around Sally's drawn figure and then at the words *to be continued* scrawled underneath. With the day yet to begin he considered his options: Modernist Surrealist Literature lecture at eleven or canvass with the SWP and the get the troops out of Ireland lot, and then the pub. Troops Out and pub, he'd quickly decided, pouring his aching body out of the bed as he reached for his pint glass of water and drank furiously.

Sitting quietly, the furore of the previous evening crept up on him. He rubbed his side, which for some reason throbbed, as snippets of the aborted party, Bob, an angry Harriet, and then a tumble-down hedge sprang to mind. Fuck it, he thought, remembering Harriet throwing his coat at him as he stumbled like a wino into the night. Reaching for the phone by his bedside, he gingerly dialled.

'Harriet?' It was the answering machine. 'Marcus here. Sorry about last night – bad day, bad night.' No kidding, he thought, replacing the receiver as his stomach rumbled.

After quickly showering, he dressed, had a cup of tea, and scrambled outside where an orange racing bike blocked his path. A distant memory of having ridden home in the darkness came back to him. Where he'd found it, or heaven forbid, stolen it from, was anyone's guess.

Having bought some cigarettes and demolished a breakfast roll from the corner shop, he decided to use the bike. Putting on his Walkman he made his way down to the misty river where he rode through the tunnel and headed east towards Stratford.

The lyrics were new to him and mixed up and out of sequence in his mind as he tried to remember the words of the songs now exploding in his head. With the ferocity of Pulp bursting his eardrums, he felt like a child riding a bike for the first time, accompanied by a soundtrack which strangely complemented the rough edges of the wet East End of London through which he now flew. Bought the day after the murders of Dean and Dave, it was a must-have; after all, it had been the soundtrack to Dean's death and as close as he could possibly get to Sally. Her random selection of tracks in the car was his catalyst and complete satisfaction in the surreal reality of murder. Each and every one of them his 'Common People': Dean, Dave, and Sally, all his *lucky numbers*. He'd spotted Jack Hogan and his lanky sergeant instantly, waiting in their car outside the campus, deep in conversation, drinking coffee. Cycling past them, he'd decided to dump the bicycle outside the swimming baths and walk back down. Dangerous, but wasn't everything he did; wasn't all life a risk, he mused, as he quickly stepped into the entrance of the old library. Even after the initial shock of seeing Hogan in conversation with Sam Richards, he relished just how close everything was getting to its terminal end. Like himself, he knew that Hogan could smell the blood, and now as he and Pencil drove past him on the blind side of the road, as Hogan proudly smiled to himself, he understood that they were both following the same scent, like sniffer-dogs with their noses to the air.

Strangely invigorated, he'd even screeched like a bird on his way back to the bike, which unbelievably was still there, and rode straight back down the Mile End Road, past the university, to the Globe pub where he'd decided that an afternoon's moderate drinking was the only option left to him. And there was always the possibility that Sam Richards and the SWP might show up to fuel his hatred and desire to do more than he'd glorified in already.

Where were all the students, he wondered, looking at the old mock train station clock screwed to the wall. Ah, seminars (where he should have been), he concluded, finishing off his first pint of the day and lighting a cigarette. Just then he spied a young boy in an Arsenal shirt eyeing up the bike he'd left precariously slumped up against a lamppost outside.

'Go on, take it,' he muttered to himself as the boy looked left to right before greedily climbing on to the bike and pedalling away like the clappers.

'Beautiful,' he said, taking a long-satisfied puff on his fag, 'fucking beautiful.'

As the afternoon slowly slipped away, the odd group of students began to arrive, mainly those he knew by sight and a couple on his own course who merely nodded in his direction. These he tended to distance himself from due to his chosen alias. So far, he'd managed to distance Tom from Marcus and as he never socialised or even bothered speaking to his fellow students, he managed to avoid suspicion, just being perceived as aloof. There was no sign of Sam Richards and his cronies.

Three pints later, Marcus was totally miserable. Like a kid with no one to play with he felt desperately alone. He'd tried Harriet a few times on the payphone at the end of the bar. On the third attempt, she'd answered only to hang up upon hearing his voice. Not a victim in sight, he'd reached a low point. Ordering himself a double brandy he slumped back down and listened to the jukebox blaring out 'Gangsta's Paradise', which seemed to be constantly playing everywhere you went. This was soon followed by Simply Red's 'Fairground'. Harriet was right: he really was immersed in plebdom, so much so that his own previous privileged life was becoming a little blurred.

'Tom! All right, mate!'

Well, thank heavens for small mercies, he thought, as Charlie Harper, who seemed to be in a hurry, poked his head around the door.

'Come in; have a pint,' called out Marcus desperately.

'Can't, it's me old mum's birthday; me and me sis are throwing a surprise party.'

Good old Cockney knees-up, remembered Marcus, who wanted to sneer at and degrade Charlie's altruistic gesture towards his *old mum*.

'Got to look after your mother; best woman you'll ever meet,' he said, thinking of his own silent, detached, hardly ever smiling mother who'd wanted to pack him off to boarding school as soon as he was born.

'Look, 'ave you got a pen?' said Charlie, ready to take off as he constantly checked the numbers of the buses as they trundled past in case he had to run.

'No, but go on,' said Marcus, excited and intrigued at the prospect of a possible invitation.

Giving him an address, directions, and a time, Charlie spied his number twenty-five bus. 'It's the Russian fella I was telling you about,' he said quickly, 'going away for a month. Scalextric! Fuckin' A!' he added for good measure. 'Gotta go; see you then!'

Before Marcus could answer, he was gone, sprinting for a bus. 'Can't wait,' he said passively as a multitude of possibilities and scenarios flooded his mind.

With the effects of two days' drinking and being a little out of practice on the hunting front, he was a bit slow to begin with, but as the walled jukebox began to buzz and a song he'd never heard before exploded from its speakers his imagination moved up a gear. Spinning and re-tracking in time to the repetitious demonic wall of noise, his thoughts spiralled.

'More brandy,' said an inner voice, 'and make it a double.'

Extra fuel; shocking images; broken faces, bodies, and screams sucked violently through the eye of a needle!

Closing his eyes, he could still hear the cries of Dean Waters pleading for his life above the sound of his pounding Walkman, as he pressed deeper into Dean's head, gouging his eyes, trying to hook his fingers around the nose bone, all the time hitting him with his other fist. And Dave, poor Dave, screaming, howling like an animal, as he forced the biro into his eye, as it seemed to suddenly stop as if it had reached the back of his head, the end of the pen snapping with the sheer brute force . . .

Remembering the beautiful silence which had followed as he cleaned the blood from his arms and face, Marcus smiled. As if still there savouring the moment, still smoking that cigarette, he took a long satisfying breath.

Still waiting, he pressed the buzzer again. Maybe he was too early: five thirty. He definitely said five thirty, he thought, checking again that it was apartment six as the speaker suddenly sprang to life.

'Yeah?' crackled the intercom. Loud techno music throbbed in the background, no doubt the amphetamine to the Scalextric.

'It's Tom.'

'Come up!' Charlie shouted above the din. 'It's fucking mad here.'

Another old Cockney knees-up, thought Marcus, who for some reason couldn't get the line out of his head.

Having spent the entire day in bed after two days of poisoning his liver, Marcus now felt as if intoxication had cleared a lot of the rot from his mind. It was as if he was returning to work after a long layoff, restored, refreshed, and ready to put in an afternoon's graft.

'Wow!' said Marcus for good effect, scanning the bachelor pad of a filthy-rich Russian oligarch, whose idea of high culture and wealth was to cram as much gold, high-tech merchandise, and opulence into one expansive entertainment pod. Dimmer switches, fifty-two-inch TV screens, multi-player music combos, contrived art, mostly of great leaders: Napoleon, Wellington, and Nelson, with the odd Athenian landscape (all in gold frames) brought together in one gaudy vision of quasi-high culture.

'Have a look at this, bro,' Charlie said, excitedly leading Marcus by the arm up a spiral staircase into the main hub of the building on the second floor as he winced at the touch. 'This you won't believe.'

He hadn't been exaggerating, the whole area was covered in a black track surrounded by Grand Prix stands, advertising boards, and manicured rolling green hills and trees, in the middle of which sat two white leather recliners with control panels built into the arm rests.

'The Russian loves this stuff,' said Charlie, clambering into one of the white seats as Marcus reluctantly followed. 'Here,' he said, handing Tom a red racing car, 'thought you'd like the colour, being a socialist and all.'

A socialist, thought Marcus, he'd certainly done a good job of fooling everyone!

'Put it in there,' Charlie instructed as they both placed their cars on the track. 'It takes three minutes to get to the finishing line; but first look at this,' he continued. 'Press this button here,' he said as both seats slowly elevated to a lofty position above the track. 'Brilliant, ain't it? You can see the whole track from up here.'

He really is obsessed with this, thought Marcus, wondering how long he would last sitting in the middle of a toy Grand Prix track with a Scalextric freak.

'Geezer!' shouted Charlie, banging the arm rest as his car flashed past the finishing line for the fourth time.

He's not like Dean and Dave, thought Marcus, admiring Charlie's wiry frame, bulging muscles, and obvious athleticism, built like a lean, light-middleweight boxer. Not someone he could bully into submission without a fight. He'd have to keep his spite and sarcasm in check and grasp the opportunity when it arose.

'Can I have a look around?' he asked earnestly, as if on a play-date.

'Sure,' answered Charlie, rising from his seat, 'do you want a beer?'

'No, thanks, just the tour for now,' he smiled.

'Come on,' said Charlie, tipping Marcus's elbow as they got up, 'you've got to see the cheese room — it's really fucking freaky.'

That's twice he's touched me now, Marcus thought, sensing a growing anger and an adrenalin rush pumping through his veins – *touch me again and I'll—*

'This fella is worth millions; no, probably billions,' Charlie stated, his eyes as wide as saucers.

Pupils dilated: he's pumped with something, thought Marcus. Speed, yeah, probably speed, he's speaking a hundred miles per hour. A bit mean with his drugs, he mused, spotting a hefty onyx ornament of a phoenix and considering its weight, reach, and proximity.

'Look in here,' said Charlie, opening the thick oak door, 'this is trippy.'

Switching on the bright industrial lighting, you had to take a second to make sure you were still on the same planet, as mounds of stacked cheese in a room the size of a tennis court loomed into view. Cheeses of all colours, volumes, and varieties mounted on wall-to-wall shelves like draughts pieces, each one swathed in creamy hessian, and stacked to the lofty ceiling like a huge mouldy army. If you liked cheese, then the harmonious odour of rich dairy magic would smother your senses and lift you to a higher level as it sucked you into its heavenly stench.

In the centre of the room stood a heavily scarred table with various wooden and marble blocks littered upon it. At the far end lay a huge ornate cutting board with attached cheese wire, which extended into a long razor-sharp guillotine.

'Amazing,' announced Marcus, wanting to show a bit more enthusiasm, 'what a lot of cheese – could have a good old cheesy knees-up with that lot,' he laughed, the first bit of sarcasm trickling from his lips as he smirked.

Far too high to see it, the comment completely bypassed Charlie. His pupils no longer dots, but black oval buttons, he muttered something about not knowing Russians liked cheese so much and that his old mum hated the stuff. Marcus detested him a little bit more every time he referred to his 'old mum' as the stinking, sweaty, airless stench made him want to commit the vilest of violence and smash through the mouldy atmosphere and wreak shameless, merciless havoc upon Charlie's stupid cranium.

'Can I cut some cheese?' Marcus asked brightly, picking up the wire.

Hesitantly, Charlie looked around at the vast array of untouched blocks. 'Can't start a new one,' he said limply, not really wanting to disappoint his guest.

'Ah, just a little piece,' said Marcus, picking up one of the smaller slabs as Charlie reluctantly nodded in agreement. 'If you've ever used a cheese wire it's one of the most satisfying feelings and sensations you will ever experience,' he began, placing a new creamy round ball on the board and caressing it, marvelling at its plump, soft, cool texture and its uncanny resemblance to dead human flesh. 'As the wire touches the surface, before it cuts,' he demonstrated holding the taut wire tight, 'now and after: first the perfection and then the disfiguration as it changes appearance. Like this,' he said, making the first incision. 'Slice, slice,' he continued, expertly slicing two even pieces of gouda and watching as the split cheese expanded, fell and then slumped on the slab. 'Now that's a beautiful thing,' he said as Charlie, mesmerised and stoned, looked on.

'Here,' he said, staring deep into his button eyes and passing him the razor wire, 'try it,' he insisted.

★

Time: 19.01.

The glass panelling on the side of the apartment disintegrated and shattered into tiny pieces, showering the rooms in a hailstorm of glistening particles, sucked into the building and then violently blown out, like a hyperventilating vacuum cleaner.

After the initial explosion, the flat appeared like it had been placed in a bottle and vigorously shaken and then turned upside down as dust and diamond-like glass covered the floor like a fresh snowfall.

'Yesssssssss!' shrieked Marcus, running from the cheese room, his shirt ripped from his back, covered in white dust and streaked with blood. Howling like a banshee, he danced around the apartment, turning, jumping, his arms splaying around his body like he'd just scored a goal. Spiralling over to the gaping hole where the side of the building used to be, he stopped and gazed with wonder at the devastation outside. As a gentle wind blew into the room, he did a double-take as he stared out at the mangled steel beams of the building opposite, which seemed as if a fast Intercity train had smashed into the side of it, and sent a writhing viper into spasm as it ripped through the structure. To his left a hanging desk, only held together by a computer cable, dangled down one side of the building as office paraphernalia flapped out of the windows and paper flew gracefully in the air.

Taking a step forward towards the edge where a glass panel used to sit, he felt as if he was facing Armageddon as the floor above creaked, the surrounding walls temporarily swayed, and time lost its essence and meaning as if it had been torn to shreds.

The eerie silence that followed appeared to last an eternity before being interrupted by a chorus of alarms and distant sirens as reality reappeared.

A distant cry for help from another building nudged him back into the now. Whatever had happened and however invigorated he'd been by it all, he knew it was time to flee the bombsite. Spotting his dusty overcoat still draped over the sofa, he quickly put it on and left.

Chapter Twenty-three

Desperate for a new angle, Jack had paid a visit to a criminal psychologist, Anthony Bell. A rather strange individual, Jack had been told, who rarely made eye contact unless you made a sudden movement, Bell was also viewed as one of the best in the business. Jack had been warned though that he was a bit of a slow starter, and that he'd have to pick through much of the mass of probabilities presented, which Bell had the habit of not putting in any general order.

'Class discrimination, also known as classism: prejudice or discrimination on the basis of social class. It's complex, because it includes individual attitudes, behaviours, systems of policy, and practices,' said Bell, hardly blinking, staring off into the distance somewhere above Jack's head.

Jack had been fiddling with a paperclip, listening impatiently, at the same time wondering if all Bell's stating the obvious was going to be eating into his precious time, and how long it would be until he got to the point.

'What I'm trying to find out is whether there might be a psychological reason for extreme class hatred. Is that possible?'

211

'Not really,' began Bell, pushing his glasses up to the bridge of his cherry-red nose. 'Take racism – an extreme form of hatred. I think most psychologists would believe that racism is a cultural and social problem, not a matter for individual pathology.'

'So, how should we be viewing this; why the out-of-control hatred and violence?'

'OK,' began Bell, briefly making eye contact, 'take the people behind the Holocaust, the Final Solution: psychopaths, maybe, men and women with borderline personality disorders, some perhaps just unpleasant, bigoted, or with below average intelligence, prejudiced enough to commit the vilest of crimes, though with the majority not having any real, clear mental illness. Yes, there were exceptions. But what I would say is that if you look at a personality like Hitler, who by his own account felt belittled and, though he wouldn't admit it, in awe of the Jewish artists he encountered in Vienna, perhaps that might be a clue or a pathway into the mind of the individual you are looking for?'

'You mean, it's a social reaction to perhaps an incident in the perpetrator's past?'

'I would say so. From what you've told me, I'd say that this person was possibly a victim of either an act of violence or an injustice by or from someone of a particular social class, which has resulted in an extreme response. More than likely they're an individual with a borderline personality order, who is experiencing paranoia and impulsive, extreme anger.'

'Would you say sexual abuse as well?'

'Quite possibly.'

Jack had put down the paperclip and was now pensively gluing it alltogether. After a rocky start, intentionally or not

Bell had presented him with a clearer understanding of their suspect.

'You see, with perpetrators of hate crimes, the offenders may not just be motivated by hate, but also by fear. This can lead to the dehumanisation of a particular group.'

'So, there was probably a spark to this hatred – something that really pushed them over the edge?'

'I'd say so.'

'Well, that's encouraging.'

'But I'd say there is probably another angle worth considering,' Bell added, picking a book off the shelf and passing it across to Jack. 'Nietzsche, and the concept of the will to power, the superman or over-man, the *Ubermensch*.'

'Someone who sees themselves as a super-being?'

'Taken to an extreme, yes. The Nazis used Nietzsche to good effect to achieve their aims.'

'To justify them.'

'Perhaps.'

'Is it something we could run with?'

'Definitely something to consider.'

'And psychopaths: I mean, they often view themselves as superior?'

'Definitely, but also consider the narcissist, someone inflated by their own self-importance and a deep need for excessive attention. Like the psychopath, they have a complete lack of empathy for others. I would suggest this person craves attention. It's as if they want to be celebrated in some way.'

'For their crimes?'

'It's as if what they are doing is in a perverse way a service to others.'

'For the good of all.'

'Why not? Evil often comes in the guise of a common good.'

He thinks he's a superman, thought Jack, now pulling into the station compound.

It had been a good idea to visit the psychologist that morning. There seemed to be some clarity that he was at least moving in the right direction. Entering his office he found both Pencil and Evans busying themselves in a strangely quiet, industrious way.

'Are you two all right?'

There was definitely a tension between them, the type that is more evident when each person tries to pretend that the other one is not in the room.

'Yes, sir,' they both chimed flatly.

They clearly weren't all right. You couldn't really call it a lover's tiff, because that part of their relationship was complicated. It was more of a breakdown in Terms of Contract, of not playing by the agreed rules. Although Jack didn't know it, Pencil had fallen for her and had made every excuse in the book to avoid the tripartite sex games, leading to a suspicious Erika demanding that Evans immediately end the arrangement.

'I've got the photofit, sir,' said Evans, glancing past Pencil to where Jack now sat. 'They're on your desk,' she added, wondering why he hadn't noticed.

'Well,' said Jack, flicking open the file and flattening its spine, 'he's a lot different to the real Tom Gray. 'But he looks familiar,' he finally said, though not familiar enough, he thought tracking backwards and forwards through his catalogue of mugshots and not tripping over a single one. It was almost a good likeness, not that Jack caught it: the confident air, steady stare, and chiselled, square jaw, it was all there, but masked by the floppy black quiff.

'The couple from Stratford, Luke and Lucy, have my number; they said that they would call if they spotted him,' added Evans.

'Good,' said Jack, remembering how young and innocent they'd appeared. 'And what about Sam Richards?' he asked directly to Pencil.

'Gone off the radar, keeping a low profile, sir, apparently staying with a friend in Dorset. I'd say we might have scared him off,' he said, avoiding eye contact with everyone in the room.

'Well, if he shows up, stuff that photofit right up his nose.'

'Yes, sir.'

'So, nothing else?' asked Jack, glancing back and forth between his detectives who clearly were no longer communicating. *Have that chat, Jack,* came the inner voice tapping him on the head, *have that conversation.*

'OK,' he began, slapping the file back down on his desk, 'it's like this.' He now had their attention. 'Whatever's going on between you two stops here when you walk through that door! It's obviously starting to affect your work. Got it?'

Red-faced and a little ashamed, they didn't try to wriggle out of it, instead repeating 'Got it' and managing a smile of sorts in each other's direction, enough to placate Jack's well-acted-out frustration.

In truth, Jack was finding it harder to remain grumpy for long these days. Like everyone else in authority he knew that he had to have that hard edge in his arsenal if he wanted to get results, but he was finding it harder than usual because his personal life was so good. No, perfect. That morning after their elevenses at the Hitchcock Hotel, they'd walked some more in the forest, out past the gypsy camp (reminding Jake again about the dangers of going AWOL), and had filled their notebooks some more with now migrating flocks of birds making for warmer climes. Although having only planned to keep in touch with the station, and with Skuld threatening a shopping expedition, he'd decided by late afternoon to make a surprise visit. If it had been a week earlier, he may have found his two detectives in a compromising position.

Telling-off over, Evans followed up on her poster campaign and Pencil excused himself, saying that he had to speak with one of the mechanics about a loose ball-bearing in one of the unmarked cars. If you put it all together, they'd hit a bit of a brick wall and were scratching around for scraps of evidence. At a stretch they were going over old ground, hoping that Tom Gray would miraculously resurface.

'So, are you and Detective Sergeant Sharpner OK now?' said Jack, breaking the silence as he watched Pencil through the window as he crossed over to the compound.

'Yes, sir, it was nothing,' she blushed.

'It happens,' he began awkwardly, 'you know, complications and falling-outs at work.'

It was the first time in a long while he'd thought of his deceased partner Chris. The fatal shooting was never far from his mind, though he'd learnt to brush it to one side as soon as it appeared. Now as he looked at the fresh young face of Evans, he thought of the brief fling he'd had with his partner. It had been a big mistake; both of them caught up in the moment, that after-work situation, staring at a finished bottle of wine and talking shop, when camaraderie becomes a little blurred and is replaced by physical attraction as the barman calls last orders and you both think it's a good idea to have a nightcap some-place else. In hindsight it had been too soon. He'd still had some way to go to starting another relationship. Luckily, their work-ing relationship was such a good one that their mutual respect allowed them to continue as before. Until the fatal day it was simply a one-night stand with a happy outcome which had been pleasantly ironed over.

'It's fine now, we'll get over it,' Evans said, wondering how much Jack actually knew of their love triangle.

'I've been there,' said Jack, not going into details as he sub-liminally drew a line under their conversation.

Boom!

Boom!

'What the hell?' said Jack, standing abruptly with Evans and moving over to the window. They stared out at the London skyline for an answer which didn't readily come.

The bomb went off just after seven p.m. The shock wave of the blast was felt as far away as Barking. Before reacting to the bang they'd visibly seen the whole room shudder and slightly shift to one side then back again. Outside, dazed officers were now racing to their patrol cars, while shocked admin staff looked to one another for an explanation.

'What do you reckon, sir?' said Pencil, now alongside them as they watched the bellowing smoke in the distance.

'IRA,' replied Jack. He'd witnessed blasts at first hand before, the most recent being the NatWest Tower bomb in the heart of the City.

'They're on ceasefire, aren't they, sir?' asked Evans.

'Were,' said Jack, shaking his head and trying not to dwell on the mutilation that may have occurred just a few miles away. Distant alarms began their chorus of mayhem across Tower Hamlets and the mangled South Quay.

'No point in rushing to the scene,' began Jack, reading his detectives' minds, 'Anti–Terrorism boys won't want us getting in the way.'

Switching on the *Channel Four News*, they, like everyone else that day, watched the events as they unfolded. It was indeed the end of the IRA's seventeen–month ceasefire. Miraculously, casualties were low, although the deaths of two newsagents were already being reported. Like a lot of Irish people, Jack felt an unfathomable shame for the actions of others who claimed to represent them or in his case his parents. It was at times like this that he wished his name wasn't Hogan, as he imagined altered expressions or changes in the way his colleagues spoke to him. *Bastards*, he thought as he pushed out his chest as if forcing the paranoia to one side.

'News is coming in that it was a truck bomb, sir,' announced Pencil breathlessly. He'd been listening in on police radio and appeared to be caught up in the whole drama.

That's all we need: more car bombs, thought Jack, remembering how previous IRA activity in the capital had interfered with routine police work and to some extent murder cases as well.

'More bloody chaos,' he said at last, looking at his watch and remembering that Skuld had said something about going shopping up west in Oxford Street in the late afternoon. She was taking Jake along with her to get him the new trainers he'd been asking for.

A cold shiver at the base of his spine travelled frenetically to his hot, itchy neck as his head began to throb. Indecision ransacked his reason. What if there was a second bomb, he thought, feeling the panic set in and threaten to drown him. Late afternoon shopping, thousands of people, optimal casualties . . . *Fuck!*

'Sir?' It was a young officer he hadn't seen before. 'Phone call.'

It was Skuld, they were on their way back home, thank God.

'Jack, problem with the Central Line: we had to get a bus to Stratford and we're now going to get a cab home – something about a bomb.'

'Be careful, go straight home,' he said just as the pips went.

A little sweaty and relieved, he took the coffee that Pencil had made him and slumped down at his desk as the various alarms in the distance slowly ran out of steam and were replaced by the deathly sound of emergency sirens. He felt helpless, as if he could cry. Why, he didn't know, but it certainly had something to do with his son and the woman he loved being away from him, when there were people on the loose who wanted to kill and maim. Maybe it was a consequence of events, but Mandy flashed before his eyes, her helpless dead face peering up at him, her arms outstretched for him in the same position where she'd taken her last breath, pleading with him to save her.

Tears in his eyes, he turned his face away as he fought to keep himself together. The lump in his throat got bigger, threatening to rise and set him blubbing. Like at the funeral, as he'd tapped the side of the box, as if knocking on the casket was a last gesture to his wife, before he'd collapsed with his sobbing son in his arms, he now let his knuckles do a *rat-a-tat-tat!* on the desk as he swallowed hard in an attempt to untangle the expression he didn't want his colleagues to see.

Finishing off his coffee as if it were a large whiskey, he battled with the mangled images swirling around his mind, threatening to swamp the progress he'd made and pull him back into the past where the demons now happily danced.

'Please don't,' he silently pleaded as his wife's coffin was lowered for the third time.

'Sir?' It was Evans. 'You OK?'

'Yeah,' he lied, relieved to hear a voice from the present as he rubbed his well-fought-tear-touched eyes.

'Guv, I know it's not perhaps an appropriate time, but I was wondering if I could nip off early. Have a few things to sort out at home,' she added, the strain showing on her face. She desperately needed to do some patching up with her girlfriend who'd become suspiciously jealous.

'Of course, go; I'm sure DS Sharpner and I can cope,' he answered, really wanting to thank her for returning him from the clutches of the dead.

'Sir?' It was DC Gallagher, poking his head around the door. Remembering his good work with the Barnsley connection, Jack waved him in.

'Anti-Terrorism; they've found a body,' he began excitedly, 'not related to the bombing. Treating it as a separate murder scene. They say it's pretty gruesome – so it could be relevant,' he added breathlessly. 'Address,' he started again, reading from his notepad, 'Bell Tower Wharf Apartments, South Quay, flat six.'

'Could be him?' said Jack, glancing at Pencil who already had his coat on and his car keys ready.

Police work: accumulating evidence, piecing it all together, following leads, profiling, guess work, surveillance and then perhaps worst of all waiting for the suspect to make their next move and ultimately kill again. Jack knew, they all knew, it was the one thing they all regrettably needed to happen. It was a double-edged sword. Unfortunately, somebody would die, horrifically, but the perpetrator would most certainly, eventually, make a mistake.

'Sir? It can wait,' Evans started, taking off her raincoat, but Jack stopped her.

'No, you go,' he said firmly. 'I'll call you if we need anything.' In his mind, Mandy smiled at him on their wedding day, her face full of love, wonder, and hope for their future together. 'Come on, Pencil, before she handcuffs herself to the bumper,' he said as both his detectives reddened, perhaps remembering some previously acted-out fantasy.

Heading for the door, Mandy waved him goodbye.

'Some bomb – it's a big one,' said Pencil glancing nervously at his boss as they drove towards South Quay.

'Doesn't seem real, does it?' said Jack, staring out the window at the devastation and the strangeness of an utterly changed skyscape which had morphed into something disturbing at the tick and then click of a timer.

'It's like that scene from *War of the Worlds*, where the aliens begin attacking the humans and the buildings are set on fire,' said Pencil.

Jack didn't answer, instead focusing on the glittering glass which crunched beneath their tyres as they drove. Looking out at the rubble still strewn across the roads and pavements he wondered if people would ever stop slaughtering one another and whether one day he'd stop pursuing them.

Checking the red rims of his eyes in the passenger-side mirror, he somehow managed a smile as he tried to convince himself he was OK, that he was back in the public domain as DCI Jack Hogan.

'This must be it,' said Pencil, being waved on by a big burly Transport Police officer as they pulled up beside an ambulance. 'Bell Tower Wharf,' read Pencil slowly as Jack ignored him again and quickly sprang from the car.

'It ain't pretty, sir,' said the glum officer, lifting the police tape to let them by, 'some mental bastard, that's for sure.'

'That's just about everyone nowadays,' added another PC who appeared equally as gloomy.

'Paddies,' came another voice, from where Jack didn't know nor acknowledge.

'Sounds like our man?' said Jack briefly, nodding at the officers who could easily have been a double act.

'And now we have the bloody IRA to deal with again,' said the more miserable of the two officers as Jack felt the urge to get as far away as possible from them.

Looking at the entrance of the building, it wasn't possible to have guessed at the destruction within, and at the back, where large sections appeared torn away as if by a tornado, flapping in the wind like stray paper in a shredder. The layered glass and dust covering the surfaces of the interior gave the impression that a large iced cake had shattered into a million silent pieces.

'This way, sir, it's in the cheese room,' said the officer guarding the crime scene. 'You might want to put these on,' he added, handing them some shoe protectors, 'there's a lot of blood in there and it's a bit slippy.'

The blood on the floor was still flowing as they walked in, trickling steadily from the end of the table where a young man's near-decapitated corpse hung awkwardly, slumped across an ornate cheese board, his head only just attached, held together by the spinal cord, the muscle and fibres ripped from it as if the butcher had been trying to pull the face off the skull with the help of a boning knife. The cheese wire had almost severed the neck, leaving the head hanging as if it were about to topple off.

Both Jack and Pencil looked at one another. There was no need for confirmation: Jack knew it was their man's style, his trademark, trying to get to the brain and making sure that it ceased to be, broken and smashed of all knowledge.

'No stamp,' said Pencil, pointing at the forehead which had moved towards the back of the head, no doubt in an attempt to remove it.

'Hold on,' said Jack putting on some latex gloves and pushing aside the torn T-shirt, 'he's put it on the heart.'

And there it was: the star with the skull in the centre, just visible beneath the sticky blood and dust.

'Sir, the stomach,' said Pencil suddenly, his breath quick and laboured.

'Let's see what we've got. Give me a wipe.' Cleaning away the blood, he continued, 'Right, what do we have?' he said, dabbing the carved handiwork. 'F and an O,' he started, having to swab the skin of blood each time he located a letter, 'a P and a D, and then nothing. He didn't have time to finish it.'

'Fopdoodle,' said Pencil.

'Yes, same as before, but the nutter's practising his tattooing skills now.'

'Why didn't he finish it?'

'I'd say the bomb went off – interrupted his English lesson,' said Jack, with the growing realisation that they had probably already met. 'Better check this one's pockets, might be the same as before,' he said with Dean Waters in mind.

'Think you're right, sir,' said Pencil, pulling out the screwed-up piece of paper and reading it aloud as Jack visibly turned white.

'*Remember, the only just war is class war,*' he read.

The same words Jack had said to Marcus Bennett-Woods at Queen Mary and Westfield College a few days earlier.

'Jesus!' said Jack, slapping his forehead violently and wanting to hide, 'it's that smart-arsed bastard from the university.'

'Richards?'

'No, Bamber Gascoigne, bloody Marcus Bennett-Woods, representing Queen Mary and Westfield College,' spat Jack, angry with himself.

Jack knew you always felt sick when you at last put a face to the murderer and the crimes they'd committed; even more so when you've felt and smelt their breath a few feet from yours, when that person smirks and mocks you, all the time exercising their power which is slowly running out, but is nonetheless a yard ahead of you in the game.

Looking at the newest victim's contorted, creamy-coloured face, Jack felt his stomach sway and move to one side as he struggled to keep down the burning bile which was forming at the back of his throat. 'Keep it together,' he told himself as Mandy reappeared and shook her head as if telling him '*no*' and not to go down that road again – the one he'd taken before.

'Sir?' It was the officer who'd shown them into the cheese room. 'We've got an ID: Charlie Harper. His mum's the cleaner for the Russian who owns the apartment.'

'Student?' asked Jack knowing the answer.

'Yes, sir; at Queen Mary and Westfield. His mum had his student ID pass with her for the positive ID.'

'Mum's a cleaner ...' began Jack steadily, 'he really hates ordinary people, doesn't he?' he concluded as the words from the message echoed once more in his head, *the only just war is class war*, as Evans's photofit became grotesquely framed within his mind.

Chapter Twenty-four

The blood-red sky above the Admiralty buildings, slowly slinking into evening, loomed ominous, brooding as if the slashed cloth of Christ had been strewn across its domes. From the murky Thames to the Observatory on the hill, which humbly hung above the splendour, a brush stroke of a simple wooden bench accompanying it, his eyes followed the line of the darkening water-coloured path downward to the soothing slosh of the river. This was his home, his nest, his Land of Hope and Glory.

He spotted them straight away, tangled up in each other, leaning up against the barrier of the entrance by the *Cutty Sark*: the boy arching backwards as he held the woolly hatted, scarfed, and mittened girl tightly in his puny arms. The oil lantern by the sign which gave the opening times lit up their childish faces as they played at being the adults they were.

As Marcus emerged, dusty, dazed, and still invigorated by the blast from the tunnel, the last thing he wanted was to go back to his rooms and sit alone. Instead, he wished to tell the world of his ultimate superhuman power and what he'd just done;

wanted an audience to divulge his crimes to. Of course, he couldn't. Maybe he should go home now, he thought to himself as Lucy pushed her hands deep into Luke's coat, which shrouded her like a cloak, and placed her head in its mauve knitted hat on his chest as they both appeared to sigh and smile in total innocence. He could just walk past and pretend he never saw them, he mused, temporarily glued to the spot at the entrance to the tunnel, his hands thrust deep into the pockets of his dusty overcoat. The torn, soggy, blood-stained T-shirt now clung to him like a sticky candyfloss stick. Doing up the top button of his coat to conceal it, he pulled up his collar and strolled casually over to the happy couple.

'Hi-ya!' It sounded kind of corny and a little misplaced given the circumstances. At first, they didn't recognise him due to his appearance and it took a couple of takes before the penny dropped. Luckily, he'd wiped the blood from his face and hands before leaving the apartment. The bruise above his right eye was just beginning to purple and turn into a perfect rounded black eye, courtesy of a rabbit punch from Charlie Harper, who as Marcus had guessed, could look after himself. It was the only blow he'd managed to get in though as Marcus had grabbed the back of his neck. From then on, as Marcus forced his head to the cheeseboard, the quick slip of the wire had put paid to any ideas Charlie had of fighting for the rest of his life. His feet flapped around like a helpless beheaded fish and the strain of the cheese wire continued its slow journey until it found the white of the neck gristle, the muscle falling from it like cooked meat from a carved bone.

'It's me, Tom Gray, poor old Dave's mate,' he said, smiling as the colour drained from them. 'We met at the campus and then at the Globe; you didn't want to smoke a few joints with us – remember?'

They remembered all right; they also remembered their meeting with DCI Hogan and more recently with DS Evans, and her insistence that the suspect shouldn't be approached under any circumstances, that they should contact her ASAP if they spotted him. And here he was, grinning in front of them, the very face they'd eagerly given a detailed identity kit image of.

Frozen to the spot, the boy held the girl even tighter as they both fought to say their first words.

'Come on,' said Marcus, 'you look like you've both seen a ghost,' he laughed. 'Oh, it's the dust, isn't it – you need an explanation?' he began. 'Back to me roots, innit? I'm a working man now, got a part-time job labouring on a building site. Hard graft, but it pays for the beer,' he added, wondering if they'd ever speak at all, while at the same time relishing the fear they were transmitting. With a more serious expression on his face he stood for a few seconds, his primal eye searching their faces for clues and coming up each time with fright and flight.

They know, he concluded, witnessing the girl's lip quiver as she attempted to speak.

'Oh, yeah,' she wavered, 'Tom.'

'D … Dave's mate,' stuttered her boyfriend, regretting that he'd left it so long to say anything.

'That's it,' chuckled Marcus, 'was worried there for a minute that you didn't recognise me,' he said cryptically with emphasis on the *didn't recognise* bit, spat with a hint of violence.

'We're just sightseeing,' managed Luke, almost stuttering again on *just*.

'Just finishing up,' interrupted Lucy.

'I could have taken you on a tour of the place if I'd known,' began Marcus, now toying with them and not letting them leave like he knew they desperately wanted to. 'Well, History is my second subject,' he continued, 'like the *Cutty Sark*,' he said patting the side of the ship, 'a tea clipper built on the Clyde in 1869 for the Jock Willis Shipping Line, one of the fastest clippers of its time.'

Like a cat with a barely alive mouse between its paws, he played with them, now pointing towards the numerous old Admiralty buildings beyond and giving a brief history of many of the taverns to their left, which the press gangs used to use to obtain their crews for the King's navy.

'Did you visit the Royal Observatory?' he asked emphatically, now very much the tour guide. 'It's the historic prime meridian of the world.'

'No,' they both said innocently, where a lying *yes* may have given them hope of an escape route.

'Come with me, then,' he said enthusiastically, 'one of the best views of London.'

'We've got an exam tomorrow,' tried the boy, who knew it sounded lame as soon as he said it.

'Won't keep you long,' said Marcus firmly, 'we'll just climb to the top, have a look and then you can go.'

Looking at each other, Luke and Lucy mutually agreed that they probably didn't have any choice, and that they'd do as he wanted and then quickly slip away.

The poor frightened lambs, he thought as they briefly disentangled themselves, only to clasp hands tightly and reluctantly follow him in the direction of the Observatory which loomed on the hill beyond.

'Opened in 1676, the Observatory played a major role in astronomy and navigation,' he said breathlessly as they climbed the hill.

'Right,' they both said, eagerly hoping that the history lesson would soon be over.

'Do you like Conrad?'

Learning that they barely knew any of his work, Marcus proceeded to tell them about the novel *The Secret Agent*. 'The anarchist in the story blows himself up outside the Observatory!'

The greyness and bluey shadows in the park were now slowly on their way to darkness. The few people who'd been milling around close to twilight had now disappeared, most of them descending the hill to the pubs and restaurants, while others who daily used the park as a shortcut after work trudged upwards towards their homes in South East London.

'Beautiful, isn't it?' said Marcus as the silvery Thames zigzagged below them, lit by thousands of sparking lights from East to West, while above them each little star showed the way to one of the oldest capitals in the world. As the moon became full, like a huge dinner plate above their heads, he thought of Conrad (how could you not!) and then the Second World War, the German bomber pilots who'd follow the brightness of the moonlight on the water as a runway back to their bases after leaving London in flames.

'Let's just sit a moment,' he began, 'before you go,' he added, sensing their trepidation as they obeyed and sat at a safe distance from him, looking out at the sprawling city below, stretching out as Conrad had seen it, like an ancient waterway connecting everyone to the past.

'So,' said Marcus out of the greyness, his features barely recognisable in the darkness. 'Been to the Globe lately?'

'Not since seeing you there,' replied Luke, still gripping his
girlfriend's sweaty hand and trying not to let his voice falter.

'Umm,' Marcus hummed, letting the ominous sound linger
in the silence and evening dampness as he inhaled deeply and
his chest moistened. 'Haven't found Dave's killer yet, then?' His
voice like a preacher man, full of doom and hellfire, made them
flinch and the girl's legs go to jelly as she felt sick. Wishing
they'd stayed put, both of them now wanted to run and hide.
Their limbs numb with fear, they seized up as if they were
glued to the spot where they now sat. 'I'd say he's quite close by,
wouldn't you? The killer, I mean,' he said, lighting a cigarette as
they both agreed. 'They say, so I've heard, that most victims
know their killers.' He was enjoying himself and was only just
getting going. 'Imagine,' he laughed, 'if I was the murderer and
you were unwittingly sitting up here with me on this lonely,
now deserted hill – wouldn't that be weird?' he said in a way
that demanded an instant response. They both replied that *it
would be strange all right.*

'And do you know what the strangest thing is, to use your
word: strange? Is that you probably know – I mean,' he continued slowly, 'the killer. And to me that would be weirder
still – that you knew,' he laughed, 'you sitting next to me and
knowing who put poor old Dave to rest – so to speak. That
would be funny, wouldn't it?'

'I think we should go now,' said Lucy nervously, going to
get up.

'Dave; poor dead Dave,' he began again in a more serious

tone, 'there was nothing I could do about him, you know. He should had followed his dad to Dagenham, maybe got himself an apprenticeship, shouldn't have ventured where his type doesn't belong. Oh, you're not going to go, are you?' he said at last as the girl flopped back down, her legs unable to rescue her.

'No, but soon,' stammered Luke, putting a protective arm around her as his bladder reminded him that he needed a pee.

'That night at the campus bar, did you notice how he ignored me, as if I wasn't there, every time I asked him a question? Did you?' he enquired again as they both nodded in the darkness. 'Thought he was better than me; thought I was just there to buy him drinks and supply spliffs. I mean, really,' he continued now using his confident posh voice, 'do I sound like a pleb? Well?' he shouted as the couple stiffened and prepared to run for their lives. The first tears of panic came to the girl's eyes as she let out a sob in the darkness. 'Don't cry, little one,' he said, shuffling closer and placing a comforting arm across both their shoulders. 'You don't have to worry. I know what you are; there's no need to fear me – you're different to Dave; more like me.'

As a flock of crows suddenly cackled overhead, heading for their beds in the trees on the other side of the park, Lucy pulled herself away from him, deeper into her boyfriend's embrace. Retrieving his arm, Marcus now sat dangerously passive, as if ready to pounce. 'I thought you had to go?' he said simply. 'Go on! Run!' he suddenly roared as the terrified couple sprang to their feet. 'Run! Run!' he laughed, getting up and pretending to pursue them as they precariously ran and slid down the hill towards the park gate and freedom, Marcus now standing with his arms outstretched like a bird perched on top of the world, legs apart.

'*Wah! Wah! Ewah!*' he shouted after them, flapping his arms, as the bed-bound murder of crows above briefly joined in.

Lying down on the ground he now gazed up at the twinkling stars above and the Observatory which lay to his left. Looking at its silvery dome and exact alignment to the stars, he thought back to the explosion and the total cosmic energy he'd felt at the time of Charlie's timely death, when the blast collided with the sheer brilliance of it all. Pulling up the collar of his coat he swayed back and forth for a time and then let himself roll down the hill, tumbling like a child who'd just discovered the thrill for the first time, until he hit the flat ground at the bottom.

Standing and enjoying the dizzy spell, which made him want to spin like a top and do it all over again, he gazed back up the hill at the moon which was now just peeking behind it, giving the impression that it was trying to hide its smile. Marvelling at its sheer beauty as it towered over him, he could have stayed rooted to the spot for ever had it not been for the spoiler of reality.

Leaving the park and crossing the road he could just make out the scared couple running towards the tunnel. 'Have to fly,' he said to himself as if the desperate escape in the distance had something to do with his imminent departure. 'It's time,' he concluded, scanning the rest of the street and making sure he hadn't been spotted.

Soon back in his rooms, he changed his T-shirt, grabbed his rucksack and began packing a change of clothes, a couple of Conrad novels, a complete works of Shakespeare and a chef's knife set, neatly folded and tied, courtesy of a Russian he'd never met. Everything else can stay, he thought, looking round the room. Sitting down on the edge of the bed he remembered every blow: up and down, swinging like a blacksmith's hammer to the anvil, deadly thuds which echoed around the spinning room as he tasted blood for the first time, spurting like a leaking pipe from Dean's lopsided face. Every memory of Dean, Dave, and Charlie, were now one, a sacrament to be honoured and knelt before. Smiling to himself he grabbed his notepad off the floor and began writing.

Job done, he took one last look at the drawing of Sally, threw the notepad on to the bed, slung his rucksack over his shoulder, and quickly left. Like a bird flying its nest, he didn't look back but headed east.

Chapter Twenty-five

The only just war is class war. It was there right where he'd left it and it wasn't ready to leave. Nor were the numerous pictures of Mandy and Chris relentlessly flicking on and off in his overactive brain. Although nowhere as bad as before when he nearly lost everything, he felt it was now more like the slow, nagging neurosis of a depressive who'd forgotten to take his medication, continuously niggling away like a stretched hernia.

Alone in his office, Jack tried his hardest to keep the wolves at bay; thought of the number of times he'd solved or failed to crack a case, a numbers game to clog up the cruel, relentless workings of the mind which plotted to wreak havoc and misery within every passing thought.

'Police work,' he said to himself in desperation, fighting the impulse to slap himself hard in the face as he tried to think clearly. 'Please!' he reasoned, kicking the side of his desk as he fought another loop of episodes circling his head like hungry buzzards waiting for him to die.

Things had got drastically held up after the misplaced

excitement of the South Quay bombing and the discovery of Charlie Harper's mutilated corpse. Pencil had been frantically trying to get hold of Marcus Bennett-Woods' address from the university, but had to temporarily abandon his pursuit and wait as a large group of Orthodox Jews protested outside the college, not allowing anybody to pass until digging ceased beside the Jewish graveyard at the back of the university.

'Sir?'

It was Evans. Perhaps things hadn't worked out at home, thought Jack, not at all surprised at her sudden return. 'The student couple from Stratford,' she began breathlessly, 'they met him in Greenwich an hour after the bombing; he was covered in dust. They say he more or less confessed to killing Dave and that he was acting weird.'

'Are they OK?' asked Jack, now leaning across his desk.

'Said they feared he was going to hurt them; he apparently told them to run and went to chase after them.'

'So, he's probably still there?'

'Yes, sir; they said he stayed in the park.'

Maybe he went home afterwards, mused Jack, becoming impatient at the lack of progress at the university. 'Pencil!' he shouted with urgency.

'Guv,' his sergeant called from the other room.

'We need that address, now!'

'They still won't let the admin staff in until the digging stops,' he shouted back.

'Damn it!' said Jack, thumping the desk with his fist. 'Either get the digging called off or instruct the officers there to get the staff into the building!' he shouted back, knowing that police intervention without the legal go-ahead would be difficult.

Feeling his blood pressure rising, Jack took a deep breath and mentally began counting down from fifty. By twenty-one the call came that the diggers had given in to the bus loads of demonstrators who'd arrived and got dangerously close to the heavy machinery for their own safety. Protest called off, they soon had Marcus Bennett-Woods' student number and postal address: Flat One, 96 Britannia Court, Greenwich.

'Arm up,' instructed Jack, grabbing his raincoat off the stand behind him and instinctively tapping his breast pocket.

'Yes, sir,' they both replied, acknowledging each other as they did and perhaps putting their quarrel to rest.

'Back-up as well,' continued Jack, 'seal the area – the park, quay-side, and Thames tunnel – but keep the armed response boys on standstill,' he added, not wanting to get too carried away, but still needing to tick the right boxes.

'Greenwich is a bastard to get to from here, sir,' stated Pencil, picking up his car keys. 'Thames Police might lend a hand – will get us there a lot quicker.'

'Good point; what's the nearest base?'

'Near Albert Docks, about three miles from here.'

'I'll phone ahead, sir,' said Evans, already dialling the number. They of course already knew the area well. It seemed as if they would forever be criss-crossing the scene of Dave Wilkins' vicious murder. 'Sir, the area is sealed off across the river, they're expecting us,' called out Evans, pressing her police radio as they piled into the car and Pencil sped towards the docks.

'If he's still there, he won't get out,' said Jack, holding the handle of the passenger side tight and wondering where the evening would lead.

★

237

The horrible mist blowing in from the river was making driving difficult, not that Pencil altered his speed as they raced towards the inky Thames. After passing under a dark flyover they were all relieved to see the lights of the police port and the dazzling rear bulbs of the patrol boats.

'Never been on a police boat before,' said Pencil excitedly as they pulled up abruptly beside it.

In a matter of seconds they were aboard, standing on the drizzly deck and heading for the dazzling lights of Greenwich pier, every inch a maritime spectacle of former naval superiority, welcoming them in like so many who'd gone before them, returning from the tropics and the far reaches of the Empire.

With the boat secured they quickly scurried towards land. 'Sir, it's only a short walk,' said the officer meeting them at the gangplank. 'Above the chip shop there,' he added, pointing beyond the police cordon.

'No lights on,' said Jack as they walked the hundred yards to the stationary squad car blocking the road.

'The back is covered, sir; no one's gone in or out,' stated the officer letting them through.

'Keep it casual,' said Jack, taking the lead as the others tried to keep up. 'Pencil, you go round the rear; me and Evans will get the front. When we smash in the front door – burst in,' he said waving on the officer waiting with the battering ram. 'Didn't think you'd need one,' added Jack, winking at his detective who walked ahead of them towards the fire escape at the back of the building.

Please, Mandy, not now, pleaded Jack to himself as he tried to focus on what might be behind the door of flat one, and not his young bride who'd joined him on the doorstep. Smiling, she obeyed and faded from his mind.

'Ready?' he whispered to Evans.

'Ready.'

'Officer, smash it in.'

A sucking sound, a violent shift, and then the bolt of the battering ram being released and they were in. They heard Pencil crashing in at the back as he dramatically yelled 'Police!' and then an eerie silence descended, the type which curdles the stomach and plays with the mind. They all began to wonder if the maniac was hiding in the building, or if there was a booby-trap waiting to maim them.

'Sir, no one here!' yelled Pencil as they made their way to the top of the stairs. 'Looks like he's scarpered.'

'Those bloody diggers,' cursed Jack, thinking of the time they'd lost in getting the address.

'Sir, in here,' said Pencil, already in the bedroom which showed signs of being left in a hurry. 'A weirdo cave,' he stated, using a term often used by Jack upon entering a psycho's lair.

'You're not kidding,' Jack agreed as the naked sketch of Sally peered out at him from the wall. Now disfigured, the artist had applied what looked like gashes to the torso, slashing it with red marker pen. He'd also added pink to her hair and stamped the class war symbol menacingly on the eye of her side profile. Reading the caption scrawled underneath, *to be continued*, no one could fail to put together the storyboard daubed before them.

'Christ,' said Evans, 'do you think . . . ?'

'Got to be,' said Jack.

'The pink hair's a bit of a giveaway,' added Pencil, his head hitting the single bulb blazing away in the middle of the room.

'Sir,' said Evans, handing him the notepad which had been left on the bed. 'It's addressed to you.'

Detective Chief Inspector Hogan, welcome to my humble abode. I want to share something with you, something that I saw in your eyes, perhaps deep down in your soul.

Shocked at the intimate tone of the writing, Jack swallowed hard and bit his lip before continuing.

I think you are haunted; that you have real doubts about something, and that maybe your ghosts have plagued your judgement before and that they will do so again. It's only a hunch, Mr Hogan, but I think you know I'm right.

To catch someone like me, you will have to kill me or fail.

We will meet very soon, Mr Hogan, and when we do, I will look you straight in the eye and you will know what you have to do, and if you don't, then you will fail like your type were born to.

'He's trying to psych me out,' said Jack dismissively as he handed Pencil the note, his face red with a mixture of anger and a growing feeling he'd been found out, that just maybe Tom Gray, aka Marcus Bennett-Woods, really had seen the ghosts in his eyes.

'Right nutter,' said Pencil in solidarity, hiding some concern for his boss as he handed the note to Evans. She digested it passively, as if it were a shopping list.

'Nutter,' agreed Evans, throwing Pencil a worried glance.

'Our clientele, all right,' replied Jack, a grey, weary, frightened look sweeping across his face.

'Judging by the clothes on the floor and the open drawers, I'd say he quickly packed a bag and fled,' said Evans, changing the subject as she saw Jack's troubled expression appear, his mask sliding to one side and then back again in a split second.

'Pencil, phone ahead to Hackney, get them to seal off Langley Road; we'll get back over the river and then put the boot down,' Jack said mechanically.

Rattled for sure, Jack tried to appear in control as he gave orders and made judgements, even if those very judgements had been questioned and serialised in Marcus's letter, which had been intended to unnerve him.

'Oh, and try Sally Drayton's phone number – she might be in,' he added as they quickly made for the dark, grey river and the searchlights of the river police, which lit up the sky.

Chapter Twenty-six

Marcus guessed that the lock to the door of 52 Orwell Gardens had been broken and that his SWP membership letter had been opened. He was not surprised; knew it had already happened and that his trail had been found. Stepping into the entrance, he peered down into the hole where the rushing water ran under the condemned house. Picking up a pebble and throwing it in, he waited for the plop and the tinkling echo which followed. Crouching down, he reached into the hole and felt for the rusty pipe from which he magically pulled out a key on a piece of string. Wiping the key clean, he stood and kicked the rest of the junk mail into the hole, then turned and left the building, slamming the broken door behind him.

Out in the street, Marcus lit a cigarette and looked about him. Sure that there was no one watching, he did a quick U-turn and ducked down the steps of the basement flat next door to flat four: a dirty, dank entrance filled with litter and dumped rubbish. At a glance the damp basement appeared derelict and uninhabited. The grimy windows and torn off-white net curtains gave the impression that the last occupier was probably long dead and the flat left to rot. The red pixie boot plant pot on the doorstep was the only decorative feature left from the person who once lived there. Kicking aside a rubbish bag and some empty whiskey and gin bottles, Marcus let himself into the low-ceilinged hovel. The tiny hall led directly into the small main room, where peeling green and beige wallpaper hung from the moist blackened walls to the filthy red carpet.

Putting down his rucksack and a bag of groceries Marcus slumped down into the battered, moth-ridden brown sofa set in the middle of the room. The doors to the kitchenette and the one bedroom were left open and had more light in them than the room in which he now sat. The rays of light pouring down from the outside street lighting above exposed the dust particles and the thick atmosphere of the rooms, which stank of mildew. The streams of light produced a dusty, foggy glow. Blowing smoke rings above his head, Marcus turned to the bluey brightness of the solitary bedroom and smiled as if ready to begin a story.

'It's done,' he began. 'I don't know if anyone's ever said it, but the end part is easier than the beginning. A good novelist, so I'm told, knows the end of their story before they start. Really gifted ones write backwards. Imagine committing the last murder and then working back to the first, wouldn't that be brilliant? I mean, you'd never get caught. Though there's no fun in that: not being captured. What would be the point in killing?' he laughed.

Stopping abruptly as if hearing an intrusive noise or movement, he waited a moment before stubbing his cigarette out on the carpet with his foot and continuing.

'Class bounty hunters,' he muttered, as if a forgotten stream of consciousness had caught up with him and burst through his vocal cords. Just like in that scene in *Planet of the Apes*, where the gorillas round up the humans who are attempting to educate themselves, he thought, enjoying the temporary silence and heaviness in the air as he listened to his excited breath and the beat of his heart.

The sound of a heavy goods lorry pounding past shook the basement as Marcus lit another cigarette. 'Well, that's it: it's done,' he repeated again, 'the final countdown,' he said, thinking of the eighties song. 'One, maybe two more and it's all over, the legacy is set.'

A sudden movement made him stop again, something like a restless mouse gnawing out a new home in the skirting board.

'Come!' came the order as a shuffling sound edged closer from the bedroom.

'I said come!' Marcus roared again.

Peering out of the dust-laden rays of light stood a dishevelled figure in a stained red and yellow shell suit, wearing a pair of oversized cheap white trainers. Bent over, his head lowered, the figure slopped forward, dragging his feet as he went.

'Pick up your feet!' came the command as the figure obeyed. 'Sit!'

Squatting down and embracing his knees, the young man kept his greasy head lowered as if awaiting the next instruction.

'Head up!'

Gazing up with heavy dark rings under his eyes and a grey, sweaty, pimply complexion, the man held Marcus's firm stare.

'Tom – you can speak now,' Marcus said casually.

'Yes, sir.'

'Here, put my cigarette out,' he said, holding out the smouldering butt as Tom slowly crawled forward and took it from his master's hand and stubbed it out in an overflowing ashtray beside him. 'Oh, and pick that up,' he added, pointing to the one he'd ground into the carpet previously.

'Yes, sir.'

'Tom,' he continued as the poor creature retreated to his crouching position, 'it's over; it's time; this is the end.'

'End,' mouthed Tom, not sure whether he should.

'Yes, Tom, it's finished.'

Having prematurely aged, Tom Gray appeared a lot older than he was. His heavy stoop told the whole story, that he'd been a captive for some time; an obedient slave who never ventured out unless told to run an errand to the corner shop (though it very rarely happened). The day he'd begun his solitary existence was when he ceased to be. After their first chance meeting, Marcus had taken him under his wing, given him shelter and gained his trust and confidence. Gradually the relationship changed. After the first beating, then the second and third, Tom was at his mercy, made to sleep like a dog in the corner of the room with a dirty old blanket for comfort. Otherwise lost, homeless and vulnerable, the new master–servant relationship had been quickly established. The dog had been whipped into submission and was at the mercy of its owner.

Things changed dramatically the day Marcus got refused a place at Cambridge. His application had been late and his father's name and influence was not what it had been. This he accepted as entirely his own fault. His second choice, Goldsmiths, refused him on the grounds that a large proportion of new applicants who in the past would never have gone to university were now applying in their droves and the college wanted to give places to them (though they didn't say as much) — a kind of positive discrimination in play. Luckily, Queen Mary and Westfield College had offered him a place, but the idea that those not as worthy as himself had been given places which traditionally would have been rightfully his and those of his class grated on him greatly. It was an epiphany, from which point everything would change utterly. His frustration now never far from his fists, he took it out even more on poor Tom, who'd by now had stopped going out completely due to the bruises that covered his face and body. After a drunken night during which he nearly beat his lodger to death, he latched on to the idea; the pure realisation that maybe he was the one who was destined to stop the rot. As Tom cried himself to sleep in his corner, Marcus decided that he'd have to become one of them if he was to be effective in pursuit of his prey. It was then that he became Tom Gray.

For the next three weeks he searched the derelict buildings of East London for a lair. When he spied the basement in Stratford, he knew it was only the beginning. It would be where he'd hide the real Tom Gray, while the new one met and hunted down the sons and daughters of the working class, who now threatened the institutions he held dear.

'I've brought you some groceries,' he said, throwing the carrier bag in Tom's direction. 'There's some Mars bars, crisps, and Fanta.'

'Thank you, sir.'

Delving into the bag, Tom pulled out the crisps and asked if he could open them. Given the go-ahead he scoffed them greedily, like a famished animal. Coming up for air, he started on the chocolate.

'You really are a hungry little piggy today,' Marcus said, smiling and pulling out a pack of cigarettes. He skimmed them like a flat stone across the carpet. 'There's something I have to do,' he continued in a more serious tone as he reached into his rucksack and produced the set of knives. Unwrapping the white satchel on his lap, he took out a cleaver and ran his finger along the edge. 'Definitely this one,' he said, placing it on the arm of the chair. 'And maybe the boning knife as well,' he added, putting it next to the cleaver. 'Oh, and I nearly forgot: the reliable old carving knife, and *this* is a real find,' he continued excitedly, taking out the cheese wire, 'thanks to a rich Russian cheese monster,' he laughed. 'Beautiful, isn't she?' he said, stretching it to its full length of a metre. 'You don't have to answer, I can see you're hungry.'

Taking out the sharpening iron he began honing the knives. Holding the iron rigidly in front of him, he expertly flashed both sides of the blade of the carving knife in a quick rhythmic movement, as the chime of clashing, grating steel rang around the room.

'Did it never cross your mind that this could be for you?' he asked, making a playful stab with the knife as Tom opened a can of Fanta which sprayed all over his shell suit.

'Yes, sir,' he replied, wiping himself down with his cuff.

'Do you want it to be?'

'No, sir.'

'Come here,' he commanded, 'right there,' he said, pointing in front of him and handing him the iron. 'Now, hold it tightly with both hands; that's it,' he continued, taking the carving knife and proceeding to sharpen it. 'One slip and you lose a finger or two,' he laughed, moving the task up a gear as steel vigorously struck steel and the blade appeared to blur in the flurry of it all. 'Right, let's try it out,' he said, now finished and

247

a little breathless. 'You can give me that.' He said, motioning towards the iron. 'Good boy, now give me your hand.' Reluctantly, Tom did as he was told. 'Do you like cheese?' Marcus asked, taking a small block from his bag. 'Of course you do,' he said, not waiting for an answer. 'Here, place it in your hand; that's it – perfect. All right, let's try this beauty out.' He took Tom's outstretched hand, lifting the knife and then slowly letting it cut through the block of cheese till it sliced into the skin beneath.

'Oops, too sharp,' he smiled, watching Tom's palm suddenly flood with blood. Pulling the knife away violently, he let it slash a bit deeper and Tom let out a little whimper. 'Oh, it's only a scratch,' Marcus added, wiping the blood off the blade on the cuff of Tom's still outstretched arm. 'You can keep the cheese – the Russian won't mind,' he said, casually signalling for his captive to return to his original position.

'As I was saying, Tom,' he began again, 'it's all over. I'm moving on; you're going to be on your own from now on.'

Whether there was a flicker of recognition in Tom Gray's dead eyes or not, he listened intently, clutching his bloody hand.

'I mean totally alone; you see, I don't need you any more. The Tom Gray I took from you has done his job. I no longer need him. So, I'm giving him back to you: Tom Gray, meet Tom Gray,' he concluded comically.

In the silence which now engulfed them he looked at the broken thing before him and wondered what the future held for him. What would he do? Could he survive?

'I've written some instructions for you,' he began, tossing him a sealed letter. 'There's an ATM card in there with a PIN number. You remember me taking you to the cash machine once – don't you?'

'Yes, sir.'

'Every Friday, go there, put in the code, and draw out a hundred pounds. It will be there for as long as you need it.'

'Yes, sir.'

'My old dad has upped my allowance,' he said lazily. 'You, of course, never had that luxury.'

Tom merely nodded, knowing that not to could result in a violent reaction and an unnecessary beating.

'You're free, Tom Gray. You're free!' Marcus began laughing to himself. 'I'm no longer your master – you can leave, you can stay, you can do whatever you want with the rest of your life.'

Remaining passively glued to the red carpet, Tom bowed his greasy mop and began to weep.

'Come on, Tom, don't cry,' Marcus said, now standing over him and patting his shoulder. 'Look, go down to the corner shop and get us both some beers,' he motioned, handing him a ten-pound note. 'Come on,' he said, lifting him to his feet. 'Oh, and this is yours,' he remembered, handing him the key, 'you truly are free, Tom: a free man with a key to his castle.'

'Thank you, sir,' Tom managed, taking the key in his grimy, sticky, bloody fingers and holding Marcus's steady gaze.

'Now go!' demanded Marcus, with what appeared to be tears in his eyes, 'go before I change my mind,' he concluded, patting Tom's arm and giving him a gentle push as he obeyed and shuffled towards the door.

Waiting for the door to close, Marcus quickly placed the knives back in their case and returned them to the rucksack, grabbed his coat, wiped the tears from his eyes, and followed Tom Gray out into the night.

Chapter Twenty-seven

'I love *Schindler's List*, don't you?' said Pete, repeating snatches of the dialogue and doing an exaggerated impersonation of the Nazi camp commander who was admiring Oscar's expensive clothes at the bottom of the bed.

'How can you love *Schindler's List* – it's so depressing?'

'If you've watched it as many times as me and you have a natural propensity to find German accents funny, then you will,' yawned Pete, flicking the remote to a documentary about footballers' wives.

'I suppose I'd rather watch the Nazis in black-and-white misery than soccer bimbos,' stated a sleepy Sally, slipping down deeper under the duvet and nestling into the side of her boyfriend like a limpet on a rock. 'Lights out soon,' she announced, knowing that Pete always needed a countdown when engaged in his favourite pastime.

'Give me five more,' he said, giving her a squeeze while keeping one eye firmly on the TV mounted on the table at the foot of the bed.

It seemed longer than a week ago that Sally had moved in.

Even the cat appeared to have taken the transition in her stride, marking out her territory in the back garden and adjoining alleyway with that horrendous smell which reminds you why you don't like cats. Now with her tiny yellow Fiat Panda back from Forensics, the whole Tom episode was slowly sailing away into history. Staying at Pete's was the ultimate cosy coupledom you could hope for. Pete was the perfect housekeeper, preparing breakfast, providing a laundry service, and a hearty dinner upon her return from college each day. Though his habits hadn't changed that much, he now tended to get all his chores completed early so as to catch the matinee films on BBC Two, which usually finished just as he was getting hungry and Sally was due to return. It was bliss, a perfect arrangement. If Pete could have lived the rest of his life within the confines and daily routine of domesticity and daytime TV, he would have given himself entirely – that was, if the dole didn't get too suspicious. They'd recently introduced a number of new job initiatives – Job Club being one of them, which Pete had managed to skip on the technicality that the work he was constantly available for didn't really exist. So far, so good, as no bones had been thrown in his direction. As for Sally, she was in the last year of her Art and Design degree and was hoping to scrape a 2.1, as were most students in her cohort. To get a First you had to avoid the pub and live in the library. 2.1s were, to pardon the pun, strictly second best but increasingly achievable.

It seemed that Sally had everything she needed, and that the future promised the same. Even her compulsion to tell Pete everything about Andy Murrow had all but disappeared, as if time and her resistance to cave in had torn it to shreds. If anything, the whole Tom scare had established a sense of stability, enhanced security (Pete) and a general feeling that things could only get better.

'Pete?'

'Yeah.'

'We're on five now – blanket street.'

'Are you sure, Sal?' said Pete, who'd flicked to a late-night discussion on the probability of life on Mars. 'I thought we were still on three.'

'Defo five.'

'Ok,' he yawned, pressing the off button as they kissed, and the room fell into beautiful darkness at the click of a switch.

Fail as your type were born to, pondered Jack as the police patrol boat moored at the Albert Docks. The cheeky bastard – if it's a class war he wants then he's picked the wrong fight, he thought in an attempt to distance himself from the psychologically revealing part of the note, the part that had him pinned down as haunted, vulnerable, and unable to make clear judgements.

Keeping the past at bay wasn't going to be easy. The incident with Chris was never going to be blown away, not even by Jack's gun, which Marcus had suggested was his only get out of jail free card.

I won't be part of a sicko's final chapter in which he goes out in a hail of police bullets, he thought as he stepped on to the gang plank; '*or maybe you will have to?*' said the distant voice of Chris, who was making gunslinger shapes with a set of toy pistols.

'Sir?' It was Pencil with the police radio at his chin. 'She's not there – must be at the boyfriend's.'

'How far is it?' asked Jack, glad to be hearing other voices that weren't just in his own head.

'Not far from Sally Drayton's, just a couple of streets away.'

'OK, extend the cordon; no one in or out. And tell them: no headlights. I want the street dark. If he's there I don't want him agitated,' he said as they made for the car.

Singing an old hymn from his days at boarding school, a rare happy memory caused him to smile as his voice bellowed theatrically. Stopping at the chorus as he was about to begin it, Marcus whistled the tune instead to the marching time and pace he'd launched into since leaving Hackney station. Collar up, dust in his tight cropped hair, and an aluminous orange rucksack draped over his shoulder, he swaggered with confident determination like someone returning late from work, who'd perhaps had a particularly good day.

Shipley Road, Bell Road, North Avenue, Shaftsbury Road, Tower Road – streets that meant nothing. Apart from the last one, Clifton Road, which as he interrupted his whistling and glanced at the sign, held significant meaning and as he read the street sign aloud, had a chilling ring to it.

Turning over on her side, Sally was halfway through a recurring dream in which she stumbled upon a cinema and climbed the steps to the brightly lit, glitzy entrance. Once inside, the lights went out as she desperately tried to find her seat before the film began. Guided by a pull she couldn't explain, each step filled her with an overwhelming dread and fear, the worst feeling ever, mixed with pain, sadness, guilt, and an evil within stabbing away at her side as she felt as if she was about to choke.

As she reached her seat the whole dreaded sequence began again as hands reach out, touching and grabbing at her as they tried to pull her into the darkness, accompanied all the way by a thick, tight nausea as the auditorium became greyer and darker and then completely jet black as she began screaming from the pit of her soul until she awoke, rolling and hollering in the middle of a night sweat.

'Pete! Pete!' she yelled, opening her wet bloodshot eyes and then wishing she hadn't.

The bedside lamp was on as she turned over, petrified, towards him.

Pete, black tape criss-crossed over his eyes and across his mouth, wriggled beside her. His neck red with bloody lacerations, he sweated profusely on the saturated pillow, the cheese wire cutting further into his skin every time he moved his torso. Clipped into a slip knot like a lasso around his neck, the end of the wire had been expertly secured to a pulley attached to the brass bedstead at his head. If he were to fight for his life his head would come cleanly off. His arms were tied above him, he was like a trussed, basted chicken waiting to be cooked. His brown and beige trim retro underpants were his only dignity. In the middle of his chest was the ink stamp of the class war logo, violently splurged across his skin.

'Pete! Pete!'

'Hush, Sally; hush,' came the voice behind her as she began to panic at the absurdity stinging her eyes.

Slowly turning her head, she looked at the solitary figure

254

sitting on the edge of the bed bedside her, holding a piece of cord in his hand.

'You really are a sound sleeper, Sally; bit of a snorer too,' he smirked. 'Don't do anything stupid,' he said, holding up the cord which she could now see was part of a construction which led like a spider's web to the wire noose where her boyfriend lay. 'One tug and he's gone, Sally; just one pull of the string and Anne Boleyn's head rolls,' he said smiling.

The face she knew, but the posh, clipped, confident accent she didn't. 'Tom,' she eventually stammered, her wet pyjamas clinging to her as a chill shot up her spine and made her shiver uncontrollably.

'No, Sally, Tom's back in Stratford – remember? You dropped him off there. He saw you peeping.'

'Who are you?' she managed, gripping Pete's hand beside her and fighting the urge to scream.

'The name's Marcus,' he said, throwing her some matches and then popping a cigarette in his mouth. 'Do be a good girl and light it for me – you see, if I use this hand,' he added shaking the cord, 'we may have a few problems to deal with.'

Picking up the matches she'd dropped, her shaky hand quickly obeyed him as she now sat upright in the bed, straightening her top and bottoms.

'Nice colour pink. Like the polka dots – very cute and fluffy,' he remarked, nodding at her legs as he took a long satisfying lungful of his lit fag.

'What do you want?' she asked, as the colour drained from her face and her heartbeat accelerated.

'Thought I'd return this,' he laughed, putting his hand in his pocket and producing her silver earring. 'Here, put it on,' he said as she shook her head.

'I said put it on!'

This time she did as she was told. His booming voice made her want to vomit.

'Tom said you left it in the alleyway, but I found it in the car – you should be more careful,' he added with a grin. 'I must say, the boyfriend's quiet – poor chap.'

The sinister part wasn't so much that he wasn't strange Tom from the party, but the fact he sounded like a completely different person to the one she'd travelled with in the car. His appearance had also added to the macabre, his close-shaved hair and ragged attire giving him a ghostly kind of look.

'Why are you doing this?' she said, now clasping her hands tightly together as Pete moaned in pain beside her.

'In war there are casualties,' he began, nodding sardonically towards the logo on Pete's chest, 'and as it says: *the only just war is class war*. Heard of it first on a demonstration; it seemed apt, though I've turned it on its head somewhat,' he said, pretending to pull the cord with his other hand. 'No, no, don't speak,' he told her as she went to plead with him again. Leaning across her, he put a finger to her lips as she jumped. 'Save your words. I know the questions you want to ask,' he said soothingly as if beginning a bedtime story.

Her knees visibly knocking together, her expression pleaded with him as she swallowed the words she wanted to say: '*You're not going to kill me?*'

'Hold this,' he said, handing her the cord, 'don't let it slip and don't pull it.' He laughed, standing up. 'Here,' he continued, motioning for her to pass it back as he tied it loosely on to the bedstead behind her head, like a cowboy fastening his horse outside a saloon, before sitting down. 'Sally,' he began again as if speaking to a young child. 'I'm not going to harm you – not now.' He started placing an unwelcome hand on her trembling knee. 'You see, I saw you doing it. That's a bit cheap, isn't it?' he corrected himself, 'I mean, ever since I saw you make love to this peon here,' he spat, reaching above her and giving the cord a gentle yank, enough for the wire to widen the slit in Pete's throat as he groaned.

'Don't speak,' he said again as she went to reason with him. 'Actually, this might be better.' He reached for the roll of black tape and, ripping a piece off, roughly plastered it over her mouth, then proceeded to fasten her wrists and ankles as she defiantly wriggled and then gave up just as quick. 'It's what they do in the movies, Sally: the pretty girl always has to be bound and gagged . . . On my way here tonight, I had every intention of killing you. I was filled with hatred for you – that was until I saw you deep in sleep, your eyes twitching; no doubt having a nightmare. Then I remembered how I was initially attracted to you and how I wanted to take you. You see,' he continued hesitantly, 'with your type, the females are enticing; it's like they put a spell on you. And you, you have pure beauty and it wasn't unusual for a man of good breeding to take lovers, mistresses, even wives from your class and improve them – teach them the finer things. And then I saw you, naked, arched over this giant pleb, and it turned me on – oh, yes,' he purred. 'But it also meant that I could never take you as a lover. Not now,' he added sadly, stroking her thigh as she began to cry and shudder. 'But him!' he suddenly spat violently, 'he was always going to suffer, but you, no, you're just going to have the memory of that suffering. When Roman generals conquered a town or village, they'd always make the women and children watch as their men were put to death. It's a lesson, Sally, a price that has to be paid. But there's a twist,' he said, picking up the duct tape again, 'you're not going to *see* the act of revenge, you're going to hear it, as your mind pictures the act and the cries of pain and suffering echo in your ears for all eternity.' He placed an X of tape over each eye as she was encased by the fear of darkness, submerged into a random world of uncertainty and blindness as if sprung back into her nightmare.

'May the generations that follow you speak of this day,' he started getting to his feet and pacing around the room, 'that they know their place, like your fathers' before who knew theirs; that the blood of those who are slain this year of nineteen hundred and ninety-six, remains a reminder of their foolish aspirations. May each cut and blow be the mark which sets them apart and diminishes them, as they once again truly grasp their lowly standing in the fabric of order,' he concluded, removing his coat and slipping off his T-shirt as he thumped his naked chest with his fist.

Silence, rustling, swishing and footsteps: they all circled her as the shaking intensified and the feelings of helplessness overcame her as she was paralysed by the evil which threatened to mutilate and pummel the love of her life, whose shallow breathing began to frighten her.

'So, Pete.' His voice booming like a sudden bell tolling made her jump. 'It's time. Now, I know you've been listening very carefully,' he began, holding the carving knife in his hand and resting its tip directly on the ink spot in the middle of Pete's chest as his heartbeat increased. 'It's OK, I'm only practising. I once tried to place my hand into an eye socket and pull out a brain. Made a complete balls-up of it. You see, I've never had time to perfect it – I was learning on the job. That's it,' he said, changing the subject, 'just a little nick. Hurts less, doesn't it – when you can't see what's going on?' he stated as a tiny trickle of blood oozed from the stamp on Pete's chest as his limbs and body stiffened. 'I've never sliced up a live specimen before; well, apart from a bit of engraving,' he chuckled. 'It's good to get started, before the real work begins. And the cheese wire? Well, that's an entirely different gig: it's the weight and the tautness which does the work,' he said as Pete moved his head to one side and the wire cut a bit deeper.

'Now, Pete, are you listening? No, don't shake your head – that's not a good idea. Just squeeze my finger if you understand,' he added, taking his captive's hand. 'That's it: good. Now, I'm going to take the plaster off your mouth and if you say one word, I swear to God, I will chop her head off. Do you understand?' he said calmly, 'squeeze if you do? That's it: good. Now, don't get me wrong, you can shout and scream as loud as you like. In fact, the louder the better; but you don't speak to her – yes? Squeeze. Yes. You're a quick learner, and so far, the perfect victim ...' He suddenly ripped the plaster clear from Pete's mouth, and the captive let out a gut-churning cry as all the previously bottled-up fear and pain was released in one haunting, animal howl.

'That's it, you let it out, old son,' said Marcus, mockingly patting Pete on the shoulder as Sally began to sob uncontrollably, the sounds she was trying to make muffled by the plastic tape which made her hyperventilate. 'There, there, let it all go,' he continued, as Pete's cry gradually became a dying whimper and his breathing more controlled.

Untying the cord from the bedstead, he now looped it around his own neck and fastened it securely, then pulled away slightly to take the slack of the wire waiting to splice deeper into Pete's neck.

'Pete, I have to say – and it pains me to – but you're very brave,' he announced, lighting another cigarette as he watched the blood trickle from the small cut on Pete's pale chest every time he exhaled. 'Don't worry: the cavalry will be here soon. Unfortunately, we have to wait for them. I hate to see an animal suffer – even your type – but I'm afraid we must have witnesses to what will be my final parting gift. It's just the way things are done. Cigarette? Your last, I guess,' he laughed. 'Go on, squeeze,' he said, offering his hand. 'Oh, a non-smoker; how boring,' he concluded, blowing smoke into his face.

Pete's grip remained limp and clammy as he drifted in and out of consciousness.

Chapter Twenty-eight

'Guv, you all right?' asked Pencil, a little unnerved at the tense silence which had been circulating in the car as they sped from the Albert Docks to Hackney.

'Yeah, I'm fine,' replied Jack flatly, as he gazed despondently out at the damp London nightlife passing him by in a depressing drizzle.

The intensity of the situation had lent itself to his quiet demeanour as he ploughed through the numerous heinous scenarios and dramas which may be awaiting them beyond the Hackney Empire, where a different sort of drama had already been acted out two hours previously, in the form of *Who's Afraid of Virginia Woolf*. Passing the theatre, he remembered being there with Mandy and Jake for their first ever pantomime as a family, and how they'd had pie and mash afterwards. Now the café was gone, along with a lot of the shops which were either for sale or left derelict.

Fitting the lack of street lighting in darkest Hackney, his mood was bleak and a long way from a positive ending, which for an experienced detective was never, ever an alternative, but a consequence of what has to be faced. The Americans called it collateral damage; Jack called it *the shit that happens*, the stinking crap that you would most certainly get smeared on your shoe as you attempted to uphold the law. There were of course happy outcomes, but they always came with a price, whether physical or mental, the scars remained for ever. And then there were Mandy and Chris to contend with all over again – the never-ending sequence of misery, which for the recipient was torturous, tedious, and something you instantly bored of, as it hacked away unchecked at your sanity. Jack knew the odds, understood the probability that an image would flash before his eyes, would do so within the looming minutes and hours, that they would intensify when the stakes were at their highest.

As the sweat poured from his brow, he considered his options and came up with what he'd intended all along since the episodes had returned. Checking his passenger mirror, he watched intently as Evans gazed off into the distance. Giving a sideways glance at Pencil, he slipped his hand into his breast pocket and pressed one of the pills out of its foil-coated plastic holder. Then making a double-check of his two detectives he surreptitiously popped it in his mouth and swallowed hard. It was low-strength Diazepam, nothing serious, the dosage enough to get him nicely through the next twenty-four hours.

He'd never in his years in the force had to make a chemical choice. OK, he had been a self-medicating drunk before, but he'd never strategically approached a dangerous situation with the view to using a drug to clear his mind. He was sure that if he hadn't done so now, the next few hours may have proved to be catastrophically fatal. Sooner than he'd anticipated he was strangely calm: a familiar feeling. His mind felt as if it had been chemically scrubbed from top to bottom, each nerve-ending in his brain gleamingly clean and bright, empty enough to be filled with pragmatic reasoning.

With a pleasant feeling twirling around the top of his head, the car appeared to effortlessly glide to an airy halt at the road-block at the top of the cordoned-off street. Maybe he'd taken too much? he thought. Though as soon as the idea formed in his head, the reasoning he believed had just put a cautionary arm around him as quickly abandoned him, as he forgot and wondered what he'd been thinking in the first place.

'Clifton Road, sir,' announced Pencil, turning off the ignition. Jack wanted to say *cool*, but just nodded instead. 'It's the dilapidated townhouse next to The Full English Café,' he concluded, pointing beyond the luminous yellow police tape.

Out of the car, Jack stood for a while, hands in pockets, the collar of his navy-blue raincoat pulled to attention as a mild gust of wind gently swished into his face and ran soothingly through his hair. The magical Victorian street before him remained still and silent, as if all its inhabitants were floating in their dreams, circling their houses in the night sky. Thinking of Jake and Skuld, he felt the warm glow of the drugs fully kick in as he wondered what they were doing, before realising that they too were probably safely tucked up in bed.

'Sir?' It was Pencil again.

'Yes, Pencil; I'm ready,' he replied instantly, as if a clean, clear white light had been suddenly switched on.

With an aura of inevitability and a new spring in his step, Jack led the way, giving instructions as he went. It seemed as if vulnerable Jack was happy enough to be led by reliable old Jack, who had become weirdly electronically charged and focused.

263

Stopping abruptly, he addressed his detectives. 'This isn't going to be easy,' he began as if the words he spoke were clinging to him, not wanting to escape his mouth, locked within a dark cavern in his throat. 'I'm sure we're going to be entering a stand-off of sorts,' he added slowly. 'Are you ready for that?'

'Yes, sir,' they both replied, glancing nervously at one another.

'Whatever happens, it falls to me. You know what I mean?'

They knew exactly what he meant: the unwritten rule, that judgements, choices and ultimate decisions for right or wrong rested with the boss.

'All I want is that you follow my lead. Watch the eyes: focus on the sudden change and read the game. To use an old football analogy,' he added with a smile, 'watch the ball.'

With both his colleagues at his side he felt like a sheriff with his posse. Like him they felt that strange, innate solidarity officers feel when they walk into the unknown together.

'Think Bobby Moore: best reader of the game ever,' said Jack, slightly more relaxed.

Reaching the steps of the house, they surveyed the ground-floor flat. The one light on in what they supposed could be the bedroom or sitting room was most certainly their destination. Noticing that the door was still ominously ajar, they guessed that their man was already inside.

'We all go through the front,' whispered Jack, pulling out his gun as both Pencil and Evans followed suit. 'There's no need to cover the back – he's not going to want to escape,' he concluded as he gently pushed open the door.

Once inside the high-ceilinged hallway, they could just make out the muffled sobbing of a woman as they located the room where the light seeped under the door. Signalling to Evans and

Pencil to get either side of the entrance, Jack gingerly put his hand on the doorknob. He heard what sounded like a professional butcher sharpening his knives, as they clanged, clattered, and scraped. Hesitating for a second, he held back.

As Pencil's boots creaked on the loose floorboard and the clashing sound of metal intensified, the tension in Jack's wrist and fingers became electric. Sensing the now or never pressure forming in his grip, he looked to his colleagues, winked, turned the handle and threw open the door.

'Police!' shouted Evans as they piled blindly in.

'Oh, Detective Chief Inspector Hogan,' said Marcus Bennett-Woods, turning casually towards the sudden intrusion, his sharpening iron gripped defiantly in one hand in front of him and his boning knife in the other, 'there's really no need for amateur dramatics – you'll scare the poor lambs,' he said, gesturing with his knife, pointing at the trembling Sally and deathly white Pete. 'And we've all been so looking forward to seeing you and you have to make an entrance like that,' he smiled.

It had been like when the opening curtain goes up to reveal the brightly lit stage set of the first act of a play. From the darkness of the hall to the sudden light, they'd been stunned and sickened into silence by gore. The scene hit them in all its graphic glory: the surreal criss-crossed eyes of the captives; the web of pulleys and wires which led to the sticky, bloody, gashed and swollen neck; the sacrificial bullseye on the disturbingly creamy, waxen torso, and then the star of the show: the bare-chested, crop-headed, dusty man with a noose tied securely round his neck. Briefly glancing at his image in the wardrobe mirror, which appeared to flash back at him like a spotlight, Jack shivered at the absurdity of all, at seeing himself pointing a deadly firearm.

'Quite a scene, don't you think?' Marcus laughed, detecting the horror smeared across their shocked faces as their eyes recorded every sickening detail, struggling to comprehend it all in one vile swoop. 'Really, Mr Hogan,' he continued slowly, putting down the sharpening iron by Pete's side, 'do you actually need all those guns?' he said, nodding at both Evans's and Pencil's outstretched arms as Jack glanced from side to side and then at his own gun slightly trembling in front of him.

'Come on, Mr Hogan – cat got your tongue?'

He'd been stunned into silence, as they all had, paralysed and struggling to put it all together. Awkwardly, he waited, waited for all his experience to swell in his mind, for the coping mechanism, which hadn't been switched on yet, to catch up with him and force him into action.

'You really are a disappointment, DCI Hogan, you're not the hard-staring bastard from the interview room,' Marcus said, unaware that his words were just about to switch Jack on.

'Put the knife down,' Jack said calmly, much to the relief of Pencil and Evans, who'd feared a 'Chris scenario' developing again.

'Oh, he speaks,' said Marcus patronisingly. 'What, this?' he laughed, waving the knife around in front of him like a pirate with a cutlass. 'I don't think so – do you?'

Jack knew the routine: ask, reason, and ask some more until you've exhausted all avenues, until you get to the part where they tell you what they intend to do or want.

'Let the girl go,' he reasoned.

'Oh, Mr Hogan,' Marcus started before following another train of thought, 'or maybe we should use first names, unless you want to continue with the Irish one?' he added spitefully.

'OK. I'm Jack.'

'Well, *Jack*. Good working-class name, Jack.' He almost spat the words. 'You know I can't let her go – she's the leading lady,' he added. 'You can't have the death of a lover without the heroine swooning all over the body, surely?'

It was going nowhere, Jack knew as much, but he had to keep it going. 'Then let one of my colleagues remove the tape.'

'What, the big freaky gangly one or the blonde power dresser?' he laughed, pointing to each one in turn with his knife.

'Either,' answered Jack, playing the game and feeling Pencil's penetrating stare behind him; he no doubt wanted to rip the sicko apart.

'No can do, Jack,' he said with a swish of his knife which was beginning to irritate the DCI. 'Common name: Jack. Oh, and an Irish surname – *interesting* profile – I'm sure there's a story there?'

So that's your game, thought Jack – the baiting's begun.

'I wasn't sure to begin with, Jack, but you're one of them, aren't you, and I'm guessing born of Paddy immigrant parents?'

OK, time to play a bit, thought Jack, ignoring the jibe. 'You mean working class, Marcus?' he said, finally getting into his stride.

'Well done, Jack, or should I say Sherlock?'

'Working class and proud, is that what you want to hear?' he replied, visibly adjusting the grip on his gun.

'Well, class warrior,' spat Marcus slowly, his mood suddenly changed, 'tell those two monkeys behind you to lower their guns – the only gun I want to see is yours.'

Nodding to his detectives to do as they were told, Jack stepped back into the game. 'So, hit a bit of a nerve there, Marcus – being working class and proud; you don't think that's possible, then?' he said, smiling for the first time. 'I think that really bothers you. Being surrounded by bright, deserving, ordinary people – you're threatened by that.'

Maybe he'd gone too far; perhaps he was pushing him too quickly? A bead of sweat ran down Jack's forehead.

'It's irrelevant what you or your type think,' Marcus replied casually, sticking his finger in the cut on Pete's chest as the captive gave a sickening groan. 'I don't think that's a good idea, do you?' he said, holding the cord around his neck and going to pull it as Evans went to go to Pete's assistance.

'Look, Jack,' he continued as Evans retreated, 'perhaps I should explain a few things about what's happening here. You see the cheese wire round the pleb's throat and the cord around mine all connected, right? One pull, or if my full weight was to suddenly slump, his head rolls, plain and simple. You can see what his wriggling has done already,' he said, motioning towards the saturated, blood-soaked pillow and sheets. 'Oh, yes, Jack, I can see you looking at the chest; well, that scratch is where the dagger goes, where the heart stops, the final act when you then pull the trigger and kill me,' he said, looking deep into Jack's steady eyes.

So, that was the twist, thought Jack, weighing up his options: one, the lunatic goes to thrust the boning knife into Pete's heart. Two, he shoots Marcus, who falls with all his weight over the body, the pulley slips, the wire tightens, Pete's head comes off. Either way Pete dies, as does Marcus, who gets his wish and his blaze of glory.

He's good, thought Jack. Here was a man who'd orchestrated his own end and that of his victim down to the last detail. A catch-22, where the winner holds the knife and the cord of death, and the loser the gun which he has to use – no, has been *ordered* to use by the master himself.

'And when does all this begin?' said Jack flatly, buying time and taking the game further to a state of red alert, to the part where the detective has to engage in mind games or try to appeal to the assailant's better nature – the latter being the only option open to him.

'When you make your move, Jack,' Marcus said, smiling, loving the drama unfolding as Sally began to cry and shake uncontrollably. 'Shut up! Shut up!' he suddenly snapped, his eyes blazing, as Evans went to move forward again. 'Are you bloody stupid?' he shouted, holding the cord tightly again as she stopped short of Sally, unaware that she had uncannily moved things up a notch or two. 'Back! *Abschaum!*' he barked as Evans retreated.

Seeing the anger in Marcus's eyes, Jack contemplated the kill as he waited for the flicker; the real twitch of intent which he knew wasn't far away. Change of tack, he thought, as the muscles in his tired arms tightened.

'I bet your dad would be really proud, what with him being a diplomat and you his only son?' There – there it was: a flicker in Marcus's eye, that movement that spelt that pain had been delivered and that it had troubled him – the knowledge that Jack had been uncovering and sifting through the layers of his life. And of course, the personal jibe, aimed to unsettle him, just as his letter to Jack had.

'Been doing your homework then?' he replied, tapping the boning knife annoyingly on the steel of the bedstead.

'A bit,' began Jack. 'I also learnt that your mother didn't want you either – packing you off to boarding school aged six. Is that how your type treats their children, Marcus?'

'Oooh, that hurt, Jack,' Marcus laughed, now pointing the knife at him. 'If I'm not mistaken, I'd say you're trying to upset me!'

Jack didn't reply; the sparring had moved on rapidly to the part where talk had exhausted itself and the only thing to cling to was the faint scent of the end.

Inspector Hogan, welcome to my humble abode. I just want you to know that I saw something in your eyes the other day, something dark, deep down in your soul. Maybe you did, thought Jack, as the letter randomly flew off to another compartment of his mind.

As if the sound was turned down, Jack silently surveyed every line in Marcus's face. The younger man no doubt did the same of him. Like two gunslingers waiting for the twitch, they watched and contemplated.

No plan in sight, Jack shifted uneasily on his heels as Marcus began to casually whistle 'The Lord of the Dance'. Sally sniffled and Pete moaned a bit more.

Why boxing? he wondered, as Mandy did an Ali shuffle in front of him and Chris put up her fists and led with her right, before laying a playful left hook on his arm. A message maybe? thought Jack, his mind now white and clean again. Mandy and Chris blew him a kiss and waved goodbye.

Rocky Marciano, Marvelous Marvin Hagler, Jack Dempsey, they all led with the right. Hagler would jab away; would come at you, jabbing away with the left, then suddenly switch to his natural right. Then that jab would fly off to one side, his opponent's gaze following the glove and then bang! The left would come: boom! Crash! Straight on the jaw and they'd hit the floor.

'Are you ready, Jack?' said Marcus, breaking his reverie, holding out the knife and checking the slack of the noose round his neck. 'I think we've done enough talking, don't you?'

This was it, knew Jack, although there was one more shot to call.

'Ever heard of a southpaw, Marcus?' he said finally as his knees temporarily wobbled and his chest tightened.

'Come on, Jack, don't mess around,' Marcus replied loftily as the old familiar smirk arrived on his face. 'Time's running out – you know what you have to do.'

'Jack Dempsey, Marvin Hagler – heard of them?'

'No, only Jack Hogan,' he said, decisively staring deep into his eyes as he raised the dagger high above Pete's marked chest. 'Good!'

It really did all happen as if in a dream sequence: you caught the change of expression in your hand, you blew the dice and threw it up in the air and hoped that it landed on a six, each take, every minute detail, turning, shifting, becoming incomprehensible in a disturbing cycle of timeless motion.

Jack threw his dice. A sudden forty-five-degree turn, he saw his own reflection in the wardrobe mirror again and shot two rounds into his forty-five-year-old face. The glass disintegrated into crushed ice. Seeing the rapid swing of the arm to the right, towards the mirror, Marcus instinctively followed the manoeuvre as the glass shattered beside him. Dropping his gun, Jack sprang at the knife, holding it firmly, while holding up Marcus's head with his other hand, as Pencil rushed to his side and helped hold the weight of the trunk of Marcus's body, which struggled to slump and fall. Instantly dropping his head, Marcus's sweaty face was plastered on to Jack's cheek as their eyeballs met and locked: an eye for an eye, a primal glance of hatred and fear – it was all so familiar as humanity sought to hold the stare of pure evil.

'Gotcha!' shouted Jack as Evans pounced and released the wire around Pete's hideously swollen neck. It was only an instant but there was a heavenly sigh and hush which made you want to drop to your knees and pray. The near–total silence, only the scuffling of shoes, it was holy, it was eerily sacred because life had been saved. The kind of sudden nothingness that would make you want to unashamedly weep.

'Not too bright, your type, are they?' snarled Jack, pulling Marcus's arm roughly around his back as Pencil laid on the cuffs. 'Southpaws lead with the right, Marcus. Lesson number one for novices: never follow the glove if it flies to one side. Always focus on the left that's coming up straight for you.'

'Bloody amateur,' goaded Pencil, yanking Marcus's arm violently up to his shoulder blade.

Not giving him the chance to speak or have the last word, Jack turned his back as the master was led away by the servant.

Chapter Twenty-nine

One year later

'My old dad first brought me here. During the week he toiled like a slave. Come the weekends he was an accordion player in a Ceilidh band. With football in the afternoons, either West Ham or Leyton Orient playing at home, he always put Saturday mornings aside for birdwatching – our time, rain or shine,' Jack said as a flock of starlings screeched above his head. 'And do you know?' he continued, watching the last straggler fly past, 'the Romanies used to pull their wagons into the forest back then and their horses would run wild. If you ever saw a horse in the street, you knew a Romany was looking for it. Then suddenly, you'd hear this strange high-pitched whistle and the horse would then gallop like the wind towards it. Some days we'd play football with the gypsy kids – though you knew they'd never played properly before, always picking up the ball and running into the forest with it. One thing they did know were their birds – particularly the sounds they made: finches, woodpeckers, skylarks, they knew all their songs; knew when they were about to up and leave and when they'd return. You see the two young women there and the

273

young boy with the shopping trolley,' he said, pointing towards the path that sprang into the forest, 'they are following the same tracks their people have travelled for generations. Like the birds above them, they come and go and always return. The camp is the same as ever. Even when they pack up, the burnt ground of the fire remains, as do their stories and memories.'

Aware now of running behind him, Jack stopped and turned around.

'Dad,' Jake shouted excitedly, catching up, his hair now swept back with lashings of gel.

'Jake – where's Skuld?'

'There,' said Jake, pointing ten yards behind him, 'she said she'd catch up as soon as she caught her breath.'

'Right,' said Jack, waving to Skuld whose tiny bump was just visible in the distance, the cause of which had made her ankles swell and her bladder become weaker, as she huffed and puffed along the path.

The young man beside him in the leather biker jacket and David Bowie T-shirt smiled broadly, all the time looking around him in wonder as if seeing the world for the first time.

'Oh, Jake,' began Jack, 'this is the young man I was telling you about: Tom Gray, the one who returned from the land of the missing.'

'Nice to meet you,' said Jake, holding out his hand as Tom hesitated for a moment before shaking it vigorously with both his own. 'I think it's really cool, the way you just turned up again and everything,' added Jake, a little embarrassed.

'Thanks,' said Tom, shifting nervously on his heels, but still smiling.

'I think my sergeant is here now,' said Jack, waving to Pencil who'd just pulled up outside the Hitchcock. 'He'll drive you home,' he said warmly as Tom stared back at the trees beyond.

'Jack,' interrupted Skuld, who'd now caught up. 'I think me and the baby need a skateboard,' she said, tenderly clutching her swollen belly as she waddled up and gave him a peck on the cheek.

'This is Tom,' Jack said again, holding out his hand in introduction.

'Yes, the missing boy – now found,' she replied, smiling as did everyone else.

The remnants of a young Tom Gray from the photograph still danced around the heavy crow's feet splayed like stainless steel forks around his mournful eyes. His stoop was gone, but not forgotten, still hiding in an East London basement lair. Continuing with routine weekly trips to the ATM and corner shop, his missing-person poster had soon made it into Mr Ahmed's grocery store.

'You're that Tom person,' said Mr Ahmed, who'd been studying his face closely for days, trying to unpick the layers of abuse sketched on his blank face. Only the missing tooth gave him away, when he'd managed a rare smile when the shopkeeper dropped a jar of pickled onions on the floor and began cursing passionately in Hindi. Realising that Tom was watching him he caught his smile and as he did, that of the young man from the poster on the noticeboard beside the toilet rolls and disinfectants behind the counter, which appeared to be staring back at them in disbelief.

'That's you,' cried Mr Ahmed, pointing as Tom stood, stunned and confused as he tried to make a connection with his lost past and the young man gazing across at him.

When Jack, Pencil, and Evans had called around to pick him up that afternoon he merely told them that he thought he might be Tom Gray.

As they crossed the road to the waiting car, a minibus loaded with young men pulled up outside the hotel and the men began spilling out with their luggage. Saying their goodbyes to Tom, who'd disappeared into the backseat of Pencil's car just as quick as he'd appeared a little over four months ago, they walked towards the steps of the entrance as the car sped away. The young men were now directly in front of them, mostly wearing rugby tops, chinos, and yachting shoes, and radiating wealth and confidence. No doubt down for a lads' rugby weekend, thought Jack, his hands now a little sweaty.

'Sorry, luv,' mocked the last one of the troupe who'd accidentally knocked into a young waitress who was rushing up the steps to begin her shift as the rest of them laughed at the Cockney quip.

'Pint, dad?' said Jake right on cue as the young men marched confidently into the foyer.

'Do you know what? I think we'll give it a miss today, Jake,' smiled Jack, putting his arm protectively around Skuld and ruffling his son's hair as he led them away. 'Maybe we'll go for a drive. I know a nice little pie and mash shop in Leyton.'

Acknowledgements

I would like to thank: my family and friends from Ireland, UK and further afield who have supported me as a writer; Bea Grabowska and the team at Headline for all their hard work and believing in this book; my editor Greg Rees for his spot-on observations; ultimately, my wife and son for supporting me throughout this process.

Not forgetting all the creatives who have unknowingly inspired me.

Author's Note

Deadly Lesson (formerly *The Birds That Fly East*) began life as a class-driven drama that had a lot to say about institutions, the family psyche and notions of accepting one's perceived lot in society. Although the fabric of the story has many layers of interpretation, it can be one event which sparks the imagination.

I remember watching some '*yobbo*' kicking a can along the road, when a group of entitled young men began jeering him, saying he should get a job. When the youth suddenly stopped and turned aggressively towards them, I feared the worst. Instead of a fist he produced a pen from his pocket and waved it mockingly at them. I think he said he was a writer (somewhere in 1991).